ANN GREYSON

The Lonely Vampire

Copyright © 2020 by Ann Greyson

Written by Ann Greyson

First Edition: September 2020

ISBN 978-0-578-70508-8
LCCN 2020910181

Printed in the United States of America

The Lonely Vampire

Prologue

1578. Gheorgheni, Romania

A GRAY MIST lingered over the horizon of the rural town in the Szekely Land in eastern Transylvania. The light was changing in the sky. At first glance, it was a peaceful-looking scene. But the sounds of low moaning traveling through the air evoked something else — menacing, threatening. Because these spooky sounds were not coming from the grazing sheep in the yards of the farmhouses.

A dark-haired muscular man, about five foot nine inches tall, dressed in a blood stained, long-sleeved white shirt hanging over his black pants and black boots was slowly walking toward Gheorgheni. He dragged a bloody ax behind him through the mud and grass, and then across puddles of water left over from the recent rain, now turned red from drops of blood.

Trudging through the marshy land, the man was weary from wielding the heavy ax as he came to the edge of the rustic town. This was the last stop on his search for the last of the vampires rumored to be scattered about. Some were in plain sight, while others were hidden where you had to search.

His first encounter was with two children. A boy and a girl with pale complexions, both no older than eleven years, stood by a wooden fence. The little girl, holding a doll in her left arm, smiled mischievously. She had long black hair in two braids. And she wore a brown, knee-length dress over a white, long-sleeved shirt, white knee-high socks and black shoes. The boy with dark eyes and wavy hair was wearing brown pants with a matching vest over a white, long-sleeved shirt and black shoes.

To any onlooker, they looked like sweet and innocent children. The ax-wielding man knew they were no ordinary children. They were vampires.

After they whispered to each other in some strange language, they welcomed him with a wave of their hands. The vampire children weren't scared and believed they could possess the slow-moving man. They were wrong.

News of these vampires whipped the people into an all-out frenzy. By a decree of the Hungarian ruling prince, the acts of the vampire were deemed to be criminal and subject to immediate execution. It was even put into law that vampires acted against the laws of Transylvania, which belonged to the Kingdom of Hungary.

The ax-carrying man was on the move again. He came to a farmhouse, where an older female vampire with long black flowing hair down to her waist, wearing a three-quarter-sleeved red dress to her knees, was floating in the air. She growled at him while her red eyes glared with rage. When he came closer, her arms reached out for him as her bare feet dangled in mid-air. She was next to receive his ax.

There was no place left to hide for the vampires. Romanians and Hungarians everywhere united for the sole purpose of ending the vampires long-standing presence in the region that had lasted a little over one hundred years.

The man made his way toward a cave opening, seeking a vampire that he knew was hiding there. As he drew nearer, a cluster of bats flew out. He paid no attention to them, thinking they were a nuisance and just regular bats. But it was wrong of him to have made that assumption.

He kept his eyes forward as he walked onward into the cave. There he found a young female vampire with long dark hair and red eyes hovering in a corner. She was dressed in a gray short-sleeve-knee-length dress that clung to her perfectly. Her pointy nails dug into the cave wall as she hissed at him and bared her teeth that were like sharpened knives.

"There is no escaping. I will send you on your way," he told her in Romanian.

The man held the ax high over his head and headed directly toward her. With a swift downward motion, he let the ax hit her neck, chopping off her head. Her body collapsed to the ground.

Just as darkness covered the countryside, the man left the cave. A full moon rose in the distance. He continued his mission.

A bat, with black leathery wings and black marks that streaked its brown fur, flew away from the flock. It swooped down and landed behind the wall of a farmhouse. There it transformed into a beautiful woman in her early thirties in appearance. A scarf around her head covered her raven-hair and concealed her pale complexion. She wore a black and burgundy shawl draped around her shoulders over a frilly three-quarter sleeved shirt with a ruffle around the neckline, a burgundy skirt, and black shoes. She was a vampire.

Her name was Ileana Vladislava and her brown eyes were pierced with pain. A single tear fell down her cheek. Just the thought of her friends being murdered, wounded her deeply. Her mind reeled, but there wasn't time to dwell on it. She needed to save her own skin.

Ileana waited a minute or so longer, dabbed at her eyes, then looked every which way to make sure no one was looking at her. No one was in sight at all. She took off running toward the forest. In a matter of seconds, she quickly transformed into a bat and soared high above the treetops.

Claymor, the werewolf, arrived on the scene to assist in the massacre of the vampires. An ally of the people and a vampire hunter in his own right, he could sniff out vampires with his sense of smell and penetrating eyesight. What made him unique from other werewolves was a pinch of gray fur on the left side of his face near his ear.

Over the many years, the vampires had attacked and killed many of his brethren. Now there were approximately the same number of vampires as there were werewolves. This was payback for him. He was determined to rid the land of them.

When in human form, Claymor was like any other man considering that he was born a werewolf. His mother was human. You would never know his true nature. No one knew for sure exactly who he was. Rightfully so, he kept his identity concealed.

The ax-toting man found himself staring at the sky, where a full moon was in plain view. He was convinced that all vampires had been eliminated. There was nothing to worry about anymore — so he believed.

But the werewolf wasn't convinced that all vampires had been wiped out. Sniffing the air, he caught the scent of a vampire in the air near the forest. He followed the trail of the smell locating where it was most concentrated until it all faded away. The earlier rain had left the air moist confusing his senses.

Alone in the deep woods, Claymor was disgruntled. He knew a vampire – or vampires – had escaped. Rising to his full six feet three inches, he threw his head back and howled loudly at the full moon hanging in the sky. Its glow threw a blue light into the woods, casting shadows all around him.

The black-eyed, dark-haired beast sank to his knees, lifted his head slowly, and raised his hands toward the moon. Setting his jaw with determination, he vowed to continue searching for the missing vampire or vampires. After lowering his arms, the werewolf raised his head higher and glanced at the bright full moon before letting out a long high-pitched howl.

Roughly nine hours later, the bat reached a city on the shores of the Black Sea. At a little after four in the morning, all was quiet on a ship docked in the port of Constanta. A few hours earlier, the large wooden vessel had been prepared to set sail in the early morning. The bat flew at it at top speed.

Alone in the darkness on the top deck, the bat peered around with its piercing brown eyes. With its pointed furry brown ears, it carefully listened to the sounds of a bunch of chickens squawking and clucking nearby. On the move again, it flew into the compartment where some farm animals in wooden crates, including many chickens and pigs were being held.

Upon seeing the bat, the animals yelped in fear. When it took a hanging position up in the corner of the ceiling, the animals settled down, thinking they were safe from harm. They were, at least for the time being.

The bat briefly glared at the many small animals that would serve well for feeding, before closing its eyes and drifting to sleep.

Chapter 1

2017. Newcastle upon Tyne, England

I LEFT WORK in a hurry, stepping outside on a dull, late Friday afternoon in mid-August. Walking my usual path toward the tube station, down Thornton Street toward Westgate Road, I just realized that I had been working for a little over a year at Longwood Nursing and Rehabilitation Center. I couldn't be happier helping the elderly with all aspects of their daily care — or at least I thought I was happy.

I couldn't say that it was my dream job, but I was going with it for now.

When I enrolled at Northumbria University, I was interested in healthcare, but I didn't want to be a doctor or even a full-blown nurse. I remember that day I said to myself: 'Myrna Ivester, you must do something with your life.' So, I settled instead on a career as a nursing assistant.

I wondered if I was tired of seeing the same streets over and over. Newcastle upon Tyne was the only place I knew in my short lifespan of twenty-three years. Never traveling anywhere, it was like I was holding myself back from life, watching from a safe distance, and not fully participating.

In all the passing thoughts, there was one thing I knew for sure, and that was I was not satisfied with my life. Was I expecting too much of life? I couldn't say for sure. Being young most older people would say there was a whole world in front of me. It was an expression often thrown onto young people of today and no consolation to me.

Some would say I was beautiful, having long dirty-blonde hair, blue eyes, a fair complexion, and slim figure, though I didn't feel that way about myself. My lack of confidence stemmed from the time my parents died, possibly the worst day of my life.

Ever since losing my parents at the young age of five, I had been detached from watery emotion. Despite my sensitivity, you would rarely see me showing my feelings or emotions. Oftentimes withdrawn, the instinct to turn inward and shut everything and everybody out, came naturally to me.

Upon reaching the entrance to Central Station, I descended the steep stairs. As soon as I stepped onto the platform, the train appeared in the tunnel. After the Metro stopped, the doors opened, and I walked in. The train was crowded, as usual, but I found a window seat.

Staring out the window of the fast-moving train, my thoughts drifted back to my late parents. My life just didn't feel the same after their death, something essential had broken inside me. For the longest time, I wanted my mom and dad back. I knew that wasn't allowed but I just wanted to talk to them. Eventually I faced the fact that they were gone forever.

When my parents died in a horrible car accident in March 1999, everything happened so fast in my life. How I was feeling and what I was thinking. Because I remember everything about that day. I was pulled out of class at West Denton Primary School because my Aunt Eowyn, my mother's sister, was waiting for me outside on Hillhead Road. Somebody called her to pick me up. She told me I was coming over to her house for a while — and she told me why, too. My parents died in a head-on collision with a truck.

It had tugged at me for years even though I had forgotten all about that day, until this moment.

Before I caught up with the events of that time, I was already living in her house. I started a new life under the watchful eye of an aunt I barely knew. Eowyn Dymtrow was a dear soul — so kind and devoted to her family that in time I grew to love her deeply. She and her husband raised me, along with their son, as if I were another child of theirs.

The clanking sound of the doors opening startled me from my thoughts. It was good that it happened because my stop was coming up next.

As the train settled to a stop, I stood up to leave. A few minutes later, I made my way from the surface level platform toward South Gosforth Station's exit. In the process, I took my Google Pixel smartphone out of my crossbody bag for a quick call to my best friend and roommate Siobhan Mulcahy. I asked her to be ready to go when I got home.

"All right see you in a few," I said before hanging up.

The reason I was in a hurry was because tonight we were celebrating Siobhan's promotion at work, a much needed one at that. She graduated from Northumbria University with a Bachelor of Science degree in Nursing Science, and soon after got hired as a nurse at Freeman Hospital. Today she was promoted to head nurse of her department. It was not because of her wit or beauty, though many male doctors she works with found her attractive. It was because she was exceedingly dedicated to her hospital duties and deserved it because of the sacrifices she had made for her job. It seemed right to reward her as the senior staff at the hospital believed she was the best choice for the management position, despite her age of twenty-four. She was more than capable and seemed to enjoy the new responsibility.

Siobhan was well satisfied with her status in life, and with herself for fulfilling her ultimate goal. I wasn't jealous either watching her obtain all the things she wanted out of life. Even if I was dissatisfied with my life because it wasn't progressing along like hers. This was something that I didn't share with Siobhan, and I didn't suspect that she sensed it. Perhaps she thought that was the way I was. Like I just went through life without a plan.

Somehow thinking on all of this, I had spent my whole life longing for something that I didn't understand myself. And I didn't know if I would ever find satisfaction in anything I do.

These kinds of thoughts had been haunting me and giving me nightmares for days. Even at times, I had had premonitory dreams. Or, at least, I thought they were. I kept thinking it would go away. So there was no point in saying anything about it to Siobhan or anybody else either.

Stepping onto Haddricks Mill Road, I turned left and headed down the winding street that lead to my home. Perhaps I spaced out, because I didn't remember much about my near five minutes of walking.

At six-thirty that night, I was home and getting ready to go out. Siobhan was more than ready and had just stepped out of the house to go wait in the car. Now she was the one in a hurry. I couldn't blame her either.

The freehold detached house located on Lilburn Gardens that I share with Siobhan was a modest 3-bedroom Victorian redbrick with a small garden overflowing with plants of every kind. I loved the place right from the first day I set my eyes on it.

After I had dressed up for the special evening ahead, I locked up, and headed toward Siobhan's blue five-door Toyota Corolla hatchback. When I slipped into the passenger's seat, she looked at me and her bright green eyes twinkled playfully. We gave each other a fast kiss on the cheek before she turned the key in the ignition. We adored each other, and often showed it.

Siobhan tore out of the driveway on our way for an evening of fun, food, and laughter. That was the way we liked to live our lives. Even though these days, I felt like I was pushing myself through life.

Chapter 2

NOISES could be heard from the Hunan Manor, a bustling Chinese restaurant on Sandhill near the Quayside stretch along the River Tyne and with the Tyne Bridge in the background. There were quite a few people in the place as it was a popular haunt for the locals. Siobhan Mulcahy and I were seated in a moderately luxury restaurant booth. The waiter had just left with our orders of dim sum and Tsingtao bottled beer for both of us.

Looking at the glimmering candlelight from a glass votive in the center of the table, I remembered the first time we met during our first year at Northumbria University, where Siobhan had been a nursing student. I was in the hallway of the Lovaine Hall residence standing in line, waiting for the bathroom. A girl ahead of me in line started banging on the door rushing someone who had been in there a long time. It was Siobhan. Already, I liked her spunk and was caught off guard by it.

There had been an undercurrent of sparks between us after a few weeks of hanging out together. The two of us became fast friends. By the luck of the draw, we became roommates in our senior year, and we were soon comparing notes about the hospitals we would be working at after graduation in 2015.

Siobhan's cell phone rang pulling me away from my reminiscing thoughts. She grabbed her Apple iPhone from her faux leather Stella McCartney handbag, looked at the caller ID, and announced to me it was her mother calling from Middlesbrough before answering.

"Hi mom," she said joyously. "Thank you, thank you. Dad told me earlier that you would be calling me to congratulate me as well."

Siobhan was born and raised in Middlesbrough, a large post-industrial town in North Yorkshire, but fell in love with Newcastle upon Tyne while attending the university. Most important, she was blessed with a good sense of humor despite the fact that we both came from an Irish lineage.

I turned my gaze from Siobhan, who was still talking on the phone at this time, to the Chinese waiter dressed in a white, long-sleeved shirt, black bow tie and black slacks. The tall and lanky man with a thin receding hairline, bushy eyebrows, a Fu Manchu-looking goatee, tufts of gray hair on his face, and dark, beady eyes under dark-rimmed spectacles, was pushing a cart with plates and stacks of little bamboo baskets toward us. His peculiar appearance kind of creeped me out.

The wonderful aroma of delicious food approaching our table caused Siobhan to take a quick glance over her shoulder. She looked pleased when she saw the dim sum was on the way.

"Mom, I have to run. The dinner is coming," she said quickly. "Talk to you later. Bye."

The waiter dropped the bamboo baskets of food on our table to serve ourselves and then said, "If I can assist you with anything else, you be sure to let me know. Enjoy your meal."

As the waiter backed away, he bowed his head once before leaving for the kitchen.

I dug in immediately and stated, "Let me do the honors. This is your night."

Before she could say anything, I had already opened a basket.

"Myrna, you're too kind."

Quickly I served us both hearty portions of steamed and fried lobster dumplings, jumbo shrimp teriyaki and fried wontons. When our plates were full, I decided to say something.

From across the table I raised a beer bottle to propose a toast and said, "Here's to your promotion."

"Here, here! After almost two years working there, it was about time because I'm really a good nurse. And don't think I'm full of myself when I say that either," Siobhan said and clanked her bottle into mine in a toast.

I found myself smiling at her enthusiasm for her job. She was very upbeat as if it were the best thing that ever happened to her. Everything in her life was going exactly the way she wanted. She looked proud and beautiful, and I loved seeing her that way.

"Don't worry. I don't think anything of the sort. On another note, now you'll have some extra money to fix the stereo system in your car, that you keep postponing."

"How about I finance a new car?"

"Great idea Siobhan, I'm with you on that."

"My dream car is the F-Type Jaguar."

"Isn't that really expensive?"

"Yeah. But I still want to do it," she told me and went back to her plate.

"You go, girl, that's the spirit."

We both laughed and kept chowing down on the wonderful Chinese food in front of us.

Siobhan wielded that kind of energy almost all of the time. Most people, including myself, liked her for that reason. She was the most put-together person I had ever known.

"So, what do you think of this place?"

"I really like it. The food is awesome," I answered.

"So, my nurse friend Alysa was right?"

"Yes, she was right to recommend it."

"She's going through a tough time right now."

"What's going on?"

"Her boyfriend left her. And now she can't afford to pay the rent where she's at."

"We have extra space. Did you invite her to stay with us?" I inquired.

"I wanted to wait to ask you before I said anything. And I am waiting to see if she gets a better offer."

"Before inviting her to stay with us, I'd like to meet her first," I said, a little bit wary.

"Of course. But I know you will like her."

Just as soon as our plates were empty, Siobhan looked rather emotional. But I didn't think it was because of the alcohol. We only had one beer.

"Myrna, I want to thank you for a great evening," she said emotionally.

"That's what friends are for, sweetie."

"I'm glad to call you friend."

"I feel exactly the same, Siobhan."

"On a serious note. Now that I have more money from my raise at work, do I have to pay for this?"

I laughed when she said that.

"Come on Siobhan. I told you earlier that it was my treat, didn't I?"

"You did. But I had to ask. Just in case," she said with a look of relief.

We walked out of the restaurant arm and arm singing "Shut Up and Dance," a song by Walk the Moon we liked a lot during our last year at university, on the way to Siobhan's car.

The quiet streets shimmered under the glare of overhead lamps. The still air was filled with the faint odor of tobacco. Following the smell, I barely glimpsed out of the corner of my eye the light from a burning cigarette. Holding it was a tall, thin man with a hound's face and a curvy mustache. The man wearing a black top hat, long black tuxedo jacket, black slacks and black shoes was leaning against a wall in the shadow of a streetlight. He was holding a wire leash to a cute little monkey.

The monkey with a thick tail, and a coat of rich brown fur, made occasional squeaking noises and clutched the man's pants leg with his little furry hand.

As I was walking fairly fast, I failed to mention it to Siobhan. Yet, I couldn't help looking back to see what he was doing.

When I made eye contact with him, he quickly glanced away. He dropped the cigarette and let it burn out on the ground. Then he turned his back to me and started to walk away, pulling on the leash.

"Come along, Jasper," his English precisely delivered despite the thick Croatian accent.

I wondered if one day I would look back on this. That happy image of the two of us strolling down the street. What some people would call a Kodak moment.

Chapter 3

IT WAS an early Saturday morning, slightly before five — still dark. Deep in the woods, a low moaning sound was coming from the passing wind through the trees and shrubbery. It wasn't the witching hour — that time between three and four in the morning where supernatural phenomena was most likely to occur, but it was creepy enough, at that. Because there was something supernatural in the area near Jesmond Dene Road.

Many years had passed since the development and landscape design of the woodland park gifted in 1883 by Sir William George Armstrong for the benefit of the inhabitants of the city. The beautiful golden and crimson azaleas and rhododendrons in Jesmond Dene was a constant, visible reminder of the legacy of the wealthy industrialist and owner of Sir W.G. Armstrong Whitworth & Co. shipbuilding and engineering business.

In the tranquil haven of a narrow wooded leafy valley near the Ouseburn River in the surrounding grounds of Jesmond Dene, a handful of black bears were grunting and feeding on grass and clover. It was a rare treat, seeing bears in these parts. At least Ileana Vladislava thought so — as she quietly watched them. And for what purpose?

One might describe her as a hunter of sorts.

A shadow fell upon a large tree trunk lying on the ground where, on top of it, stood Ileana. She was in a hunting stance. Carefully she observed the animals, anticipating when she would make her move.

Grey wagtails chirped noisily and flew by the bears. One wagtail began to pester a bear nibbling near a pine tree. He grunted as he shook his head about, trying to ward off the pesky bird. Soon enough, the bird flew away to join a flock of its kind on the moss nearby.

Such distractions served a good purpose to what waited in the darkness for the unsuspecting bears. There was no way the bears could tell they were being hunted.

The slim woman, about five foot four in height, dressed in a simple black T-shirt and black leggings, didn't appear to have the strength to overpower a big, sturdy bear. No human should have dared touch him. But Ileana was no ordinary human, but a supernatural being with exceptional abilities. A vampire, yes, that was a fitting word to describe her.

From time to time, Ileana glanced about, over her shoulder, and looking right and left to make sure that she was completely alone in the woods — as she liked it. She was. It was important to her that no one else was there to see her.

Vampires always hunted in darkness in the early hours before dawn or at night. Being sensitive to bright light, Ileana was rarely out in the daylight, but she could endure it using a high factor sun protection cream.

The question remained: Why was she stalking animals instead of humans?

The answer was simple: she was afraid. The reason was easy to understand. It was all about the past, many hundreds of years ago.

All these years later in England, she had refrained from contact with most people, engaging in a few obligatory pleasantries, and not attracting attention to herself.

Her biggest fear was inside her, what she was capable of. She was determined to avoid the temptation of attraction to other human beings, for which she would desire to draw their blood from them. Establishing a vampire colony, was a risk she couldn't afford to take. There was a werewolf out there, somewhere, with a grudge against vampires.

She remembered all too well the terrible events in Transylvania. She had lost everyone who'd ever meant anything to her. It was like a witch hunt.

Ileana was the last vampire, from Old Romania. And she was lonely.

When it came right down to it, she was no different than anyone else. Deep down inside her, she carried the same desires, same longings as most people. If she ever found the right person, meant to live the kind of life she was living, would she act on it? Could she hold back her desires?

A bear wandered lazily from the pack, sniffing at the dirt, and chewing on some grass. Ileana kept her eye on that one. Now that the bear was isolated, she was prepared to go after it.

Emerging from out of the shadows, after so many years she still appeared to be in her early thirties. She was eternally young and would retain the age at which she became a blood-sucking vampire. And that was precisely what she was about to do. She was going to suck the blood, rather the life out of the bear.

Blood was the essential source of life for her, crucial to her survival.

She was hungry for the blood of the bear, who didn't sense her. He had turned his back toward her and was heading deeper into the woods. And that was the moment. She ran amazingly fast, almost flying in her haste to get to the bear. And almost like her feet weren't touching the ground.

Moving sluggishly slow, the furry beast was easily reached. There was a brief struggle, but within a few minutes the bear was down on the ground. It was no surprise that the animal was no match for her supernatural strength.

Grabbing his head with both hands, she jerked it to the side. She hissed, buried her fangs in the bear's throat and succeeded in fastening them in the soft flesh beneath its fur. Pleasure came, rising and quaking through her body. The bear gasped and grunted in her ear, and it caused a commotion when it gave a howl of rage.

Completely in the moment, she went for the kill, and lost herself in it.

After satisfaction, she wiped her mouth on her shirt, and then twisted her head in every direction, watching for signs of anyone looking at her. As far as she could see, no one was watching her.

Her fiery-red eyes turned back to the rendered powerless, but not yet dead bear. It was running out of time because she was going to take a lot more blood than imagined.

It wasn't enough that she was hidden in the shade of some nearby trees, once again, she paused and glanced around to see if anyone was looking her way. There wasn't anyone there.

Ileana fished out a needle attached to a plastic bag from her small crossbody bag. She inserted the needle into a vein in the bear's neck and filled the bag completely full of its blood.

There was no chance for the bear. Not long after she had collected the blood, the animal died. It let out a final bloodcurdling scream of terror before passing into the other world.

There was no pity in her eyes. It was her only means of survival — a true example of survival of the fittest. Without a doubt, she was the fittest.

The bear appeared to have died of natural causes.

Certainly, no one was going to check. There was no reason to. People didn't go wandering in the woods to give autopsies to dead animals. No one seemed to care about dead animals. Ileana was confident about that.

Little did she know how wrong she was.

Chapter 4

"IT'S THAT NOISE AGAIN," Lorraine Krag said, turning to her husband, Arthur, as he came in the living room and found her standing by the window.

Not more than five minutes earlier, she had distinctly heard some animal let out an unearthly scream somewhere out in the night. By the time she had gotten out of bed and made it to the window, no other noise followed.

To appease herself, she pulled the thick beige curtain to the side and stared out the window. The suspicious expression on her face said it all. The idea of an animal being abused ambushed her thoughts at every turn.

Still dressed in her sleep attire, it wasn't unusual for her to be awake at this time in the morning. She and Arthur were early risers, up at 6:00 a.m. each day. Still, she was upset that the whining scream of an animal struggling for life had pulled her out of her sleep.

Lorraine was a haughty British woman with a prominent nose that matched her nosy personality exactly. A slim redhead with some gray starting to show, now in her mid-sixties, she wasn't aging gracefully.

"What noise?" Arthur asked in an emotionless voice, then shrugged his shoulders.

Subtly, she turned from the window and cast a defiant glare at him. She knew he wasn't interested in anything she said.

Arthur shot her a puzzled look, then he simply sat down in a beige suede chair, still holding *The Journal* newspaper under his left arm that he had just retrieved from the little cement stoop at the front door.

He could tell from her expressive hazel eyes she was irate. Sometimes, little things got her going. It was just her personality, and she displayed it often and willingly.

She was yapping again. "Those horrible sounds of an animal in agony I hear almost every week."

It was typical of her to fuss about one thing or another. He was in no mood for any of it. Trying his best to ignore her, he opened up his morning paper. After glancing quickly, he stopped on something that caught his eye.

When they had lived in the city of Norwich, in the English county of Norfolk, she always found something to bicker about. Now living in Newcastle upon Tyne, she found things to complain about — again.

Lorraine turned back to the window for another glance. As she caught sight of that castle in the distance, she felt a mixture of horror and fascination creeping over her.

Her thoughts returned to the sounds of an animal in distress. The sounds that were gone. Something inside of her wanted to grab a pair of binoculars and go outside to explore the environment. But she knew Arthur would try to stop her. And she wasn't in the mood for his discouraging words.

Dissatisfied again, she shook her head as she closed the curtain, turned toward her husband with a frustrated look on her face. "Listen to me, Arthur!"

The sixty-eight-year-old, average height, stocky, man with wavy salt-and-pepper hair wasn't listening. He shifted in his chair then crossed his right leg over the left one and turned the page of the paper. He filled his mind with the news of the day, trying to wipe her nagging from his mind. It was a way of coping and dealing with the situation without getting bent out of shape.

"Hello? Earth to Arthur!" Lorraine announced with a high-browed look as she folded her arms across her chest.

After a moment of awkward silence, he shook his head at her. "Yes, dear. The animals make strange sounds all the time. I've told you time and time again to pay no mind to it."

Her arms fell to her sides in exasperation. Deep down inside she knew something was wrong. She wasn't sold on the idea that it was some random occurrence.

She wasn't backing down either. "There is something not right around here. I'm telling you since the first day we moved here. It has something to do with the strange lady of that castle."

This same debate had raged on for the three months they had been living at 6 Jesmond Dene Road, and this morning the words chosen were no different. Her growing suspicious about the caretaker of the castle across the way was driving a wedge between them.

Arthur raised one brow and added, "You're the one who wanted to leave the city of Norwich. You said you were tired of the construction noises disrupting your thinking. Now you're complaining about the noise here."

His comments stirred up so much anger inside her. "That's just a coincidence, and you know it. Give me a break already."

When she was in an agitated state, her habit was to raise her voice at the end of each sentence. It came out as if she were asking a question instead of making a statement.

The impassive expression on his face made her blood rise beneath her skin. Slowly, she started to pace the room. In the process she looked over and gave him the evil eye. She could be spiteful and scary when she was mad.

A look of surprise covered his face. Noticing that did not go over well with her, he decided the best thing to do would be to tone down his comments.

The desire was there to protest and plead her case. Exhausted by her nervous pacing, she stopped because there was one more thing she wanted to add.

"It just doesn't sound right. The animals are suffering out there. Abusing them is unnecessary and inhumane."

"There are hunters killing animals for sport all over England. There is no reason to be alarmed."

"I didn't hear any gunshots."

"Maybe the animal was attacked by another animal. This kind of thing happens all of the time," he said while reading again, or pretending to read.

At this point, she looked all huffy and puffy. Sometimes her temper got in the way of her judgment. This was one of those times.

"I plan to one day get down to the bottom of this," she said, straining to keep her voice calm, but eyes raging.

Watching her like this, he was beginning to lose his patience. "Lorraine, if you mean what I think you mean, forget it. I'm going to stop you right there, because you want to put your nose in where it doesn't belong. You don't want to cause trouble. Do you?"

She came back with a sharp remark, "Why would I do something like that?"

It struck her right then and there. Lorraine would wait until he wasn't around, such as when he made a trip to the store. She decided in the back of her mind that she would check out the area around the castle for any unusual activity. Only that would satisfy her curiosity.

"Please don't do anything you might regret later on," he added, uncrossed his legs, and then folded up the newspaper.

"Sure, Arthur, sure," she finally relented, "I will be in the kitchen. I'm going to make you some Earl Grey tea and start the breakfast."

"What a good idea. I could really use a cup."

Lorraine looked at him with a sharp eye. Before she could reply with a smart remark, it occurred to her that she didn't have anything prepared to say. Then she looked one last time toward the window and made a frustrated face.

"We'll see about that," she finally muttered putting in the last word.

And with that, she stormed toward the kitchen leaving the room in a huff.

Chapter 5

I WAS ONE WEEK SHY of turning twenty-four. It was a dreary Wednesday morning, after long night of rain, just a few days since my celebratory dinner with Siobhan Mulcahy.

At a little before eight o'clock, I came out of the shower wearing a gray towel wrapped around my body. I stopped in front of the mirror attached to my dresser. Then I twisted my thick hair into one long, fat braid fastened with a rubber band and hung it over my right shoulder.

The sound of a door closing startled me for a second, until I realized that it was Siobhan. I felt relieved when I remembered that today was her day off. Most likely, she closed her bedroom or bathroom door on the way to the kitchen.

About a minute later, I opened a drawer in my dresser and took out my work garbs, a flowered short sleeved shirt and bright pink pants. I especially liked the shirt because of the two deep pockets in the front that was perfect for stashing things like a pen, or an emergency pair of gloves.

As I dressed, suddenly something inside me was telling me that I needed to change my life. Was I tired of the same routine? It was a question I asked myself because lately I felt torn up inside.

It seemed like such a long time ago when I was offered the job at Longwood Nursing and Rehabilitation Center. At that time, I was thrilled to accept it.

Nowadays, I just didn't feel the same way I used to. Oftentimes I found myself questioning whether I made a good decision when I took the job. Was it a crutch to hold me back from living each day to the fullest and experiencing all that life had to offer?

Just last night Siobhan said to me that I hadn't taken enough risks in my life like a lot of young people. With certainty, I felt she was right about that.

Then I thought, perhaps I felt this way because my birthday was coming up soon and I didn't have a clue about what I wanted. I tried to reassure myself that I was just having birthday jitters. But I was sure I was going through an emotional crisis.

Recognizing that line of thinking wasn't productive, I needed to put it on the back burner for now. So, I put on my Jimmy Choo crossbody bag, grabbed my keys, and headed toward the front door.

After locking up, I darted over to my white Honda SH125 Mode scooter and gingerly sat myself on it. I treated myself to this two-wheeler in 2016. It was a belated gift from me to me, eight months later, for graduating from the university.

Honestly, I didn't have enough money to buy a car outright and didn't want to lease or finance one. So, I settled on a scooter which was affordable, lightweight, compact and fuel efficient. With time I had grown to love it more and more. Even with my helmet on, I felt like such a free spirit driving it on the open road.

I drove at a steady pace. It usually took me about twenty minutes to cover the distance. I enjoyed the ride, except in rainy weather, I preferred to take the Metro.

When I got to Thornton Street, I turned toward the parking lot right next to a HSBC Bank that was designated for employees of Longwood Nursing and Rehabilitation Center. After I turned off my bike and put down the kickstand, I walked to the employee back entrance.

At the secure double doors, that led into the main corridor of the facility, I swiped my access card across the reader. The doors opened, I stepped inside and headed for the office area to clock in. Right on time. Nine o'clock.

My shift ran until five, with a one-hour lunch break occurring between noon and 2 p.m. and two ten-minute breaks. My duties included checking patients' vitals and tucking them comfortably in bed, fluffing their pillows, distributing food trays, and feeding and bathing them. Ninety percent of the residents were over the age of sixty-five and not in the best of health. And I did my best to accommodate them.

Before I could open my locker and put my things away, Joyce Gunn came into the women's locker room and said, "Myrna, I'm so glad you're here! I need your assistance, immediately! It's an emergency situation with Stan Brightman again."

"Is he all right?" I asked, a bit worried.

"He's in a state of anxiety, wandering up and down the corridor and trying to leave the premises. He believes that his daughter is waiting for him at home," Joyce told me frantically.

"He seems to have developed a habit of doing that lately."

"You get along so well with him. I think if you read him a book, it will calm him down."

"I'll be right there," I said as I shoved my bag in the locker.

"Thanks, Myrna! You're a doll!" she said, smiling her big, toothy smile and walked out of the room.

Joyce Gunn was my supervisor and she instilled in me a real interest in the job and the company. Well, sometimes she did. On the whole she was a pleasure to work with.

A black woman of mature years, who stood about five feet five inches with short-braided hair and a skinny figure, Joyce looked marvelous since returning from medical leave six weeks ago. Her bout with lupus was thankfully months behind her. The purple flower-patterned scrub top with light purple scrub pants she was wearing really brought out the color of her large moon shaped eyes.

I walked down the corridor, thinking how the day had started off a little shaky, Stan Brightman in a state of agitation. Hopefully this wasn't an omen of things to come.

Apparently, an orderly had brought Mr. Brightman back to his room because he wasn't in the hallway. When I poked my head in his room a big smile came over his face as he looked in my direction. Standing beside the bed, he also looked a little bewildered. At any rate, he appeared to have calmed down.

"Good morning, Stan, how are you today?" I asked as I stepped into his room.

Most patients shared a room, but because of his medical condition, he was given a private room. In fact, a dozen rooms on this one hall were private.

"Who are you? Are you here to take me home?" he asked, becoming emotionally unhinged.

"No. I'm Myrna Ivester. I work here," I said in a pleasing voice.

His brown eyes stared intently at me. The five-foot-eight tall, wavy-white-haired man with a small nose seemed tired from his earlier ranting. He really was a sweet old Jewish man who couldn't help his occasional outbursts.

"I've seen you before," he said a little more coherently.

"Stan, why don't you sit down on the bed? How about I read you a book?"

"Oh, I don't know. Maybe I should just leave now," he said, still confused.

"How about I read for a little while?"

When I came closer to him, I noticed a spot of his breakfast stained on the front of his blue long-sleeved pajama top — something yellow. Probably eggs.

"Will you take me home after?"

"As I've told you before, this is your home now."

He sat down on the edge of the bed and simply asked, "You're going to read? The one about magic and witches?"

"Yes. You remember. *Harry Potter and the Deathly Hallows*. It's my favorite *Harry Potter* book by J.K. Rowling."

Even in his state of dementia, he understood some of what was going on.

Just then, an orderly, dressed in a white smock top and loose fitted white pants, appeared at the door, and asked if I had things under control and I assured him I did. The well-built, blue-eyed young man gave me a quick smile and left without another word.

I grabbed the book from the shelf in the corner and pulled a stool over to sit next to him. After I sat down, I began to flip through the book looking for the chapter I'd been reading before. Then I started to read.

Chapter 6

WHEN I GOT HOME, Siobhan Mulcahy wasn't there, which wasn't unusual. And I knew not to worry. More than likely, she was out shopping or running errands for herself, something she did on her days off from work.

I turned into my bedroom and dropped my crossbody bag on my bed. Then I went into the bathroom to freshen up.

As I came out of the bathroom, I thought I heard the sound of a car horn outside. It sounded different than the horn of Siobhan's Toyota. So, I just ignored it thinking it was a car passing by.

Going about my business, I walked toward my closet for a change of clothes, until the sound of the horn came again. I stopped in my tracks, halfway to the door of the closet.

"What in the bejesus?" I asked quietly under my breath.

Someone was pressing their car horn insistently. The noise was beginning to irritate me. Whoever was out there was obviously in a hurry.

Quickly leaving the bedroom, I bolted through the living room and went straight to the window next to the front door. I wanted to see who was causing that ruckus.

Peeling back the curtains, I looked through a grimy windowpane. Immediately, I saw a new gray two-door Jaguar coupe parked in front of the house at the curb instead of in the driveway. Siobhan was sitting in the driver's seat. She got her dream car.

When Siobhan saw me open the front door, she waved at me, then stuck her head out the window. "Myrna, isn't it gorgeous?"

"Siobhan, it's awesome," I said, rushing up to the driver's side door.

"Let's go out for a spin. How about some curry? My treat."

"This car is expensive. Why don't I treat?"

"I'll gladly take you up on that," she said, chuckling.

"It's a deal! Let me just change out of my work clothes," I said and ran back into the house.

Back in my bedroom I stripped off my clothes and threw them in the laundry basket in the closet. In a rush, I put on a lacy white camisole to go under my sheer tan cardigan and slipped on a pair of tan corduroys and black sandals. Lastly, I grabbed my crossbody, turned off the lights and hurried to the front door to lock up.

Eagerly, I went to the passenger side of the Jaguar. The first thing I noticed was that the black leather interior smelled new. Just as you would expect in a brand-spanking-new car. It was the epitome of luxury.

"This car is hot!" I exclaimed.

"I got a good deal on it," she said as she drove off.

"You have to explain that one."

"Earlier today I went over to the dealership to look at this 2017 F-Type model advertised on their webpage that I found surfing the Web on my iPhone. I went crazy for it. I put down five thousand pounds from my savings account for a down payment. And I was allowed three thousand three hundred pounds trade-in for my 2014 Toyota Corolla. Not to mention a four-hundred-pound monthly car payment for the next five years."

"Still, it's a bit pricy," I added.

"The good news is that on Friday I will get my first paycheck with the salary increase."

"I just thought of something. Now with the car of your dreams, maybe you can find the man of dreams," I said changing the subject.

"Easier said than done. Wishful thinking Myrna."

"Nothing on my end either," I told her rather depressingly.

"We're young and exploring. There's no hurry."

Or so we told ourselves. And more silly jokes started popping up and kept us laughing the rest of the ten-minute ride to the restaurant.

Siobhan pulled into the valet parking lot on Forster Street directly across Mango Grove restaurant. Despite the fully comprehensive insurance policy and InControl secure tracking service to protect the Jaguar from theft, she was still worried about losing it. I could empathize with her having just bought it. Plus, I wouldn't want to be walking home should anything happen to it. So, I was with her on that added bit of protection.

By the time Siobhan pulled the key from the ignition, I was already out of the car. I came around and found that she was still sitting in the driver's seat with the door open. All the while the attendant stood there smiling holding out his hand. Waiting.

"Let's go, Siobhan," I urged her.

"Okay. I'm just enjoying it," she said as she climbed out of the car and handed the man the keys.

In return he gave her a numbered ticket to retrieve her car later. Then we set off toward the restaurant.

To my surprise, Siobhan's favorite Indian restaurant, Mango Grove, wasn't all that crowded for a Wednesday night. The sheer aroma of the place made my stomach growl. After a long day's work, I was famished and couldn't wait to order one of their fabulous vegetarian cuisine dishes.

After the server set a pot of tea on the table and left with our orders, Siobhan and I started chatting away.

"Are you going to show off your car to people at work tomorrow?" I asked and took a sip of mint tea.

"You bet I am," she said all giggly.

"I'm really glad you got it. It's nice to see you treat yourself for a change."

"Yes, the times are changing right before our very eyes," she said all giggly again.

"For one of us, at least."

Siobhan looked at me queerly for a moment after I said that. But what I had said wasn't far from the truth. My true feelings about my humdrum of a life slipped out accidentally. So, I laughed a little to defray the tension. Then she laughed a little.

"Myrna, that sounded pathetic."

"I agree with you. I don't even know why I said it."

Right after I said that, I swiftly shifted the conversation elsewhere. After all, this was Siobhan's time to celebrate. And there was no need to change the mood.

Dinner came and went fast. Before I knew it, we were getting her Jaguar from the valet and hopping into it gleefully.

Before she pulled out of the lot, she looked across at me and asked, "Shall we take the long way home?"

"Yes, definitely. I'll crank up the radio. Now that you have a working stereo system again, I figured I may as well put it to use."

"And I'll crank back the sunroof to get some fresh air."

Siobhan hit a button on the dashboard and the sunroof whirred back, filling the Jaguar with a rush of cool air. Then she drove out of the lot and turned north.

Reaching over, I flipped on the radio right in the middle of the song "Something Just Like This" by The

Chainsmokers & Coldplay. We both liked it a lot. She turned in her seat to face me. After making eye contact with me, she reached for the radio and turned up the volume. She glanced up at the sky before bringing her eyes back to the road.

I slid the passenger seat as far back as it would go. My legs were stretched out in front of me and crossed at the ankles. My head lolled back against the headrest of the seat and I looked up through the panoramic sunroof to see a full moon surrounded by clouds.

Chapter 7

A BOLT OF LIGHTNING struck the ground only two yards from the dark and mysterious 19th century castle, simply known as Wightwick Hall. It was a place on Jesmond Dene Road that had long been a part of the history of the city of Newcastle upon Tyne. Rain started falling soon after, and a cool breeze swept through the area. Water trickled down a flight of stone steps into the darkness, reaching the bottom of a bolted wooden door to the cellar.

Ileana Vladislava was hanging upside-down from the ceiling of the cellar. A small, black spider came from a frayed web in the corner and began to crawl on her foot. It slowly made its way up her leg, under her gray leggings.

The tickly feeling of the critter's fuzzy legs startled her from a deep sleep. Her eyelids flew open to reveal her red orbs, faintly glowing in the dark — the signature trait of a vampire in the grip of a rage.

She started to rustle about and slipped her hand down her leg to remove the culprit who had disturbed her peace. When she reached it, her fingers flicked the pest off her body.

The anger in her eyes dissipated. Her eyes squinted, and a grin came on her face. She made a mental note to remind herself to brush out the cobwebs and spiders in the room. It was not the first time the pesky creatures had bothered her rest.

Now she was wide-awake listening to the sound of the torrential downpour. Feeling it was time for a gander about, she came down from the ceiling.

As she came out of the cellar and walked up the stairs with her bare feet, she felt a bit of weakness in her body. Suddenly a chill went through her. She hugged her arms around herself for warmth. Next came a familiar pain.

First thing was first, Ileana was thirsty, for blood. As luck would have it, plenty was stocked up.

At the top of the stairs she opened the door to the hallway and strolled on the oak floor. Once in the kitchen, she opened the refrigerator door and took out a bag of blood. She took a lead crystal wine goblet from the overhead cabinet by the refrigerator and poured the blood to the rim. Placing a straw in the glass, one of those bendy types, she took a quick sip. Then she left with it, heading toward her study.

Ileana climbed a spiral staircase before reaching the study, while the storm still flashed and boomed beyond the castle walls. She felt comforted by the sound of the rain which was a steady drone on the castle roof. The first thing she did when she entered the room was look out of the window.

Admiring the rain and claps of thunder, it seemed like it would be just another day tempered with loneliness. Thoughts of how she was living her life flashed through her mind — spending most of the time inside her castle, looking out a window.

She purchased Wightwick Hall in 1929. It was a beautiful residence, but there was a feeling of emptiness in the place because of its size. It was larger than the mansion in the Gosforth area where she had resided for thirty years before. The cellar and a finished basement with media room were in the lower level of the castle. The large library, dining hall and the kitchen were on the first level. The study, six large bedrooms and four and a half baths were on the second level. A small attic, and a giant greenhouse with an ample number of skylights in the roof were on the third and top, level of the castle.

And, of course, there was always her past, the way she had lived in Transylvania, when her life was at its best. The mere thought of that time sent chills through her heart. It was long, long ago, but she remembered so well, and was scarred by the deaths of her vampire family members.

Ileana set aside the rambling thoughts. With music, books, and movies sufficient to fill her time, she ceased thinking about the past. And with that thought, she turned from the window to glimpse her tastefully designed study.

The clock that hung above the inglenook fireplace told her it was ten past eleven. She walked over and put her glass on the carved limestone overmantel, then went toward a square oak cabinet with twisted legs and a turntable on top. It stood at the left of a Victorian turquoise velvet buttoned back armchair with turned wood legs.

She played music. Today's selection was "The Dance of The Knights" from Sergei Prokofiev's *Romeo and Juliet*.

The record began to play.

After picking up the glass, she sat down on the Victorian armchair, and rested her left hand on the edge of the armrest. Leaning her head back, she let the instrumental music surround her. The fingers of her left hand began to tap the armrest as she was enthralled by the music.

When the song was over, her intense emotions subsided. Ileana leaned forward, sipped the rest of the blood to her heart's content and felt fulfilled afterwards.

With a deep sigh, she leaned her head back again and shut her eyes, enjoying the feeling of the blood flowing through her. She took a deep breath and meditated while the processes in her body worked themselves out.

Before long, she was back in the kitchen again. She proceeded to rinse the glass in the sink. While a steady stream ran from the faucet, a flash of lightning crashed across the sky. The sound caused her to look out the window above the sink. In that second, from the corner of her eye she saw a shadow move beside a tree in her direct view. She sensed it was a person, but who?

After a moment to ponder the mysterious stranger outside the castle, it suddenly came to her who it might be. She was convinced it was her nuisance of a neighbor, Lorraine Krag.

Ileana knew this too well because she had seen Mrs. Krag staring toward the castle from her living room window several times. But why today, in the pouring rain?

The last time she saw Mrs. Krag spying on the castle, Ileana took it upon herself to discover who the woman was. She decided two could play at that game. At the wee hours of the morning, Ileana had crept around the Krag's house and found her name and husband's name on the address label on a newspaper on the stoop outside the door of their house.

Why she had specifically picked out Wightwick Hall, was because it was a place she could disappear in, secluded, and ignored by other people. All of the nearby houses were unoccupied. The house at 6 Jesmond Dene Road had been empty for six decades, or possibly more. Three months ago, the estate agent of the property lowered the price of the house and in came Mr. and Mrs. Krag.

As she stared more intently out the window, part of a brownish-yellow raincoat could be seen sticking out from the side of the tree. Sensing it was Mrs. Krag made her blood boil. Probably, she thought Ileana would never notice. Lorraine Krag just wasn't a very bright woman in the eyes of Ileana Vladislava.

Ileana bared her vampire teeth in a sneer. That made her feel much better. Still, she kept her cool and turned off the faucet. She didn't let on that she had seen Mrs. Krag and would ignore it this time.

Besides, she didn't have time for such trivial matters. She shoved the thought of Lorraine Krag out of her head and focused her attention back on the glass in front of her that she was drying with a white towel.

As far as she was concerned, when it came to vampires, people didn't believe in such things. So, she wasn't worried in the least.

Her story was simple. She was a woman who lived in a castle, which was common in England, a caretaker of a large estate for the purpose of managing a greenhouse as a connoisseur of horticulture. It was a plausible explanation, well-rehearsed, and it couldn't be contradicted.

After putting the glass away, she felt it was time to return to the cellar. The spiders weren't something she cared to worry about. Ileana Vladislava was too tired.

Chapter 8

A DISTANT THUNDER was heard while an occasional flash of lightning broke for an instant across the sky. Wightwick Hall was ten paces away and the proximity and sight of it made Lorraine Krag's skin tingle. At twenty minutes before one, peering from behind a large tree, there was a stern look on her face. Thoughts about her earlier actions were upsetting her. Unfortunately, things didn't turn out the way she had hoped they would.

Why was Lorraine Krag spying on Wightwick Hall under the pouring rain?

That morning, just before nine o'clock, her husband Arthur was dressed in a light blue polo shirt buttoned to the neck under a dark gray Nautica windbreaker with matching twill pants and loafers for a trip to the Tesco on Acorn Road to purchase some groceries and household necessities and then a stopover at The Longbow Tavern for lunch. He didn't invite her along and she had no interest in joining him.

Not long after Arthur had left, she was in her living room, peeking out the window at the castle from behind the curtain, wondering if it was empty. The fact of the matter was, she was convinced the woman wasn't there. For the past four days, she'd not seen hide nor hair of her.

The rain started to fall right before her eyes. When the telephone rang, she picked it up from the mahogany end table in the room. It was Arthur. He called from his cell phone to say when he entered The Longbow Tavern it started raining hard. He decided to wait out the storm which was expected to be of a short duration. At most, he thought a delay of a couple of hours.

So, she made her move. To put her mind at ease, she wanted to find out for sure whether or not the castle was empty. Maybe even to sneak into Wightwick Hall if everything went to plan. The thought of what might be going on in that castle and its strange occupant blinded her to reason.

She got dressed and took off, wanting to make the most of the little time that remained to her.

The rain hid her well. And the black galoshes and khaki-colored hooded raincoat she was wearing blended in with the surrounding trees and foliage. So, she thought she could remain as inconspicuous as possible.

Lorraine had scrutinized every inch of the castle and its grounds. Even she snuck around, peeking into windows of the castle, watching for some movement. Nothing.

A flash of lightning struck behind the castle provoking her to look in its direction. She saw a flight of stone steps leading to the lower level. Her curiosity got the best of her and she couldn't leave it alone.

Lorraine Krag smirked to herself at her own cleverness. "This is exactly what I was looking for."

The closer she'd got to the steps, the more she felt like she was being drawn to it, by an invisible yet powerful force. As she moved even closer and snuck a look down the stairwell, it was a pure miracle that she heard the music. Right then she stopped herself from descending the stairs. She stood there for a moment listening just to make sure she wasn't imagining things. The faint sound was coming from a window above her. The moody notes of Sergei Prokofiev spilled out into the foggy air.

That was when she ran over to a tree, practically stumbled into it because the wind and water whipped at her face, partially blinding her. The sharp pangs of rain smacked her in the face with ferocity. She was not at all pleased by this.

The rain had gotten heavier. Long drops of water pattered on the hood of her raincoat. And droplets of water cascaded down her neck and seeped through her raincoat. Lightning flashed in the cloudy sky. The flash of light jolted her. She moved a little to her right and a gust of wind mixed with rain hit her in the face. Hiding as she was, she was wet and miserable.

After she brushed some droplets of rain from her eyes, she looked up at a window directly across. That was when she saw the reflection of a woman through it.

At the last possible second, she quickly shifted her body behind the tree to conceal herself further. What she didn't know was that part of her raincoat was in plain view.

"Doesn't she ever go anywhere?" she questioned with a whisper.

She kept a watchful eye, thinking she had not been seen. After another minute or so, she couldn't see the woman anywhere.

"There's something strange going on with that woman," she muttered under her breath.

If only she could erase from her mind everything that had just transpired.

Now it was raining hard, and she was drenched and tired. She turned her eyes away from the window of the castle and held onto the trunk of the tree, resting her body against it. A red squirrel came out of nowhere and scampered up the trunk passing close to her face, startling her even more. She was so frustrated by it all that her face twisted up with fury. Could things get any worse? she thought.

"Stop and take a deep breath. Just breathe a little bit. Smell the flowers if you can," she spoke to herself, trying to calm down.

Today things didn't go well for Lorraine Krag. And she was bitter coming up empty-handed.

"Well, Lorraine, it just wasn't in the cards," she whispered bitterly to herself.

For an added bit of security, she performed one last scan to confirm she wasn't being watched. The last thing she needed was to get caught trespassing.

An icy shiver ran through her body as she leered at the castle with her beady hazel eyes one more time. However, after a few more thoughts about it, the way she felt must be because of the cold rain that was pouring down on her.

Enough was enough for her. Lorraine turned and started to move away from the tree. She walked most of the way home, rather slowly with her head down. There was no looking back on that castle. She didn't even care that the rain was coming down strong. It just didn't matter to her anymore that the light wind whisked the rain in all directions, soaking her face, hair, and neck.

"I don't know why I bother, I don't," Lorraine mumbled to herself.

Why in the world had she gone out in this horrible weather? Nothing went according to plan. She began to think her little espionage excursion was wearing her down. It was something she needed to think long and hard about.

But not that long.

She thought of the day's events, again and again, and saw it as a temporary setback. Whatever that woman of mystery was up to was going to have to wait for another time. Yes, she decided there would be a next time. She would have to devise a better plan because she wasn't giving up. Something inside pushed her on.

Lorraine Krag pushed the thoughts back with a stubborn look as she trampled toward the front door of her house.

Chapter 9

SITTING AT THE COUNTER, of The Longbow Tavern situated on Stepney Bank in the heart of the Ouseburn area on a Thursday afternoon, Arthur Krag was reading the day's paper. The relaxed look on his face was because of this much needed break from the recent quarreling with his wife Lorraine. The pouring rain gave him an excuse to linger — and linger he would. He believed that time away was good for his marriage that had lasted a surprisingly thirty-four years.

A solidly built, medium height, sixty-something man with a full head of dark hair touched with gray, wearing a white shirt and brown pants under a brown apron, came through the door to the kitchen behind the counter.

The man stopped behind the counter, swiped up Arthur's plate with crumbs of leftover bread and potato salad on it, and asked, "Would you like a scone, Arthur?"

"Why certainly I would, Allan," he answered, looking up from the paper with a smile.

"So, how's Lorraine doing? If you don't mind me asking?"

"The same old, same old."

"I am sorry to hear it buddy," Allan Palen said with a chuckle, laughing at his own wisecrack and then gave a gentle nudge with his elbow against Arthur's arm.

"Yeah, me too," Arthur agreed and laughed too.

The two men had become good friends in the short time Arthur had lived in Newcastle upon Tyne. So, they could talk that way to each other.

Allan Palen carried a very thick British accent that stood out from those around him. Divorced with two daughters in their twenties, he was an easygoing, restaurateur with a sense of humor and larger-than-life personality. Everybody in the neighborhood liked him which was why his establishment was constantly busy.

He went to the kitchen and returned with an apricot scone on a plate and placed it on the counter in front of Arthur. Afterward, he picked a napkin up from the floor, tossed it in the trash can under the register near the counter, and dusted off his apron. Before returning to the kitchen, he stopped by a customer at the counter to apologize for the slight delay of his order.

Arthur took another sip of his tea and bit into the freshly baked scone. He could never get enough of them. And he was in the mood to indulge. Nobody made scones like Allan Palen, not even Lorraine even though she was a good cook and liked to cook for him. He wondered if that was why he stayed with her. That could even be why he married her. He didn't exactly remember.

The years went by so fast and his memory ran short. What was apparent was that Lorraine's personality had changed over the years. He attributed her mood to the fact that they didn't have children. They tried many times but were unsuccessful in their attempts. For most of his life, he had been busy with his career as a senior investment banker at Barclays while she had spent twenty years working as a schoolteacher. Having children would have made them closer, he thought.

Returning to his newspaper Arthur turned a page and folded it up. He peered out the window. The rain was still coming down hard. He did a doubletake when he saw a man behind his stylized gray Nissan Leaf, a compact five-door hatchback battery electric vehicle, parked in a space on Lime Street.

It was a tall, thin man with dark hair, eyes that were haggard, pale lips and a curvy mustache. The man appearing in his late forties was leaning against a reddish-brown brick wall near an artist's studio gallery.

Arthur thought his outfit of a black top hat, long black tuxedo jacket and black slacks was odd. The little brown monkey under his left arm was even odder.

The man just stared blankly into space as the rain fell hard all around him. Water dripped on his hat and clothes as the tiny, black edge of the roof above his head did little to shelter him and his pet from the whipping rain or the light wind blowing straight into his face. The monkey looked terrified, looking from side to side and pawing at him with its left arm.

Upon seeing a skinny black woman toting an umbrella coming from a distance, the man nudged the monkey with his hand. Then the monkey put his hand out like a beggar, as if trying to gain sympathy from the passerby. But she didn't make a donation. She hurried her step, ignoring the gesture of the animal. When she was a couple of feet away from them, the man gave a disappointing glare and the monkey gave a sort of confused look.

Arthur Krag wasn't surprised by this. On the contrary, it was to be expected. He had seen those types before. Losing interest, he turned his attention toward the front of the counter.

Allan came toward him and asked, "I guess you caught a glimpse of Viktor Pavlovic and his pet monkey, Jasper?"

"You know him?"

"Yes, Arthur. He lives nearby and is a regular of this establishment."

"So, what is his story? Not that it's any of my business, but I have to ask since you mentioned him."

Then he proceeded to tell Arthur that Viktor Pavlovic was originally from Croatia. As a young boy, he had taught himself magic and worked with a traveling circus. Somehow, he got stranded somehow in Newcastle upon Tyne. Finding himself out of work, he decided to earn his living as a street performer with his trained monkey.

"When the weather is good, Viktor earns a good lot of money on the weekends at the Old Eldon Square," Allan Palen added.

"Why doesn't he come inside out of the rain?"

"I think he does it on purpose to create sympathy in the passersby. He thinks he can get more money."

"A devious sort of fellow," Arthur said with a raised eyebrow.

"He's as strange as they come."

"The moment I saw Viktor, I should have asked you first."

"Who's on first?" Allan asked.

"For the second time, I should've asked you first."

"What's on second," Allan fired back.

"I don't know. So, for the third time, I'll check with you first."

"I Don't Know is on third."

"What's on third?" Arthur asked cluelessly.

"No. What's on second."

"I got it. You had me going there for a moment," Arthur said and laughed a bit.

Allan knew when to lighten the mood with his imitations of routines made famous by Bud Abbott and Lou Costello. Obviously he was a fan of their films.

"Just give me a holler when you're ready for the check," Allan said, with a cheerful smile.

After grabbing a white rag he had just wiped the counter with, he tossed it onto his right shoulder. Then he whistled his way to the door leading to the kitchen and pushed through it.

Arthur flicked his brown eyes toward the window for another gander at the rain. It was starting to dissipate. This could only mean one thing. He would be returning home soon. That thought put a frown on his face.

Chapter 10

LORRAINE KRAG was home again. It didn't look like the rain was going to start up again, and that meant Arthur would be returning soon.

The earlier rain had dropped to a drizzle then faded away as the bulbous clouds overhead dissipated during the time she had opened the door to the basement and hurried down the steps to put her raincoat and galoshes in the linen closet next to the washer and dryer, which she thought was the best place to hide them. The laundry room in the basement was a place Arthur rarely ventured.

Rummaging through her bedroom closet, she found her comfy thin gray cardigan embroidered with yellow flowers. Still shivering from the rain, she pulled it on over her yellow linen dress.

Lorraine proceeded to the kitchen to fix herself a hot cup of black tea. After making her favorite English

Breakfast Tea, perfect for anytime of day, she took the flowery bone china cup and saucer with her and headed down the hall in the direction of the living room.

After she took a sip of tea, her eyes fell upon the window that faced the mysterious castle. Overcome with curiosity, she set the cup and saucer down on the end table by the telephone. She wasn't done spying.

Parting the curtain, she wondered if she was becoming obsessed with Wightwick Hall. Looking at it from afar, she thought about the many possibilities as to why that woman was so mysterious. Maybe she was just a caretaker? Could it be that she didn't care to get involved with anyone? It was likely she was just some homebody.

"Oh, Lorraine, you're the homebody," she said loudly to herself and laughed.

Enough spying for one day, she thought to herself as she drew the curtain closed and turned her attention back to her cup of tea. She gulped down the remaining tea in the cup and then went back to the kitchen to wash it out.

"Best I prepare myself for Arthur," she said to no one in particular.

A little bit later she was back in the living room. She turned on the BBC radio channel on the device on the large scalloped mahogany coffee table in front of the sofa. The volume was set to a low level. She thought it was a good idea to get her mind off the day's frustrations.

Next, she scooped up a pair of knitting needles and a ball of yarn from the coffee table, and then sat down on the cream-colored Victorian sofa with tufted cushions, trimmed in dark oak with claw feet. She really wanted to look occupied. Her latest project was knitting a blue yarn scarf for Arthur. How she found time for such things was beyond her.

Almost fifteen minutes later, she heard footsteps coming toward the front door and keys jangling. She continued knitting without looking up as the door opened and closed. Footsteps came toward the living room. It was Arthur. Still she didn't look up.

"Hello, dear," he said in a cheery voice.

To further the charade, she didn't respond immediately, rather ignored him giving the impression she was listening to something on the radio. And like she was falling asleep, though she was pretending.

"Lorraine, did you hear me?" he asked standing in front of her with three plastic grocery bags in his hands.

"Good afternoon," she said, feigning surprise, "I didn't even hear you come in."

She acted as if she didn't have a care in the world. And was successful at that.

"How did you enjoy your day out?" she asked him, putting the knitting down and turning off the radio.

"Yes, I did," he answered vaguely, walking through the room toward the kitchen.

"I'm so sure," she said sarcastically under her breath.

"How was your day?" he shouted from the kitchen.

Arthur emptied the contents of the bags on the countertop. There was a little spring in his step as he busied himself with putting everything away in the cabinets. He was even whistling a bit. That he couldn't explain, but just went with it. He was in good spirits and he didn't have a problem showing it.

Meanwhile Lorraine said something he didn't hear. "It was wonderful, just wonderful. I turned on the radio because the rain almost put me to sleep."

It was important to sound convincing, that everything was just peachy keen. She wanted him to believe that she had been doing the same boring thing the whole time he was away.

"I picked up those shortbread cookies you like so much," Arthur said entering the room.

"Why, thank you dear."

He turned, and gave her a wink and a smile. "Did you hear anything of interest on the news?"

To her bewilderment, he walked over to her, gave her a quick peck on the cheek, and then proceeded to sit down in his comfy beige suede chair.

"Same old boring talking about the same old boring stuff," she said vaguely because she needed to say something, as she had just turned the radio on shortly before he arrived.

"I figured as much. Otherwise you would be telling me all about it," he said, shifted in his chair. "Was your day all right?"

She looked at him in surprise. Apparently, he didn't get that she had already told him. He didn't look as if he heard what she said earlier. Lately, he was often preoccupied with his own thoughts or wasn't listening to anything she said.

Rather than get irritated about it, she decided to repeat herself, this time in another way. Looking at it from her perspective, in her mind she thought that she was the one who got the better of him, not the other way around.

"Oh, Arthur, please. I have been sitting here all by my lonesome. There is nothing to report," Lorraine said with a devious grin and a silly giggle.

Chapter 11

TWENTY-FOUR YEARS OLD. It seemed like everything was moving so fast. It was already Monday, September 4, 2017, my birthday. I was prepared for it. So, I told myself as I dressed this morning.

Should I be traveling? Should I be engaged to some man? What type of presents did I want? I didn't have an answer to these questions because I was still clueless about what I wanted.

Before leaving the house for work, I found Siobhan in the kitchen and told her my decision. I settled on dinner and a movie. It was the only thing I was in the mood for. And she came up with the perfect place to go after work.

Around seven o'clock in the evening, there were only six other people in the Cinema 'N' Drafthouse on Pilgrim Street when Siobhan and I walked in. This indicated we'd have the place to ourselves, at least for a while, and that suited me very well.

Thanks to Siobhan, there was a VIP area set aside. One table was sectioned off in the center of the room near the 16-foot wide-screen mounted on the wall. Siobhan was good enough to arrange it all by telephone ahead of time. I considered myself fortunate to be her closest friend.

The joint, designed in an art deco lounge atmosphere, was popular with the twentysomethings for beers, pizza, and its Monday night movie series. The movie *Red Riding Hood* with Amanda Seyfried and Gary Oldman was playing tonight. It was released in 2011 before Siobhan and I started attending the university. Because we had not seen this film before, I was curious to see what I had missed because of the hype surrounding it.

"Welcome to the party. Follow me please we have a table already set up," I heard Siobhan say aloud to Aunt Eowyn as I headed for the bathroom.

I didn't bother to say hello. Rather, I decided to save it for when I returned.

On my way back from the bathroom, I peered out the window of the restaurant. My gut told me Casey wasn't coming, but that didn't stop me from looking.

Staring out into the dark moonless night, I reflected on the crazy spur of the moment decision, I had made when I asked Casey to meet me here and how he accepted my invitation. It seemed so silly of me because I met him for the first time at work earlier today.

Returning from lunch, I was hurrying past the elevator to a patient's room. Casey stopped me as he came out of the elevator and asked if he was in the right place. He was visiting his grandmother and wasn't sure what room she was in. I walked him to the reception desk to verify. In the process, we started talking and seemed to hit it off. For reasons beyond my comprehension I asked him to be my date for tonight. I didn't even know his last name. Plus, on top of that, I didn't even give him my phone number.

When I came back into the room, I saw Siobhan and Aunt Eowyn talking quietly at the table. They looked like they were sharing secrets no one else should know. Drinks had already been served. There was a glass of iced tea in front of Eowyn and two bottles of Guinness for Siobhan and me.

Though she was in her late fifties, time had been kind to Aunt Eowyn in its own special way. Apart from the merest graying at her temples, her shoulder-length hair, done up for the occasion, was as blond and thick as ever. She had aged gracefully without much change. She looked as lovely as ever wearing a forest green and dark pink plaid dress under a thin, pink shawl.

A smile broke across Aunt Eowyn's face as she flashed her blue eyes in my direction and put out her hand for me to come to her. She stood up from her chair and greeted me with a big hug and kisses on my cheeks. I felt like I did as a child and Aunt Eowyn would comfort me.

"Myrna, look what I got you. Your favorite," Aunt Eowyn said when we separated.

She handed me a Juicy Couture gift bag and inside was a large bottle of Viva La Juicy perfume and a white silk scarf imprinted with Fifi Lapin illustrated bunnies. My aunt's generosity put a smile on my face. To some degree, no matter how old you got to be, you would always be a child in the eyes of your relatives. That was surely true with Aunt Eowyn. I thought the world of her. For years she had been my guiding light.

Aunt Eowyn sat down again. I took my seat in-between her and Siobhan.

"Where's that person you said you met today? No Casey?" Siobhan asked.

"You figured that out pretty quick. No, I'm afraid not," I said depressingly.

With raised eyebrows, Eowyn Dymtrow threw in her two pence. "I don't know about men these days."

"You and me both," Siobhan joked.

My aunt took the words right out of my mouth. Men, as of late, no luck in that department. The last time I went out with a guy was on a double date in a cinema. He was a friend of a classmate from the university. I never saw the guy again, nor did I remember his name.

Since they were in a joking mood, I thought I would throw in the funniest thing I could think of and pull their leg a bit.

"I never said Casey was a him. I would have said it earlier, but you two didn't give me a chance to talk," I said in a nonchalant fashion.

When they both looked at each other stunned, I laughed again and said, "I was just kidding."

"You are?" Siobhan said, on purpose to extend the joke.

Siobhan broke up laughing when I looked at her funny.

"You girls are too much," Eowyn said and laughed too.

A young light skinned Hispanic waitress arrived with a large vegetable pizza on a round tray and carefully set it in the center of the table. She left and quickly returned with three red-plastic baskets of popcorn that she placed on the table.

"Enjoy it," the waitress said, then turned and left.

"So, what if I was totally stood up on my birthday?" I questioned and shrugged my shoulders.

"It's his loss. Drink up that beer and you'll forget all about him," Siobhan threw in.

"It's for the best, Myrna. You would have broken his heart and you know it," Aunt Eowyn added.

Siobhan took a bite of her pizza, then talked with her mouth full, "You've got that right!"

"You guys are so silly," I said, and laughed even more.

Siobhan drastically changed the topic and moved away to a different place. "You look great, by the way."

"Thank you for saying that. I needed to hear it," I replied.

The song "Castle on the Hill" by Ed Sheeran playing in the background was fading out slowly and the lights were dimming. The movie was starting. I sipped my beer and watched along with everyone else in the restaurant, which now had over twenty people. In the course of the evening, more people had shown up.

When the movie was over, the lights were popping up here and there. I was surprised by the singing of *Happy Birthday* by the guests.

The Hispanic waitress came from the kitchen into the room. She was holding a chocolate cake with lit pink candles on top.

Everyone in the room clapped when I blew out the candles on the cake the waitress had placed on the table in front of me.

"Don't forget to make a wish," Siobhan whispered loudly.

"And many more," someone yelled from the back of the room.

There were more laughs and more clapping. They were pretty rowdy.

I didn't know what to wish for, and just smiled. All the kindness so many had shown me, made me so grateful. It was a nice way to end the evening.

Tonight, in the company of Siobhan and Aunt Eowyn, the people I cared the most about, I was completely satisfied. I treasured their companionship, and the three of us had a lot of fun together.

It felt like one of those rare moments in life. Yet, I couldn't help but wonder if we would all be happy like this ever again.

Chapter 12

THAT NIGHT I had a horrible dream. I was standing in a graveyard, watching a funeral in slow motion. The problem was it was mine.

"Myrna, everything is okay. Take a breath and relax," I spoke in a low tone to myself.

Still unsettled by all of it, I wasn't ready to leave the bed yet and didn't need to either, because it was my day off from work. I tossed and turned eventually stopping to rest on my back. Then I started analyzing this strange nightmare while it was still fresh on my mind.

A vicar was at the burial site doing what he could to administer to my dead body that lay in a simple black casket with white satin trim. The tall, middle-aged man dressed in black and wearing a clerical collar was standing by the half-opened casket and a deep hole in the earth reading Scripture from the Bible.

There were no other people around.

I was gazing at my face, my hair, my neck, at all of me in view. When the priest gave the sign of the cross over the casket, I saw my body twitch, and I thought to myself, 'I'm not dead.'

Needing to make sure I was alive; I came closer to the casket. A moment later I saw my eyes blink open.

The priest closed his prayer book and slipped it under his left arm. Using his right arm, he closed the casket door with all his strength. The casket began to lower into the hole.

"Stop! I'm alive, for God's sake!" I yelled at him. "Why are you doing this to me?"

The white-haired man with sharp blue eyes ignored me — or rather my other self, the one on the sidelines, watching it all unfold. He bent down, put his hand into the soil and lifted it up. Then he raised himself upwards and threw a fistful of earth on the casket in the hole.

"Didn't you hear me? I told you I'm not dead," I yelled to the vicar again.

Still, he ignored me. It was as if I wasn't there. It seemed I was completely invisible to him. And all I could do was watch the horrible scene.

I came closer to the edge of the hole because I heard a noise that sounded like a wooden door opening. Sure enough, the casket door was open. Shockingly, my body was floating up and out of the casket.

The priest didn't seem to notice me. But the second he saw the other me ascending from the hole, my body floating in mid-air, he took a couple of steps backward and stood still.

When he took a vial of holy water from his jacket pocket, twisted off the top, and splashed it on my body, I saw myself hiss at him. He stepped away in fear, clutched his Bible to his chest, and his lips moved in silent prayer.

Something even more surreal happened. I saw myself transform into a bat.

The bat let out a horrible screech as it came closer to the priest. He put the Bible under his left arm and made a cross with his fingers to ward it off. The bat screeched loudly, flapping its wings furiously, and then flew away.

It was eerily scary, but not over.

"I told you I wasn't dead," I said to him.

This time he looked in my direction and gave me a cold stare with a defiant, lifted chin. He lifted his arm and pointed his finger at something behind me but didn't say a word.

I turned around to see what he was pointing at. About five feet to the left of me, stood a German Shepherd dog. A low growl rumbled up from his chest upon seeing me. Then he barked and growled in a manner that made my blood run cold.

Standing there, confused, I couldn't even scream. You would think at some point I might have started to run away. Truly, I didn't understand what I was thinking.

The vicar looked upon the scene with a grin. He opened his Bible and began reading Scripture, occasionally glancing in my direction.

Next thing that happened was a darkness fell all around me. The vicar was nowhere to be seen. The only thing I could see was a pair of red eyes of the dog growling at me. Now I was frightened.

In seconds, I took off, running in the pitch black. I was terrified beyond belief, trying to find my way out of the dark. I looked over my shoulder briefly and saw those horrible red eyes in hot pursuit. What did this animal want with me anyway? I dreaded to think about it.

Looking front again, I saw a dim light approaching. I ran toward it and found myself in a dark forest. I looked up at the trees so tall they touched the sky that was covered with dark clouds. Raindrops fell on my face and hair from the start of the rain.

Frantically, I looked back to see the German Shepherd still following me. I turned my head back to the front and ran faster and faster, while the rain was pouring down on me. I kept looking for a way to escape, but I couldn't find one.

It was there that the dream changed again.

Suddenly, I emerged from the forest and I found myself right back where it all started for me, in the graveyard. I was running so fast I didn't have time to stop myself from falling into the hole where the coffin had been. I kept falling and falling into this bottomless hole until I woke up in my bed.

This was the oddest dream, to date. I hoped these strange nightmares I'd been having, over two weeks now, would go away. Was it a premonition of sorts?

I turned over on my right side to look at the clock on the nightstand. It was almost eight o'clock in the morning. Turning to lie on my back, I tossed my white and purple plaid blanket to the side.

My mind returned to the dream. Perhaps it was inspired from the movie I watched yesterday. That seemed a logical explanation. *Red Riding Hood*, about a primitive medieval village stalked by a werewolf, was quite corny, to say the least. Apparently, the movie left an impression on me.

To prevent another nightmare, I must remind myself not to watch scary movies. Next time, it would be a romantic comedy for me, which would do me some good.

All thought of the matter had vanished from my mind when I smelled the scent of eggs enter the room. I rolled over onto my left side, closed my eyes, and breathed in the aroma.

Siobhan was making the breakfast as she usually did about this time of day. It was a hobby of hers. Cooking was therapeutic for her, took her mind off the stresses of her job.

In the meantime, I needed to drag myself out of bed. I was pressed for time. Siobhan left for work at eight-thirty on the dot because her shift started at nine.

Actually I wasn't hungry for anything other than conversation. I really wanted to spend some time with Siobhan. After having such a crazy dream, I would feel better talking to her. She often had feedback, some degree of insight regarding the way my mind worked. My imaginative mind might amuse her more than anything else. Well, I thought so.

Chapter 13

STANDING ON THE LEDGE of the roof of Wightwick Hall, Ileana Vladislava was staring into the tranquil wooded valley of Jesmond Dene. At around five o'clock on a Wednesday morning, the beautiful urban woodland was shrouded in dense gray fog. She loved this time of day, the pre-dawn hours, for hunting.

How else could this lonely vampire survive?

Her body ached all over from the dire need of blood. Her thirst was deep, and her eyes were glowing red.

Her intense vision caught sight of a couple of roe deer feeding on the grass. She was pleased by what she saw.

She took off fast, moving with a purpose straight down the side of the castle wall to the ground sixty feet below her. It was a sight to see how her long-nailed feet glided down the wall as if she had glue on the soles of her feet to prevent her from falling. Such was the way of a vampire.

The fog that blanketed the woods, helped to conceal her. She was crouched behind a huge rock in the almost total darkness, peering around for any sign of the deer seen earlier.

A lone kingfisher glided into a pine tree and perched on a branch way up high above. Its keen eyes took in the view. It spotted something of interest, Ileana Vladislava, something that seemed out of place in the bird's sanctuary.

For a short spell, the kingfisher eyed her as she climbed a large rock and fell into a crouch. That was her hunting position. Another look or two, then the bird left the branch and flew past Ileana's head, vanishing into the fog.

Time was of the essence. Ileana would like to get this over with quickly before the clouds evaporated and the sun blazed upon her. Additionally, the heat from the rising sun would dissipate the fog and bring her out in the open, clearly something she wanted to avoid.

She turned her attention to a buck about seven yards from her. The lone deer was leisurely grazing. It would have to do.

The fog swirled in and floated above the grass near the buck. He lifted his head to look around. Suddenly, he saw Ileana and stared intently at her. There was no reason for him to be afraid. Her face was soft and open while she was staring down from the rock. She didn't carry any weapon, nor did she display any threatening behavior such as a vicious look or strange sounds. It was an odd circumstance, as the animal had no idea the intentions of Ileana.

When the buck lowered his head to feed again, her face changed into a fierce expression. Her eyes were slightly red, and her fingernails began to protrude as she altered into full vampire mode.

The time to strike was now.

Gradually, she began her descent from the rock. While he wasn't paying attention to her, just continuing to graze.

She slowly stepped away from the rock, careful not to rouse him. As she drew nearer the buck jerked his head up quickly, sensing danger. He looked directly at her. The wild fiendish expression on her face frightened him so much that he ran off.

It was of no use because she ran faster than the buck imagined possible. Effortlessly, she chased him down and tackled him to the ground. As soon as her teeth pierced into his flesh, he yelped in pain.

Ileana was sprawled on the ground on her hands and knees. She had drained as much blood as possible from the body of the animal. Slowly, ever so slowly, she pulled her teeth out of the buck's neck. With the sleeve of her black linen tunic, she wiped away the blood of the animal from her mouth and chin.

After extracting blood from the his neck with a needle attached to a plastic bag, she quickly placed the plastic bag of blood inside her crossbody and tossed the bag over her shoulder.

Softly the wind blew now, through the trees around her. During which the sun was coming from behind the clouds. She needed to act quickly.

Rising to her feet, she blew out a big breath, and dusted off the soil from the knees of her black leggings. A convulsive, gasping sound was heard. Looking to the ground, she watched the buck take his last breath, and then expel it in a snort. He was gone.

She was fully contented with the kill. Best of all, she left no trail behind, confident that no one could trace the kill to her. For all these years gone by, she had become quite adept at covering her tracks.

Once again, she reminded herself that no one believed in vampires. And she was sure there was no reason for anyone to believe in them.

Right before she left the woods, she looked back over her shoulder and took a final look around. There was no one in sight.

In the last of the morning's darkness, she was fast approaching her sanctuary on Jesmond Dene Road, returning by the same route she'd traveled countless times over the years.

Strolling across the sprawling grounds of Wightwick Hall in the most inconspicuous manner possible, she didn't mind it all that much, that the name came with the property. The way she saw it, there was no reason to change it. It was a significant part of the history of Newcastle upon Tyne.

To Ileana, Wightwick Hall was just home, nothing all that special. The rich history of her place didn't appeal to her whatsoever. The only history that mattered to her was her Romanian past.

As discreetly as possible, she quietly moved closer to the castle's entrance.

Suddenly, she stopped near some shrubbery. She had felt a sudden chill in the air and experienced the prickly sensation of hairs rising at the back of her neck. Subconsciously there was something about it that bothered her, but she wasn't quite sure what it was. Was something out of place?

On the off chance that anyone could be watching her, not that she suspected for an instant that anyone was. And for the heck of it, she turned and took a quick look around. At that moment, she sensed someone.

Ileana took a gander in the direction she sensed the aura. She was looking at the Krag's house. Not a moment sooner there was a face staring at her.

Someone had noticed her, which wasn't good. Lorraine Krag was at her living room window, peeking out between the curtains. Ileana couldn't believe it!

What was Mrs. Krag doing awake at this time of day?

"It just couldn't be a coincidence," Ileana declared under her breath.

Ileana's mind was spinning with emotions. Her eyes began to go red. Right now, she needed to think straight. She didn't know what to do, until a thought suddenly came to her.

Ileana looked upon the woman with fierce eyes with the intention of frightening her, to death would be even better. That was how mad she was.

Sure enough, seconds later, she saw Lorraine Krag cower away from the window. Ileana felt complete satisfaction and turned her attention back to the castle. With a confident look on her face, she slipped inside through the front door. For now, she didn't have to say anything to placate Mrs. Krag.

Chapter 14

LORRAINE KRAG had just closed the curtain, feeling as though she was in a trance, and forced herself to turn away from the living room window. She scrunched up her nose at the thought of the staring match she just had with the woman of Wightwick Hall.

"How did she know I was looking? Could that woman have discovered my interest in her?" Lorraine asked herself those questions as frightening thoughts ran through her mind.

A cold chill rushed down her spine, her mind still troubled by the image of the creepy expression on the face of that woman. Standing there, frozen in fear, she spent the next few minutes, thinking about it all, attempting to decipher the strange look that had been on the woman's face. The woman's stare had been so intense that Lorraine felt a presence around her, like she was right there in the room with her. It was like the woman had peered into her soul. And she had felt it deep in her body.

Now she thought of the reason she was at the living room window just before six o'clock in the first place. Was it worth revolving all the circumstances in her mind? Could she just let what happened go and start anew? Not a chance. It was just in her nature to brood about it.

Twenty-five minutes ago, an animal scream startled her out of her sleep — the abrupt sound of something dying. Although the noises outside were not as loud as they had been in the past, the sound had a sense of urgency. It irritated her because she knew the animal was in distress.

Why did it happen at the same time, in the wee, wee hours, before the crack of dawn?

Oddly enough, the animal sounds never bothered Arthur. He never thought there was anything wrong with it. But she knew different.

This time she wasn't going to disturb his sleep to avoid the third degree from him. What was the point? She knew him all too well. He would tell her there wasn't anything out of the ordinary and ignore it and go back to sleep.

She had a sudden notion so strong she climbed out of bed with her hair a mess to check it out. The whimpering sounds that the animal made disappeared before reaching the living room window. And she couldn't see in the predawn murkiness. What made matters worse was the misty fog surrounding the castle and thereabouts.

It just didn't sound right, she thought to herself. It sounded like the animal had been attacked. If only there was a way to determine what was happening to those animals. She looked down at herself and realized she couldn't go outside searching for an injured animal wearing nothing but her pink, short-sleeve nightgown that went down below her knees. God knows what she might find out there.

As fate would have it, she poked her head round the curtain again. Straightaway, she saw that woman walking toward the entrance of her castle. Lorraine eyed her suspiciously, staring at her with a questioning look on her face. What made it suspicious was that the woman was coming from the direction of where she had heard the noise of the ailing animal. Unexpectedly, the woman stopped in her tracks and stared right back at her.

Lorraine pulled her thoughts back to the present. But she was so snarled up that it took a couple of more minutes to gather her composure, erasing that woman's face from her mind.

In her gut, she knew something was wrong, and that woman was somehow involved with it. What could she do? She had yet to discover what was going on with that woman. But Lorraine Krag would.

Was it wise to continue spying on that woman? Should she stop before something happened, she might regret?

For a moment's thought she took it under consideration.

"Not if I have anything to do with it. Might as well, Lorraine," she said, her tone rising slightly as she lifted her shoulders up and down.

It was as if she forgot everything that had happened earlier. She was back to her old self again, no longer shook up by seeing that woman.

Perhaps she was reading too much into things. Maybe it was all coincidence. It was likely that the woman just happened to be looking in her direction. It probably didn't mean anything. So she shook it off and chalked it up to her imagination.

It occurred to her she didn't even know the woman's name. How could she know her name? She pondered the thought for a moment, and then shook her head.

"Something else I have to do," she said mischievously.

Maybe Arthur was right about her being nosy by nature and inserting herself in other people's business. All the same, she just didn't care anymore. She gave in, succumbed to the idea that she was curious about that woman, and that was the end of that.

She looked at the clock on the wall. It was 6:02 a.m. What should she do now? What were her plans for the rest of the morning?

It was time to prepare the breakfast. Of course. That was what she always did at this time of day. But first a quick trip to the bathroom. She needed to freshen up, and brush and fix her hair.

Before she took a step forward, she paused to collect her thoughts. Then she shrugged to herself, and laughed a bit too, though not too loudly.

As she headed to the bathroom, she thought it was best she kept certain things to herself. As much as she wanted to confide in Arthur, she just couldn't bring herself to talk about what had happened earlier. He would say it was her fault for spying on Wightwick Hall again. He would treat her like she was a meddling troublemaker. That was just how he saw her.

After leaving the bathroom, she felt remarkably cheerful. The splash of cold water on her face had made all the difference.

In the kitchen, she set a carton of eggs on the counter. Looking out the kitchen window, she saw the rays of the coming sun cracking the sky. Almost a minute later, she heard Arthur walking toward the kitchen.

"Good morning, Lorraine," he said sleepily as he shuffled into the kitchen.

When she heard him speak, she quickly turned around. "Good morning, dear."

He was still waking up, getting his bearings as he tied the belt of his dark blue bathrobe around his body over his light blue pajamas.

She held an egg in each hand. "Sunny-side up or over easy?"

Noticeably, he seemed startled by her cheerful mood. When she realized she was sporting a smile from ear to ear, she consciously told herself to close her mouth. She didn't want to appear suspicious. Least of all, she didn't want him to ask unnecessary questions. Thereafter, she relaxed herself and put on a simple, pleasant expression.

Chapter 15

ILEANA VLADISLAVA came out of her kitchen. As she walked down the hallway, her mind filled with something she had almost forgotten during the past twenty minutes. She had caught Lorraine Krag spying on her and she didn't like it one bit.

She knew the chilling stare she had given Mrs. Krag wasn't enough to really scare her. Sooner or later, she might find out the truth about her. That Ileana couldn't afford.

The question was — what could she do about it?

Once her mind was well rested, she would have to figure out something to do — or not to do — about it. After such an eventful pre-dawn morning, she resigned herself to the cellar. She desperately wanted to hang from the ceiling and sleep.

Yes, Ileana was ending her day around 6:00 a.m. when most people were starting theirs. She slept in the day and hunted in the night. The vampire's routine went that way.

After walking down a flight of stairs to a door, she opened it, and went into the dark. Then she climbed up the wall onto the ceiling.

Her feet clung to the ceiling and she crossed her arms over her chest. When she closed her eyes, her mind traveled to a time long ago before she became a vampire. Images of her past in Transylvania had the strangest way of sneaking into her mind at the oddest of times.

For some reason she was thinking about her mother, whom she was fond of. Even though she had little memory of her. In November 1517, when she was eight years old, her mother died of influenza. A few months before she had died, Ileana remembered running in a field toward her for the comfort of her mother's embrace. Still, she could feel the warmth of her mother's arms and the slap of the tall weeds and grass against her legs.

Following that came the worst years of her life.

After her mother's death, her father lost his way and turned to booze. He wasn't mean to her, just neglectful. Some days she didn't have anything to eat or drink because he had spent almost all his money on alcohol.

She spent the rest of her childhood engrossed in household chores her father couldn't perform. It was the only way she could keep the place from looking like a pig pen. Also, as an only child, having no siblings, with whom to interact, she occupied her loneliness with the chores.

It was a hard life for a young girl. Often she cried. She hungered for something better.

Years later, she became a vampire at the age of thirty-one.

Was the life of a vampire better? She thought it was. And, after that thought, her mind slipped into a deep sleep. Yet, a tear streamed from her left eye and fell to the floor.

At half past four o'clock, she awoke to the sound of loud knocking on the castle's front door. What in the world? Could it be Lorraine Krag?

The knocking came again. That was it. Ileana quickly came down from the ceiling. She wanted to know who it was.

"Miss Vladislava, are you there? It's April Fielding," a voice called out from outside.

She couldn't make the connection. *Who is April Fielding?* Ileana thought, feeling nervous.

"Yes, this is Ileana," she said from behind the door.

"I'm from Pike Nurseries. I have a delivery for you."

"Oh, yes, thank you. You can leave it on the doorstep."

"I can't do that this time. This shipment of Dactylorhiza grandis, the Blackthorn Strain marsh orchids require your signature."

Ileana opened the door a little less than halfway, saw only a purplish pink flowered plant. "Where do I sign?"

April Fielding carefully placed the orchid she was holding in a box on the ground. In her late teens April wore lots of makeup on her face, including blood-colored lipstick on her full lips. Her medium-length hair was bleached blonde. She was wearing a three-quarter-sleeved black shimmery shirt, jeans with holes at the knees, and black combat boots.

April reached into the back pocket of her jeans, and pulled out a crumpled piece of paper. "Good afternoon, Miss Vladislava."

When she opened the door wider, she squinted her eyes from the sunlight. She wasted no social graces on April, and pried the pen and paper out of her hands.

After signing her name to the paper, she handed it and the pen back to April. "Anything else?"

"Well, yes, I have to carry the box inside."

"Proceed," Ileana said reluctantly, and opened the door all the way.

After stepping inside, April set the box down in the foyer, and looked around in awe. "This place is spectacular!"

The girl was too curious. Ileana wondered if she had lied about the delivery requiring her signature.

"Thank you for your assistance," Ileana said in a way that indicated to her that she had overstayed her welcome.

"Okay, I'll see you next time," April said, taking the cue, and walked out the door Ileana was holding open.

"Next time?" Ileana asked in a low voice as she shut the door.

Despite sleeping ten hours straight, she was still tired. After she carried the box of orchids upstairs and dropped it outside the door of her greenhouse, she walked to the cellar for some more sleep.

Fast forward. Some hours later. She woke abruptly feeling uneasy. Looking on with wide eyes, she remembered the last thought which had been in her mind before she fell asleep, the first time, namely the unhappiness of her life before she was turned into a vampire. Things she didn't want to remember.

Most important to her was the vampire's life. The vampires in Transylvania were the family she had longed for. Now they were gone. Now she was alone. But she wasn't sad, nor depressed. She was just lonely.

To ease her mind, she would watch a scary movie.

She took a short walk to the media room in the basement. The clock on the wall read 11:36. She did not remember the last time she'd slept so many hours.

Reclining into the large brown leather sofa, she grabbed the remote control from the round oak coffee table. Flipping through channels on the 55-inch flat screen TV mounted on the wall directly across from her, she found a channel showing a movie she wanted to watch.

All was silent in the castle except the sound of the television. The 1922 silent film *Nosferatu: A Symphony of Horror* had started at midnight. She was completely engrossed in the horror tale, a vampire story.

A scene in the movie made her raise an eyebrow. She had an odd look on her face, because she never slept in a coffin like the emaciated vampire portrayed by Max Schreck did in the movie. However, she could if she wanted to. Long ago, it was a custom of some vampires in Transylvania. Occasionally, she slept in a sleigh bed, which resembled a coffin, in one of the intimate guest chambers of the castle. More often than not, she slept hanging upside down from the ceiling of the cellar.

Another odd expression graced her face when the vampire in the film disintegrated in the sunlight that streamed in through an open window. She didn't expect that to happen.

A little sunlight wouldn't hurt her. She was amused by the fanciful stories of ignorant people. Although she knew it wasn't their fault. How could they find out the truth about vampires?

It was 2:00 a.m. when the movie ended. She switched off the TV and tidied up the sofa.

After climbing the spiral staircase, she walked down the hallway to her study. When she entered the room, the thought of Mrs. Krag returned to her.

Ileana shrugged as she went to the window for a look outside. She pulled aside the thick burgundy curtain and saw the Krag's house in the distance. Staring out into the dark night, she was already irritated, even though she knew they were asleep in their bed.

What was she going to do about Lorraine Krag?

The question resonated in her mind. Her fangs slipped out of her mouth. She lifted her left hand toward the direction of the Krag's house, made a claw shape with her fingers, and growled, "Ugh!"

Chapter 16

AT TEN TILL TWELVE, I was in the middle of placing a plate on a table in the residents' dining room located directly across from the nurses' station. Lunch was about to be served.

The clatter of silverware hitting the floor shook me out of my thoughts.

I looked in the direction of the noise and saw Elizabeth Guderian standing beside a dining table, clutching her chest with her right hand. She appeared to be having a heart attack.

As I ran to help Ms. Guderian, I yelled to an orderly who was standing near the kitchen entrance. "Get the doctor!"

Too late. Ms. Guderian backed away, bumping into a chair, which fell to the ground, taking her with it. The heart attack was fatal. By the time I reached her, it was obvious she was dead.

Careful not to get blood on my tan slacks, I dropped to the ground on my knees, reached forward and lifted her left arm, feeling for a pulse at the wrist. There was no heartbeat, nor any sign of breath.

There was a small pool of blood around the seventy-something black woman's head and some had splattered on her rose-colored cardigan she wore over a burgundy nightdress. Blood leaked from a gash in her head, which had hit the floor hard. Despite my nursing experience, I was a little squeamish at the sight of blood.

Joyce Gunn arrived on the scene with Dr. Ajay Patel to examine her and asked me, "Myrna, did you find a pulse?"

I nodded my head, because no words would come out — only tears.

Joyce's face was exasperatingly sad when the doctor rolled Ms. Guderian from her side onto her back. The doctor checked her heart with his stethoscope.

Less than a minute later, the thirty-something, dark-haired man of India descent dressed smartly in khaki dress pants, and a tan dress shirt and blue tie under a white lab coat, had that glazed look in his eyes, that she was dead, confirming what I had already knew. It was so sudden and unexpected, and it crushed me.

It was like I felt everything come to a halt. All at once, thoughts hit my mind like a ton of bricks.

Something inside me just didn't want to deal with it anymore. I stood up from the floor, trembling. Now that it was time for my ten-minute break, I needed to go somewhere and get my emotions in check. Still, with tears in my eyes, I quietly left the room without saying a word to anyone.

As I walked down the hallway, I wiped the tears from my eyes with a tissue I had pulled from the pocket of my white, short-sleeved, smock with a maroon caduceus embroidered on the chest pocket. Going outside for a breather was needed despite the fact the break area was where the smokers hung out. I couldn't stand the smell of smoke. But I was willing to endure it because I needed a release from the horror of seeing Elizabeth Guderian fall to her death.

Walking up the stairs toward the roof terrace of the building, I thought about how I had seen patients die before, but this death felt different.

It was easy to get attached to the patients. Even though the management advised not to. But how could I not? I saw them every day and was responsible for their care and well-being.

After having a few conversations with Ms. Guderian, I became fond of her. She was born and raised in Liberia, West Africa. After marrying, she moved with her husband to the United Kingdom in the 1990s. Her husband died the same year her daughter moved to London for work reasons, during which time she fell ill and ended up here.

The moment I opened the door of the terrace, the freshening breeze comforted me. After walking over to the edge, I put my hands on the cement railing, and took a bunch of deep breaths and felt rejuvenated.

As I stood there and looked at the buildings in the distance, I felt I needed to re-examine my life and my job because this felt like the most terrible Friday I ever had. Was this what I really wanted? I kept asking myself, because I felt as if I wanted to go somewhere else and start all over again.

It took a dramatic event to stir up feelings I had locked away. I needed something more meaningful in my life, and I sensed it was coming soon.

If it did come, I would give in to it, I just knew I would. I had been waiting for such a long time for something magical to happen in my life.

Just then I heard the faint sound of music. It actually sounded pretty magical. I could hear it coming from the Tyne Theatre and Opera House on Westgate Road. How I longed to be there watching that ballet.

It felt terrible to admit to myself that I had never seen a ballet and certainly never taken a ballet class. I felt I deserved a little fun and yet, most of the time, I never did anything except work.

It wasn't that I was selfish. I took this job because I like helping people. Siobhan and I felt the same in that manner. But she was dedicated to the job. And I was barely getting through each day, feeling that I was more or less flying by the seat of my pants, so to speak.

It was so strange because I always thought I was doing the right thing. Yet, I felt it wasn't the life for me.

In all the passing thoughts one surfaced. I was lonely. While preparing for work this morning, I fantasized about meeting someone special. Maybe I would go to a bar after work. But there was no way I would let myself do that on a work night — which meant almost every night for me.

I wouldn't be working this weekend. However, I would be busy with housework, activities with Siobhan and helping my aunt.

It wasn't like I wasn't aware that I was making excuses that kept me from having a relationship.

There was always the possibility that I was shying away from relationships because my parents died; because I was afraid somebody I love might die — that I feared losing someone again.

My other concern was that I was turned off by men. Most guys I met were boring, immature for their age, or stood me up. I wasn't sworn off men. My experiences weren't all that bad, but they weren't all that good, either.

I glanced down at the watch on my wrist and saw that the time was 12:25. Just a little more than ten minutes had passed, and I couldn't stay outside any longer. I needed to return to work before Joyce wondered where I was.

As I grabbed the handle of the door with my right hand, I turned my head around for one more look at the Tyne Theatre and Opera House. I couldn't help but listen to the music chiming from that lovely Victorian building. It felt odd, because I really wished I was there.

Once again, I felt that desire for some kind of change. A change I would gladly embrace with all my soul if it came my way.

I put the thoughts away and concentrated on work again. As it stood, I was already late. I turned back toward the door, opened it, and slipped back into the building.

Chapter 17

BY THE OFF CHANCE, Ileana Vladislava found herself in a seat in Box CC on the Grand Circle level of the Tyne Theatre and Opera House. She was enjoying a Friday matinee performance of *Romeo and Juliet*, her favorite ballet. It was one of the rarest treats she allowed herself to indulge in. She was even dressed in the way that was required for such an occasion. She wore a black cashmere cardigan over a black with white orchids silk, frilly blouse, and black dress pants.

The day before she had read in the newspaper that the Russian State Ballet would present the ballet for the next two weeks at the Tyne Theatre and Opera House. She needed to get herself there. From the telephone in her study, she called the box office and bought one of the last tickets available for the almost sold out performances.

Despite sleeping only five hours, a bright eyed and bushy-tailed Ileana watched the stage closely. It was a scene from Act One. "The Dance of The Knights" by Sergei Prokofiev played to her great delight. She found pleasure in the music more than the dance itself.

Despite a few empty seats, given how crowded the place was, she felt completely alone, as if she were the only one in the theatre. It was as if she didn't exist — technically — she didn't. Her world was made up of herself only.

The chair on Ileana's right was empty, and she didn't pay any attention to the old woman seated on her left. She didn't socialize with anyone. She made herself transparent to those around her and had learned over the years to come and go rather quickly. Everyone seemed to be engrossed in the ballet, and she was grateful no one seemed to notice her.

When the intermission came, the old woman seated next to her politely excused herself to the bathroom. For only a brief second, she spoke to Ileana who in return nodded.

The lights in the theatre blinked and a bell rang three times to signal that intermission was almost over, so the old woman returned to her seat. She merely smiled to Ileana before sitting down. Ileana nodded again in return, as she wasn't comfortable engaging with people.

The old woman was pleasant enough looking and very well dressed, Ileana thought. Her white hair was coiffed, and she wore an elegant cream-colored gown with beaded trimming and a cameo brooch at the collar, and a beige shawl wrapped around her shoulders.

The dancers returned to the stage, and the old woman peered at them through a pair of opera glasses, held by an ornate silver handle.

When the performance concluded, Ileana raised herself from the chair and left with everyone else. She walked down the stairs behind the slow-moving woman who had been sitting next to her.

Soon enough, the old woman's pace was beginning to irritate Ileana so when she saw an opening, she took advantage of it. She plunged into the lobby and let herself sway with the crowd. It was easy for her to disappear into the crowd, something she was exceptionally good at and had done so many times before.

That was when it happened. By some sheer coincidence, and with all of the hustling and bustling of the people, she accidentally bumped her right shoulder against the left shoulder of no other than Lorraine Krag.

And Ileana had tried so hard to avoid attracting undue attention.

Lorraine was flabbergasted by the incident. And of course, you would expect her to be.

She turned to face Ileana squarely and arched an eyebrow. Yet Lorraine didn't recognize her. How could she? She had never seen Ileana up close nor ever spoken to her.

On the contrary Ileana recognized her, did her best not to show it, and opted not to acknowledge her. Rather she behaved like a passerby completely indifferent to the situation and Lorraine didn't seem to think any differently.

"My word," Lorraine said, gave Ileana the once-over and openly stared at her waiting for an apology.

Lorraine wasn't going to be ignored. It was in her nature to always be suspicious of people she thought were sufficiently pretentious anyway. For the moment she focused all her frustration on Ileana, the woman who had intruded on her space by so rudely brushing up against her.

Ileana was so amused by the gaudy way she was dressed, that it took a moment for her to respond. Lorraine was wearing a blue chiffon long-sleeved dress with silver sequins all along the neckline, and a big white hat with a blue ribbon around it was in her left white-gloved hand. Ileana kept her chin down, her eye on the exit, and tried to hide her smile.

"Well?" Lorraine asked and squinted her hazel eyes, scrutinizing her while waiting for a response.

"Pardon me," Ileana said in a low voice without even a glance at her, as she was fed up with her already.

"Well, I never! Some people," she said, with her nose in the air, and swiftly turned her back on Ileana, just as easy as closing a door.

Lorraine Krag had to have the last word.

Ileana kept walking toward the door to exit the theatre just as Arthur Krag came out of the men's room. When he reached Lorraine, he noticed she looked distressed. He couldn't help but ask why.

"Is everything alright, dear?" he asked, bewildered by the expression of annoyance on her face.

"There is something strange about that woman. I just can't put my finger on it," she said turning around and watching Ileana walk out the door.

"Oh, Lorraine, that's what you say about everyone."

She glanced at Arthur with raised eyebrows and said with disdain, "Just forget I said anything. Let's get out of here!"

Outside the theatre, he followed behind Lorraine who was wearing her hat now. Lorraine was already nitpicking about the three-minute walk to the Grainger Town parking lot on St. James' Blvd where Arthur had left his Nissan Leaf. He took it all in, not getting a word in edge wise.

Arriving at the car, he unlocked and opened the passenger's door for her, allowing her to enter and sit herself down.

Just before he closed the door, he interrupted her yapping, and changed the subject by asking, "Did you enjoy the ballet?"

"What?" she asked as if she didn't know what he was talking about.

"The ballet you watched."

"It was fine, thank you," Lorraine said and immediately put on a fussy face, threw up her right hand, and locked the seat belt in place.

"I'm glad to hear," he said and slammed the door shut.

Arthur shook his head as he walked around the rear of his car toward the driver's side. He wanted to remind her what the day was supposed to be about. Even if it didn't last for more than a minute.

When Arthur got in the car, she gave him the look. He'd seen it before. Without saying a word, he just started the Nissan and proceeded to back out of the space he was parked in.

Lorraine almost said something but changed her mind.

"Hmm." It was the only thing that came out as she turned her head the other way, and simply looked out the window.

Chapter 18

IT WAS DARK and cold in the cellar. And just the way Ileana Vladislava liked it. It was around eleven o'clock on a Saturday morning, and she wasn't sleeping. Not more than a few minutes earlier, she was disturbed out of her sleep by a hairy spider crawling on her.

Using a broom, she brushed away the cobwebs in the corners of the ceiling. When a small black spider fell on her left arm, she brushed it off with her right hand. It fell on the floor and she trapped it in a corner and crushed it, pressing the weight of her body onto the broom handle. It was extreme, but it gave her great relief.

With a satisfied feeling, she put away the broom in the closet near the door of the room. Then she looked around and decided not to go back to sleep.

As she left the cellar, she took in the quietness of the castle. She wondered what she was going to do for the rest of the day. It was a question she had asked herself before. Maybe she should read something. This thought came as she strolled through the foyer, where she saw the newspaper and the scattering of mail on the floor below the front door slot, where the mailman had shoved them through.

She scooped the mail up and headed down the hallway toward the library. Once inside the room, she sat down in a Venetian chair of ebony and inlaid all over with mother-of-pearl. The chair was positioned by a dark brown cherrywood end table and a bookshelf with an ideal collection of classical novels, her very favorite books in the world. She loved the library so much that she had decorated it with expensive art and antique furniture.

After turning on the Victorian table lamp, she glanced through the letters, all promotional mail, nothing of interest. She dropped the junk mail on the end table. Then she read *The Journal's* full-page review of the ballet *Romeo and Juliet*. She was pleased with the commentary.

A couple of minutes went by and she was bored already, something that often happened to her. She closed the newspaper and placed it on top of the mail on the end table. For some time, she leaned back in the chair and stared at the bookshelves.

At long last, she stood and searched for something to read. It wasn't surprising she had already read every book there at least twice.

"Not this one. Not again," she said to herself as she looked at some of the books on the shelves.

Tired of perusing the shelves, she sat back into the Venetian chair. Her mind started to wander and before anything else she started feeling isolated and lonely. Most times she could handle it, but there were times, like now, when she thought the loneliness would overwhelm her. Its intensity was such that she felt she needed to go somewhere.

That was when another thought came to her mind. To improve her mind, she decided to go to the Newcastle City Library to look at the shelves to see if there were any interesting books. It seemed like a good idea, since she was already suitably attired, wearing a three-quarter sleeved thin gold sweater that ended mid-thigh and tan colored leggings.

But first she needed to check the weather. She stood up from the chair, went to the window and poked her head out of the curtain to look. Casting her eyes toward the sky, it was cloudy, yet, it wasn't raining. Just as she liked it, a little dark in the afternoon.

However, to be on the safe side, she pulled out a pair of sunglasses from the drawer of the end table. The sun's rays irritated her eyes, not enough to be in any danger of blinding her, but enough to trouble her. She slipped them on as she headed for the closet in the hallway where she kept a pair of sneakers.

After exiting the castle, she entered the garage. She stared at her lovely silver Bentley Continental GT two-door coupe. It was only two years old, and she fancied it. It fit well with the British people as if she were one of them. She kept it in pristine condition, though she rarely drove it. And today was no exception.

She would take the Metro to Monument Station.

Less than a ten minutes' walk, the Ilford Road Station was a comfortable distance away. She exited the garage, turned, and took the shortcut through the woods so she could cut her walking time in half.

The short trek through the woods brought her to the station's entrance. She stepped on the sidewalk, walked through an entrance toward the ticket machines, and reached into her crossbody for money to pay. After purchasing a ticket, she slipped it in another machine to enter the surface level platform.

The only other people waiting were a senior couple in their 70s — most likely husband and wife. Neither of them looked at Ileana as she crept further down the platform and positioned herself against a wall in a shadowed area under the awning, where the light did not quite reach.

While patiently waiting for the train to arrive, she stared off in a trance. Her mind was starting to drift away. Although she wasn't thinking about anything in particular.

The sound of the approaching train brought her to the present moment. Before coming to a screeching halt, the train sent a gust of wind in her direction.

As the doors opened, the subway car's overhead lights flickered on and off at the same time Ileana stepped inside. Like a blink of the eye, you could hardly see her physically enter the car. No one on the train noticed her.

Typically, Ileana sat alone in the corner of the car by the connecting doorway to the next car, the usual seat she took. Despite the distance she kept from others, she could feel their energy around her. And of all things, she kept her sunglasses on.

The train tore out of the station the instant the doors closed. It entered a tunnel and disappeared into the dark.

Chapter 19

 and I was on the Metro train on my way to the Newcastle City Library. The library was my favorite retreat, an ideal refuge from the grind of work whenever I could spare myself. Since I was a young girl, I loved reading, especially fantasy because it occupied my mind with something other than thoughts of missing my parents that I loved so much.

About an hour ago, I awoke with a feeling of anxiousness. Since yesterday I had been struggling with self-doubt stemming from the sight of Ms. Guderian falling to her death, and probably would feel this way for the next day or so.

I sensed I was at a crossroads in my life.

With questions racing through my mind, I had stayed in bed a few extra minutes. I was in a trance. Was I satisfied with my life? Once more, that nagging, and recurring question popped into my mind. Was I feeling this way because Siobhan Mulcahy was on top of the world in her career and seeing her often just reminded me that I wasn't where I wanted to be in life?

Thanks to sleeping in later than usual, I was slightly saddened that I had missed seeing Siobhan before she left. If she was off work today, we might have done something together. Then I thought, maybe it was for the best because I needed to get my head together. Some time alone with my thoughts would do me good.

That was when I decided on a trip to the library. Checking out a book to read over the next days might improve my state of mind.

I had checked the weather from the window, and I didn't see anything to brighten my day. It was cloudy, looking like it could rain any moment. Which wasn't the kind of weather I should drive my scooter in. But I think it was all for the best because of the mood I was in, it would feel good to sit back and let someone else do the driving.

So, here I was sitting on the Metro, and I thought, sometimes I feel like I was born generations too late. People living centuries ago seemed to have things easier. The simple ways of the past interested me so much that I often read fairy tales or romance classics such as "Emma" by Jane Austen. When I was at Northumbria University, I even took many literature courses just so I could read.

The quiet train ride kept me lost in my thoughts. I didn't even notice that I was twirling my dirty-blonde hair clockwise with my left index finger. It was a nervous habit I had picked up when I was a child.

My gaze turned to the face of a thirty-something Rastafarian man with dreadlocks, a wide nose, and fat lips dressed in a faded denim jacket and jeans, seated across the aisle staring at me with bulging eyes with blue contacts. There was a puzzled look on his face, as if he were trying to understand something. Men sometimes acted like that around me, unless he just happened to be glancing in my direction.

Maybe I'd caught his attention when I was playing with my hair. He seemed nice enough looking, but I wasn't interested in communicating with him.

Tucking my hair behind my ear, I tried to ignore him and stared out the window. Before I could think any more on it, the train had just stopped where I needed to get off. Surprisingly, I couldn't help but notice him looking me over as I left the train.

I traveled up the stairs from the lower level concourse of Monument Station. After exiting onto Blackett Street, I turned the corner and saw a Pret A Manger across the way on Grainger Street. The delicious aroma coming from there told me that I needed to eat. I carefully considered my sudden craving for a cup of tea and a sandwich.

The library could wait.

Stopping in my tracks, I turned on my heel and made a beeline to the restaurant. Inside, the place was chock-full of people. Unfortunately, there were no tables left outside or inside. After making a purchase, I ventured over to a stool facing the window counter.

Nobody else had said anything to me besides the clerk behind the counter. While I was eating, I drew only an occasional glance — and awkward at that — from some of the men at the tables. I was accustomed to simple flirting from the opposite sex, but nothing had come of it, I thought sadly.

Despite the crowd, I felt so alone as I sat there. You would think I wasn't there. Sometimes I felt as if I didn't belong anywhere. It seemed that people either ignored me or avoided me. It made me feel like an outsider. As I looked around the place, I wondered about all of that.

There I was again, thinking in depth, and analyzing all the things I kept deep inside.

An outside table became available, and I thought about sitting there, but changed my mind when I saw that Rastafarian man walk by. That very same man from the train. Perhaps it was just happenstance that he'd been walking too fast, preoccupied with his thoughts, or he would have seen me.

It was best not to think on it anymore. I took the last bite of my brie, tomato and basil baguette and dusted off my hands. Then I continued sipping on my large cup of organic Earl Grey tea and stared at the passersby from the window.

I finished up my tea and the rest of my rosemary and olive oil kettle cooked chips and decided to take an even longer route to the library. I just wanted a little more time to myself, more time to think.

Exiting the restaurant, I walked on Blackett Street for a stroll through Old Eldon Square. Seemed like a good place for sightseeing.

Chapter 20

 I could see that it was packed with people. There was something happening over there, maybe it was worth a glance.

When I got there, I found that the high-spirited crowd was assembled watching some live event. Apparently, this had been going on for some time.

Looking in the direction everyone was facing, I could see a man that looked like a master of ceremonies of a circus, fair, or other variety show. And he behaved as such a person in charge of an event.

Off the bat, I recognized him. It was the man with the curvy mustache. It was another odd coincidence, seeing that man who had been leaning against a wall on Sandhill the night Siobhan Mulcahy and I came out of Hunan Manor celebrating her promotion at work.

The man looked even more mysterious in the daylight. I noticed that besides having a hound's face, his nose was shaped like a bird's beak, his cheeks were hollow, and his large ears were set at right angles to his skull.

He was wearing wooden stilts under long black trousers to go with his black top hat and long black tuxedo jacket, which made his height overpowering. And again, he was holding a wire leash to a brown monkey, which he commanded to perform tricks. And it did.

"Isn't it adorable?" I heard someone mumble behind me.

The man handed a cane to the monkey. The little furry critter balanced the cane upright on the ground in front of him, and then without touching it, he moved his paws around it, and the cane danced all by itself. This got the crowd's attention, and some people clapped.

In between a trick, the monkey found time to take interest in a handful of pigeons squawking around. The monkey walked to a bird closest to him and reached out its hand to touch it. It flapped its wings and flew up to the sky causing the other pigeons to scatter.

At the end of the monkey's performance, people clapped their hands, amused by its tricks. The monkey took off its red velvet hat, gave a solemn bow, then held the hat out to the people, some of whom put money in it. The whole spectacle made me laugh.

The money collected made the man smile.

"Jasper, say thank you to the people for their support," the man said to the monkey.

"That's it," the man said, after the monkey bowed to the crowd.

The man went on to say that the money was strictly for the care and maintenance of his pet. It didn't matter because the people wanted to make a donation. And nobody was complaining.

Twice I caught the man's deep-set green eyes looking my way. A short while after that, I saw him staring at me oddly as though he had seen me before somewhere — as indeed he had. Perhaps he remembered seeing me on Sandhill with Siobhan.

The way he looked at me, it was like I was the only one in the square. He stared at me for only a minute or two and in that time, I couldn't shake his stare. It was as if I was in a trance or under some magic spell.

While I drifted off in a cloud of thoughts, I was wondering what he was thinking because it wasn't a look of attraction. He wasn't checking me out, rather it was a look of concern. Then I thought I was reading too much into it, because I suddenly felt as if everyone on the street were staring at me.

It felt very odd, until he stopped looking at me because the monkey handed him the hat filled with money.

"Hello, Viktor," a man with a Jamaican accent called out and then asked me, "So, what you think about that?"

The man with the monkey, whose name I had just learned was Viktor, turned around and just nodded his head to the man who called out his name. I whipped my head around to see the man who had also said something to me and saw that Rastafarian man I had seen on the train.

How many coincidences could I possibly have in one day? Was there a full moon behind those clouds? These questions danced around in my mind as I stood there staring at him, surprised he had spoken to me.

As far as I knew, he hadn't followed me. I was positive about that. He acted as if he didn't remember me from the train and, like, he had just nonchalantly asked me a question. And by the way he was looking at Viktor and his monkey, I wasn't even sure he'd seen my face. He seemed genuinely amused by it all.

I finally said politely, "It is some spectacle."

"Yes, I agree. I've seen Viktor here many times before. Nothing surprises me in this city."

After he said that he turned and looked at me straight in the eye, like he wanted to say something else. Then a look of remembrance came into his eyes.

After a momentary pause, he spoke again. "Hey now, I think I saw you on the Metro. Yes. I know I have."

It was pretty convincing, and it didn't seem like an act, either. So, I went along with it.

"Yes, I remember seeing you there."

"And now you're here too. What a coincidence! I hope this is a sign of good things to come. Oh, yes, I sure hope so," he said, quite jovially.

He was personable enough and easy to get along with. I decided not to think too much on this casual encounter. The more I thought about it, I convinced myself that it was nothing to be alarmed about. Still, I fought the urge to babble about anything particular in order to stop the conversation from going any further.

It was time for me to go when I noticed him staring where he shouldn't be looking, where he couldn't stop looking.

"Well, it was nice to see you again. But I must be going."

"Maybe, I'll bump into you again sometime."

"Maybe you will."

"My name is Lonnie Trigg. So please don't forget it."

"Sure thing," I said with a smile.

Weaving my way out of the crowd of looky-loos, I saw a sudden movement out of the corner of my eye and swung around to see Viktor shoot a glance at me. I turned my eyes forward again, uninterested in analyzing it. There were more important things for me to do, such as go to a library.

I was ready to escape from it all, especially from all the emotions running through me. Reading an adventurous novel, was the only way I knew how to do it. It was all I could do just to keep myself from coming unhinged.

In the distance I could see dark clouds in the sky looming just over the library. It had gotten dark quickly I thought to myself as I came closer to the building. It might rain at any time and I didn't have my umbrella with me. I could only hope my choice to wear my waist-length white Burberry rain jacket with detachable hood would be enough if I got caught in the rain. It was lightweight, waterproof, very comfy, and went well with my red and white long-sleeved, buttoned-down shirt and blue jeans.

My plan was to be at the library for a couple of hours at most, but I might stay longer if the rain comes. I would wait out the worst of it if that be the case. It was something I kept in the back of my mind as I walked up some stairs on New Bridge Street West.

Chapter 21

AT ABOUT TWO THIRTY in the afternoon, as I quickened my pace, eager to get indoors, I couldn't help noticing a well-proportioned teenage girl with bleached blonde medium-length hair sitting on the steps near the entrance of the library. What caught my attention was the graphic tattoo of a vampire chick with blood dripping from a fang on her right shoulder blade. Her grayish-blue eyes were distant, yet focused, and she turned her head slowly as if she were looking for someone.

When her glance fell upon me, she caught me admiring her tattoo, and her expression changed to one of indifference. She gave me the once-over from head to toe, pulled her cat styled sunglasses from the top of her head to cover her eyes, and turned her face in another direction. It struck me as rather odd, that she was wearing sunglasses on a cloudy day.

Without another thought about that girl, I walked through the library. I knew exactly the kind of book I wanted. Eager to find something, I started shuffling through stacks of index cards in a drawer of the card catalog against the wall.

When I felt cool air on the back of my neck, I stopped searching. Nevertheless, if someone had hurriedly walked by, when I turned around to look, no one was there that I could see. In fact, I was surprised that there were few people at the library.

When I closed the small drawer of the card catalog, I felt a breeze again. I looked over my shoulder to find a raven-haired woman leaning against a shelf holding a big book about the opera in her arms, looking directly at me. It was possible she had sent a small breeze in my direction because she was the only person in view.

The woman seemed to recognize me, though I couldn't recall where I'd seen her. Whoever she was, her brown eyes were all over me, studying me. But why?

The look she was giving me, which was hard, made me feel like I was important in some way, and this was peculiar. Even more peculiar was that I didn't even think about looking away because I was just as curious about her.

A minute later, she stopped looking at me, and placed the book she was holding on the shelf in front of her. So, I guessed it was just by chance that she had been staring at me. What else could I think?

I began to walk toward the shelves in the fiction section, thinking I'd pick up something sort of at random.

Moving quietly down an aisle between two bookshelves, I felt that somebody was watching me. To be more precise, I felt a presence nearby and wondered if someone was there.

The lights flickered above me. For a second there, I thought the electricity was out. But it all happened so fast because within seconds, the lights flickered on once again and returned to normal intensity.

Automatically, I looked up and around and that was when I saw that woman, the one who had been staring at me. By some kind of twist of fate, she was in the aisle directly across from me.

Unable to move, I froze in complete surprise. What was up with this woman? Now she was walking toward me, and our eyes met. The closer she got I could tell she was fascinated by me like she had found what she was looking for.

My brain couldn't process why she felt so familiar. Somehow on a psychic level, it was like I knew her.

She stepped into my aisle. There was nothing to be afraid of. Maybe she wanted to ask me something or maybe she just wanted to talk to me. I kept wondering.

As I stood there in the middle of the aisle looking at her, waiting to hear what she would say, the lights flickered off again. I briefly looked up toward the ceiling. As the lights came back on, I looked back to where she had been standing. She just wasn't there anymore. It was as if she just vanished into thin air.

She wasn't in the next aisle, either. I looked around the library and realized that she was nowhere to be found. Again, and again I found myself stopping, expecting to catch her looking at me from somewhere. Instead I saw a heavyset, older woman librarian wearing reading glasses with a chain attached and very white hair perched on a tall stool behind the checkout counter looking at me funnily. Probably because of the spooked look on my face, her eyes had fallen on me.

I went back to the same aisle where I'd last seen her. Now I was interested in talking to her, but she wasn't there. Where could that woman have gone off to?

So, I leaned up against the bookshelf and started thinking. The only conclusions I could draw were that she just turned around and left when she realized I wasn't the person she thought I was. Or she was going to say something but changed her mind. Outside of that, I was clueless.

Before I went back to searching the shelves, for some reason I thought of that woman again. I realized how attractive she was with European features. She was maybe in her early thirties. And there was something different about her, something I couldn't quite pin down, and it bothered me that I couldn't.

Would I ever see her again? I sure did want to.

Ever so quietly, I said to myself, "Okay, Myrna. Slowly breath in and out. Close your eyes, clear your mind, and then open your eyes again."

That felt better. And, then, at last, I returned to the bookshelf. I picked up the first book that stood out. According to the description on the back cover of "The Secret Garden" by Frances Hodgson Burnett, it was interesting enough.

I went toward the front of the library to checkout. The older woman librarian who looked at me funny before was still looking at me kind of funny. What could I say? I was just having one of those days.

The librarian slid off the stool and said, "Good afternoon."

"Good afternoon to you to," I said and handed her the book with my library card on top of it.

"Myrna Ivester how are you today?" she asked, looking at the name on the library card.

"Fine, thanks for asking."

"Is this what you were looking for?"

"Yes, that's it."

"You should enjoy reading it," she said with a wrinkled smile.

"I can only hope."

When the librarian told me the book was due back at the library in three weeks, I didn't say anymore. I simply smiled, took the paperback from her hands, and stowed it in my crossbody bag.

Bolting out the library door, flustered, all I could think about was getting out of there. That whole thing with that mysterious woman had left me feeling adrift.

The fresh air was helpful, but the darkness reminded me rain could come down. As I headed down New Bridge Street West toward the tube station, I noticed the sky had become hazier.

Feeling somewhat tired, all I was really interested in was getting back home — the sooner the better. The day had been long and odd. I tried not to remind myself that it wasn't over yet.

Chapter 22

APRIL FIELDING had recognized Ileana Vladislava as soon as she walked out of the Newcastle City Library. She remembered meeting her some days ago at Wightwick Hall when she delivered a box of orchids, for her after school part-time job as a sales associate at Pike Nurseries.

April put the sunglasses back on her head, tucking them into her hair, and stood up from the steps. Here was her chance to converse with Ileana, and she didn't want to miss it.

Holding a Hello Kitty rectangular metal lunchbox for a purse in her left hand, she rushed to catch up with Ileana who was moving at a fast pace like she was following someone. April noticed too that Ileana was caught up in her thoughts that she didn't notice her approaching.

April hurried up behind her, called out her name and waved a greeting, "Miss Vladislava, wait up!"

She could tell by the way Ileana abruptly stopped on New Bridge Street West, that she seemed surprised to hear her name in the silent air. Ileana turned her head and looked at her with questioning eyes, and appeared not to recognize her. And by the blank stare in her eyes, it was apparent she was waiting for April to say something else.

"What a coincidence finding you here. I was sitting on the steps when I saw you leave the library," April said almost out of breath.

"And you are?" Ileana asked quickly.

"April Fielding. I delivered some orchids to you the other day from Pike Nurseries," she said while walking closer to her.

"Right. Well, good day to you," she told April curtly, and started walking ahead.

"Where are you going?" April asked, walking behind her.

"Apparently, to the Tyne and Wear Metro," Ileana answered, as if she weren't sure.

"Another coincidence! I'm going there too, and I wouldn't mind the company. I am seventeen, you know. It's not safe for young people to be alone in the city."

"You are? I mean by yourself?" Ileana asked seeming startled.

"All alone here in this crazy city."

Ileana stopped walking and stared at her intensely while she thought on the matter further. She appeared to have no clue about what went on in the mind of a teenager.

Apparently, it was difficult for her to understand the desires of youth.

"Well, come along then. Better hurry, we don't want to miss the train," Ileana said and started walking fast.

April hurried her steps to follow.

"Why aren't you at school?" Ileana asked her.

"It's Saturday."

Ileana looked at her puzzled and asked, "What do you mean?"

"There's no school on Saturday," April told her matter-of-factly.

"Indeed," Ileana agreed, feigning as if she knew.

"Why aren't you at work?"

"It's my day off."

To April, Ileana Vladislava acted as if she came from another era, and she was full of quirks. Perhaps April was drawn to her for the reasons that there was something dark and mysterious about her. For now, she was just going with it and was hanging close by Ileana's side.

"Where's your library book?" April asked with curiosity.

"I didn't check anything out."

"I know what it's like. It's not easy finding something that appeals to you."

"The air is cool to be without a jacket," Ileana interjected.

"I'm really okay with it."

"Nice tattoo," Ileana said, admiring the image of a vampire.

"Thanks. I'm really interested in things like that because I'm young and exploring life."

"Your platinum tongue ring is a nice touch, too."

"I got it done two weeks ago. And it didn't hurt like I thought it would," explained April.

They reached Monument Station's entrance on Blackett Street, proceeded down a flight of stairs, and passed through the ticketing area. Then they walked down more stairs leading to the lower level concourse and platforms.

When they reached the platform for the Yellow Line service, April noticed that Ileana quickly looked past her and around her either for the reason of looking for someone or checking to see if a train was coming. She could only assume the latter, as Ileana turned to her left and walked to the end of the platform.

From time to time, Ileana looked down the platform in a way that looked like she was looking for a train. April started carrying on about something about work at length and in great detail. While inside she thought about asking Ileana something.

"Not that it's my business, but most people use their plants to make a garden. I was just wondering because I haven't seen any of the many plants, I have delivered to you outside Wightwick Hall."

Just as it looked like she was going to answer April, the light from the train appeared in the tunnel. The rumbling noise the train made was too loud. She figured there was no point in Ileana answering her until the train stopped.

Suddenly, Ileana turned and started walking down the platform. Despite the peculiarity of this act, April followed without question.

The train came to a stop and the doors opened. Ileana stepped into a car with April in tow behind her, following her to the end of the car.

Once they were seated, Ileana said, "I have a greenhouse. That's where I keep all the plants you have delivered."

"Awesome. I would love to see it," April said as the train started to leave.

"Remind me next time you come with a delivery," Ileana said reluctantly.

"I most definitely will."

From the way they were seated, anyone seated in the middle, or on the other end of the car, would not be able to see Ileana.

"Jesmond Station is coming up next. That's my stop," April said.

"This train travels so fast," Ileana said, peering around the room.

"I appreciate you escorting me, watching out for me. I hope it wasn't any trouble for you."

"It wasn't any trouble for me. I hope you get home safe," Ileana said monotonously.

"There are two more stops till the train comes to Ilford Road Station. That's where you're getting off?"

"You are quite right," Ileana agreed.

"Don't go to sleep, or you'll miss the stop."

"Thank you for pointing that out. I shall remain awake."

April lastly said, "It's been nice chatting with you. I look forward to seeing you again soon."

As the train came to the station, Ileana gave her half a smile as she stood up, walked, and stood in front of the sliding doors waiting for the train to stop so she could exit.

Chapter 23

IT WAS SOMETIME AFTER four o'clock in the afternoon when I was sitting on the train and I saw her again. Something made me look up just before the train came to a stop at Jesmond Station. That teenage girl with bleached blonde hair and cat styled sunglasses on the top of her head, dressed in a white T-shirt, black leggings, and black combat boots was standing by the doors at the other end of the car. It was the girl that had been sitting on the steps near the library. I knew it was her because of the vampire tattoo on her right shoulder blade.

Until now, I hadn't noticed her. And I couldn't help but stare at her in awe knowing that she had been in the same car with me the entire time.

The strangeness continued when I saw her turn her head in my direction, almost looking right at me. I couldn't tell whether she recognized me from earlier or not, when she stepped off of the train and onto the platform. Before I could give any reaction to that, the car doors closed.

The young girl was nowhere that I could see through the window as the train pulled out of the station.

A discomforting thought came to my mind. Was it an omen? I quickly blotted out the idea of any such thing.

Suddenly, I remembered how earlier, an eerie feeling came over me that someone was watching me while I was waiting on the platform for the train to come in. It was an odd presence that I could not explain. I wondered if I was being stalked. And if so, why?

Which now I was thinking it had to be that girl. She must have arrived at Monument Station sometime after I did, and I didn't see her among the people gathered. Still, I couldn't say for certain though that she was the one watching me.

Paranoia was starting to set in. I breathed out a sigh. It was just a random occurrence and I was jumping to conclusions, I started to tell myself. She was just a stranger passing by, like two ships passing in the night.

The overheard lights in the car flickered off, which tore apart my thoughts and brought me back in the present. Next came the sound of the connecting door between the cars being opened. A sudden rush of wind brushed my face as I looked in the direction where the noise emanated from. Strangely enough, it was the same breeze I had felt in the library.

"Get the lights back on," an irritated voice called out.

When the overhead lights sputtered and dimmed, I saw a shadow moving there — or rather someone — going through the connecting door. Not too many seconds later, the lights came back to full power. There wasn't anything there anymore, so I decided to ignore that one.

My thoughts fell on the woman that had been eyeing me in the library. I would like to know who she was. But how could I find out? Why couldn't I stop thinking about her? She wasn't a figment of my imagination either. It wasn't like me to have visions of women ogling me.

Feeling a bit out of sorts, I needed to remind myself that the woman probably thought I was someone else. Yes, that made more sense to me than any other explanation. What else could it be?

How much this was troubling me, when, out of the blue again, that creepy feeling returned. It was as if someone had me in their sights. When I looked around, I didn't see anyone watching me. Either they were good at following people without being noticed or I was losing it.

It was best that I filled my head with a story rather than give in to paranoid fears. That would be the only way to keep my sanity in what was the strangest day I had ever had. I opened up "The Secret Garden," the book I had checked out from the library and started reading the first chapter. It would occupy my mind for the duration of the train ride.

The train stopped at another station once again, but I didn't bother to look up. I kept my nose in the book and concentrated on reading every word. "The Secret Garden" was much more interesting than I had anticipated.

A few pages later in the chapter, I heard the announcement for South Gosforth Station coming next. At that point I was relieved, closed up the book, and tucked it into my crossbody bag. The good thing was that the reading had helped to distract me from the strange occurrences of the day.

I stood up and walked to the doors. While I was standing there, waiting for the train to stop, I thought about how I just wanted to get home, crawl into bed, and read more of the book. On top of everything else, I was still feeling tired.

Thinking about all that had happened earlier in the day, I wasn't sure if I should tell Siobhan. It all was so confusing to me. Actually, I didn't want to tell her, because I wasn't ready to talk about it with anyone.

Soon, I would be back to my old self again. After tonight, none of this stuff about someone stalking me would matter. All of it would be a faded memory.

When the train reached my stop, I couldn't wait to get out. The doors opened and I hurriedly stepped onto the platform. My smartphone started ringing as I approached the exit. I quickly pulled it out of my crossbody bag to check on it. The caller ID told me it was Siobhan. I answered on the third ring.

She told me not to be surprised that she wasn't home yet because she was still at work. Alysa Pitely, her coworker, had called in sick. She was putting in overtime hours and she would be home around eleven.

"If I'm sleeping when you come in, I'll talk to you in the morning," I told her before I hung up.

When I reached Haddricks Mill Road, I was glad it wasn't raining and continued on my merry way.

Chapter 24

BACK AT WIGHTWICK HALL, Ileana Vladislava was in her study, seated in a Victorian armchair. Not in a long, long time had she smiled like this. She kept seeing Myrna Ivester with her eyes open or closed and couldn't think about anything else. 'Myrna was perfect' were the words that kept ringing in her ears over and over again.

No music was playing in the study. Not this time. She needed the peace and quiet so her mind could wander freely. Her heart was thumping wildly in her chest. She thought of Myrna's beautiful face — fair complexion, wide-set blue eyes, full lips, but most of all, the very core of her lost soul.

It wasn't uncommon for Ileana to take interest in a woman. Vampires weren't restricted by gender. It didn't matter. She felt connected to Myrna, something beyond lust, rather psychological. There was a spiritual bond between vampires that went beyond physical attraction.

"Yes, her hair," she said to herself.

Myrna's long dirty-blonde hair that hung loosely over her shoulders was enough to turn anyone's eyes. So, Ileana was thinking.

It was apparent that a scheme was forming in her mind. That Myrna Ivester could be with her if she were a vampire too. There was no other way they could have a relationship.

After all this time, maybe fate was rolling things her way. It was time for two of her kind, she kept saying in her mind.

Her eyes were wide — off in her own world again.

Earlier that afternoon, she was following Myrna to Monument Station at a safe distance. She didn't want to look like a stalker. So, she had allowed April Fielding to tag along with her to shield herself from suspicion.

Sitting in the same car of the Metro train, she had noticed that Myrna seemed to recognize April. How was that so? Myrna watched April as she left the train and stepped onto the platform of Jesmond Station.

Shortly after the train left the station, she slipped on her sunglasses, threw open the connecting door and went through it to the next car. All the while the overhead lights in the cars went out, then on again. She leaned against a wall and watched Myrna through the window of the connecting door for the rest of the train ride.

Later on, she followed Myrna home.

Ileana Vladislava hadn't imagined anything like that, couldn't imagine where it might lead, from the first moment inside the Newcastle City Library where she'd seen Myrna. She remembered how she couldn't take her eyes off Myrna. She approached her, but at the last minute, she fled. It was all too much for her. She hid in the shadows, watching Myrna, and by chance she heard the librarian say her full name.

The thoughts had run through her mind over and over, but the conclusion was at hand. She had spent enough time meditating on the matter — anxious to make a decision — as she came back to the here and now.

She was filled with a desire, the like of which she hadn't felt since many years ago in Romania. For the first time since she left there, she was ready to create a vampire, in spite of the risk.

That the murderous werewolf was somewhere, hunting for vampires of Old Romania. Thus far, she had eluded the werewolf and would continue to do so.

There was no turning her back on fate. So many times, she had dreamed of a day when she would find someone who was meant to be a vampire. The day had finally come, and this was no dream — it was real.

It wasn't difficult for her to spot a person who was meant for the vampire's life. It was possible for her to peer into the soul of another human being, in the way someone would look out a window. She could see their inner thoughts with her natural skill for extrasensory perception. That and the immortal life was the vampire's gift.

Infatuation was driving her, but she didn't want to get ahead of herself. There was a question that needed to be answered. Would Myrna Ivester want to be a vampire?

The more Ileana sat there thinking about it, the more she believed it. She could sense a yearning in Myrna who seemed just as lonely as her. It was like something was missing in Myrna's life and it was that she wasn't satisfied. This convinced her that Myrna would embrace this life of hers, the vampire's life.

Or so Ileana hoped.

The plan was set. It was time to act on the desires that were consuming her. She was going to appear to Myrna in the late-night hours. If things didn't go the way she wanted, she would transform into a bat and fly away. It was simply something vampires could do.

The thought of tasting human blood once again invigorated her and reminded her that she needed some blood and she needed it now.

Rising from the chair, she left the study and proceeded to the kitchen. When she opened the refrigerator door, she found nothing inside. It completely slipped her mind that she had drank the last of the deer's blood. This was an unexpected predicament.

Leaning against the refrigerator door, her eyes were glowing red. The pain was intensifying. She needed to do something because her craving was strong.

She didn't want to hunt, for fear of being watched. Considering her nosy neighbor, she knew it was best to keep a low profile, at least for a while. Lorraine Krag could spoil all her plans.

The only option she could see was the hospital's blood bank. It wouldn't be the first time she had done it. She had taken bags of whole blood at different hospitals many times before, quite successfully.

After her trip to the hospital, hoping it would be successful, she would return to the castle, and store the blood in the refrigerator. Mostly likely a little after eleven, she would go to Myrna Ivester's home.

It was more than she anticipated, two such chances in one evening. Sensed it so strongly that it was going to be the night of nights, though; it was exciting just thinking about it.

Finally, she would give into her desires. And it was about time that she did.

Chapter 25

THE PATIENTS were tucked in their beds and the hallways were empty at the Freeman Hospital in High Heaton. The quietness at night in the hospital was eerie to Siobhan Mulcahy, even though she had worked during those hours before.

Sitting in the nurses' station in the middle of a hall, she was wearing her usual hospital garb, a white, short-sleeved smock with a small floral pattern on it, weathered brown slacks, and white sneakers. The name tag, pinned on the breast pocket of her smock, read S. Mulcahy, R.N. She tightened the ponytail holding her chestnut, shoulder length hair and began typing a few notes into the computer.

Her thoughts turned to how the scheduling of staff members for the coming weeks should be revised. Bingo! That was exactly what she would do. First thing Monday morning.

Alysa Pitely had personal issues that were affecting her job performance. And Siobhan was a little upset with her calling in sick, and for the third time in two weeks.

So, here she was, waiting for Alysa's replacement to arrive. She glanced at the clock on the computer screen — 10:27. Since nine that morning she'd been working at the hospital and right now she couldn't wait to go home.

She snatched up a patient's chart from the ordered stack on the desk. As she stood up from her chair, she reviewed the patient's history and physical progress notes

A sudden rush of air brushed past the back of her neck, jolting her out of her thoughts. It was cold on her skin and gave her goosebumps of fright. She turned around to look, thinking someone was there. But she didn't see anybody.

Her eyes moved back to the patient's chart, but she was unsettled about the strange way she was feeling. For good measure, she looked back one more time. Nothing.

Leaving the nurses' station with the patient's chart in hand, she turned left and walked down a semi-dark corridor. At the end of the corridor, she opened a door into a stairwell and hurried down the stairs to the next level. With a flash, she entered a corridor with a faint but familiar smell of disinfectant.

Her thoughts were disrupted by the sound of a door closing, not too loudly, but the hospital was quiet enough she could hear just about anything. She stopped walking.

Suddenly, the same cold gust of air that she had felt earlier surrounded her for a few seconds, and she shivered until it was gone.

Twisting around quickly, she gazed down the hospital corridor in the direction the noise had come from. To her surprise, she saw a woman dressed in a black clingy three-quarter sleeved sweater with matching leggings, and black boots leaving the Blood Issue room in the hematology unit. Then, with an alarmed look on her face, she started to approach the woman.

"Can I help you with something?" Siobhan called out to the woman.

The woman stopped walking. Then Siobhan stopped walking. It was eerie. Neither of them said a word.

Siobhan was waiting for a response. And just as it looked like the woman was going to respond. She couldn't begin to imagine what would happen next. The overhead fluorescent lights in the corridor went out, and she couldn't see anything in the darkness.

A couple of seconds later, some lights flickered on and off for a handful of seconds. Then all the lights in the corridor returned to full strength.

The weirdness wasn't over — the woman was gone.

Quietly, Siobhan crossed to the adjacent corridor. She didn't find anyone. It was as if no one had ever been there.

She decided to check the Blood Issue room. And there she asked herself, as she pulled the handle of the door, why wasn't the door locked as it usually was. Looking quickly around the room, she didn't see anything irregular.

After opening the Blood Bank refrigerator door, she thought there might be a few whole blood bags missing, but she wasn't certain. Regardless, she closed the door back up. There wasn't time to deal with it now. She needed to drop off a patient's chart.

After she left the Blood Issue room, she quickened her pace down the corridor and wondered if she had seen a ghost. She had never believed in ghosts before, but right now she wasn't sure what to believe. Maybe her mind was playing tricks on her, or maybe the raven-haired woman was never there at all.

More and more she was sure she needed a break from working too long.

After she placed the chart on a desk in an office, she decided she wasn't going to start believing in ghosts. Such a foolish notion, she thought to herself.

Not long after, she found herself climbing the dark marble stairs to the fourth floor. She was headed back to the nurses' station. When she arrived there, she found Shelagh Holton seated behind the counter, staring up at the patient monitoring board. This meant she could leave.

"Shelagh, so good to see you. Thanks for coming in on such short notice," Siobhan said to her.

"It's no big deal. How's everything going?" returned Shelagh, turning her smiling brown eyes on her.

"Since you asked, the weirdest thing just happened."

"Oh, please, tell me all the juicy details!" Shelagh said enthusiastically and stood up.

"I saw a woman come out of the Blood Issue room. I asked her a question and she stopped. The lights went out then came back on again. I went to look for her and she wasn't there."

Shelagh had been leaning against the counter listening to every word, twirling her carrot-top ponytail with a pencil.

"How sure are you that she came out of the Blood Issue room and not out of one of the adjoining rooms?"

"Actually, I'm not sure. I just got a glimpse of her."

"Maybe it was a member of the cleaning staff?"

"She wasn't wearing a uniform," declared Siobhan.

The twentysomething nurse beamed and said, "You know, when I think about it now. I've heard about stuff like that happening in hospitals all the time."

"You have?" Siobhan asked, surprisingly.

"I haven't seen anything, though, other nurses say that a lot of strange things happen on the night shift."

"Well, that's a relief. I feel better knowing I'm not the only one seeing things," Siobhan responded happily.

"Don't think about it anymore," Shelagh said and sat down on the chair.

"I'm not going home yet. I have to write up an incident report. It's the procedure. Before I leave, I'll put it on the desk for the blood bank technician to review first thing in the morning."

"There is always the chance that a patient with a life-threatening illness took the blood for their condition."

"It's a rare circumstance, but let's not rule it out," Siobhan said as they both laughed.

"Getting back to serious stuff," Shelagh quickly added, "the time has come for me to go. I have to check on some patients."

Shelagh Holton, stood up, lifted a clipboard off the desk and walked away.

It was half past eleven when Siobhan came home. She went directly to her bedroom. After changing into a lavender V-neck T-shirt and white with lavender stripes pajama bottoms, she fell onto the bed and enjoyed the stillness. She turned off the bedside lamp and dropped into sleep.

Chapter 26

AT AROUND MIDNIGHT, Ileana Vladislava had watched the lights in the house located on Lilburn Gardens go out. In the woodsy area nearby, she waited patiently to make her move. The night, that was overcast with darkish clouds, concealed her with its gloomy darkness.

Presently, it was coming up on two in the morning. The time was at hand for her to approach the house. There was a feeling of excitement from the adrenaline running through her veins.

Moving as silently as possible, she rounded the house to the back. As she approached the window with dense gray fog everywhere, it looked like she was emerging from a cloud-covered planet floating in the universe. It was too much like a scene from *Nosferatu: A Symphony of Horror*, the movie she had watched recently.

Her shadow appeared in the window. She was there.

As she watched Myrna Ivester in bed, devouring her with her vampire eyes; she could barely catch her breath. Ileana was very attracted to her.

Yes, she was going to do this!

With her gaze on Myrna, she used a vampire mind trick to place her in a hypnotic trance. She knew it worked when Myrna suddenly sat up in bed and sleepwalked her way to the window. It was as if an invisible force was pulling her toward Ileana.

Under the vampire's spell, Myrna had been whisked out of bed easily. Ileana's intention of luring her into the woods was to have her way with her, in a manner of speaking. There was no way Myrna could see what was happening in the sleep-like trance she was under. Instead Myrna's mind created a false reality.

Her mesmerizing eyes glazed over with passion for Myrna, who pulled the curtain to the side. She gave Ileana a quick glance then started to open the window, but stopped halfway, after receiving instructions to meet outside. Vulnerable — and obedient — to Ileana, she closed the curtain and proceeded toward the back door of the house. Myrna opened the door and walked to the woods.

Ileana was surrounded in fog so dense it blotted out all darkness, standing by a tree, waiting patiently. Her eyes were glowing a soft red that were magical and alluring to Myrna.

There was a bustling sound of the wind blowing through the trees as Myrna slowly walked toward her. Ileana stared deeply into her blue eyes and threw her into a deeper trance, that made her want to succumb to her.

Myrna stopped just inches away from her. She inhaled the intoxicating scent of Myrna's blood, as if it were perfume. Human blood. It teased all of Ileana's senses.

Ileana lowered her head to speak. "You're a beautiful sight."

There was no way Myrna understood the vampire language that had been whispered in her ear. Though out of practice in the art of seduction, Ileana remained confident, knowing Myrna wouldn't notice.

She came even closer to Myrna — until she stood face to face with her, just a hand's width away from her wide-eyed gaze. As Myrna fell increasingly under the vampire's influence, there was no turning away from Ileana.

Something was about to happen.

Raising her left hand, Ileana brushed back her long dirty-blonde hair that was hanging along the nape of her neck. The length of her neck was exposed, enticing Ileana to lean down and bite her there. With a shaky hand, she carefully used her fingers to locate the carotid artery. Eyes fiery red with anticipation, Ileana's fangs slipped out of her mouth.

Faint radiance from the full moon behind the clouds illuminated Ileana's vampire teeth when she said in the vampire language, "You've been waiting for this all your life."

The very long fingernails of her right hand rested on Myrna's left shoulder as her face came closer to her pale neck. And Myrna was so deeply under her spell she closed her eyes just as Ileana's fangs punctured her skin. The action caused Myrna's whole body to shudder with sensation.

And so, began the process that would transform Myrna Ivester into a vampire. Ileana Vladislava had accomplished her mission.

After draining a pint of blood from her body, Ileana's head slowly raised from her neck. When she brushed Myrna's hair back to where it was before, her eyes opened slowly. Still in a hypnotic state, Myrna was completely unaware of what had transpired.

Looking deeply into her eyes, Ileana spoke softly using the vampire language, "Go, my lovely."

The words echoed inside Myrna's head as she turned away and slowly walked through the woods toward the house.

A smile graced Ileana's bloody mouth, knowing that she had pulled it off without a hitch.

It was risky, especially knowing that her roommate Siobhan Mulcahy was asleep in her bedroom across the hall from Myrna's. Even more harrowing for Ileana was that Siobhan's bedroom was near the back door. Furthermore, Ileana pitied Siobhan for what she didn't know, for what happened right under her nose, unaware that Myrna had come and gone.

At the edge of the woods, she watched Myrna place a hand on the knob of the back door of the house Ileana quickly transformed into a bat. Before Myrna could open the door, the sounds of screeching and wings flapping in the air caused her to stop and look back at the bat.

The bat screeched loudly as it flew into the cloudy sky toward Wightwick Hall. Ileana had implanted the image of her castle in Myrna's mind, so that was what she saw. This was something only vampires could do.

Ileana knew that Myrna would return to her bedroom, crawl back into her bed, and fall into a deep slumber. Hours later, when Myrna would awake from her sleep, she might remember an image or two or nothing at all.

It was four thirty in the morning when Ileana, in bat form, flew through an open window on the second level of the castle. She landed in human form. After dusting herself off, she walked to the window and shut it.

Wearing a confident smirk on her face, she walked across the floor. As she was walking down the spiral staircase, she thought about stopping for a quick look in the refrigerator.

In the kitchen, she opened the fridge and admired the six whole blood bags she had taken from Freeman Hospital and stored the night before. At the time she stored the bags, she wasn't thrilled that she had been seen by a staff member of the hospital exiting the Blood Issue room. Ileana could only hope that the woman who had seen her thought she was seeing a ghost, from the way she fled in the cover of darkness when the lights were temporarily out in the corridor.

Now it seemed like ages ago; she had been at that hospital. She closed the refrigerator door and forgot about it entirely.

She left the kitchen and walked down the hallway toward the door that led to the cellar. Once she opened the door, she disappeared down the dark steps.

There in the complete darkness, she was hanging upside down from the ceiling. Before drifting off, she wondered what would happen next. There was no way to predict how Myrna Ivester might react. Would Myrna come to her?

Chapter 27

COMING OUT OF A deep sleep, my eyes fell on "The Secret Garden," the book lying next to me. I had fallen asleep reading it last night.

The reason I woke up was I sensed that someone was in the bedroom. It was dark. But I could feel a presence — that itch at the base of my skull telling me someone was there.

So, then how did someone get into the room?

After carefully looking around, I saw a steady breeze blowing the curtains aside, like someone was playing with them. Because the window was partially opened, I shuttered out of fear.

Utterly petrified, I slid cautiously out of bed, dropping my bare feet on the fuzzy rug. As best I could in the darkness, I checked out the room. The only light came from the LED display of the alarm clock on the nightstand. It was 4:43.

I flipped on the lamp on the nightstand. Nothing. Not a sound. Just in case there was an intruder inside my room, I checked the bathroom and the closet. They were empty. Then I walked over to close the window and peeked carefully out. Looking up at the sky I could see dark clouds. Though there were no signs of any rain.

To ease my worries, I walked around the house, turning on lights in the guest bathroom, living room, and the third bedroom we turned into an office. I also checked the front and back doors. Both were locked. I'd seen Siobhan peacefully asleep in her room too. So, I convinced myself that it was a false alarm and went back to my bedroom.

I picked up "The Secret Garden" from the bed and placed it on the nightstand. Soon after I laid out on the bed and fell to sleep.

It wasn't long after that I was having a wicked dream. A feeling of terror swept over me. As I was running in fog-filled corridors of a building of some sorts. My hair cascaded over my shoulders like a cloak. Someone was chasing me, getting closer and closer to me, which made me run faster. I couldn't see who or what it was. Thoughts of fear and confusion gripped me because I was hearing a strange voice creeping up on me from behind.

Not much later I was tired from running with knee length black boots on and hid behind a wall to catch mybreath. I hoped whatever was out there wouldn't be able to find me. Standing with my back against the wall, I took in some breaths of air and tried to shake the fear away.

Despite my fear, there was something in the back of my mind telling me that this was a dream. Somewhere in my subconscious, I knew I was not awake. Essentially, I was aware that I was inside a dream.

Still, I couldn't wake up.

The dread had subsided. But just for curiosity's sake, I peered from behind the wall. More importantly, I just wanted to know who was chasing me. Glancing down the fog-filled hallway, I swung my head from side to side trying to see everything. But I didn't find anyone there. Instead I heard a voice in the darkness. It called out my name in English and spoke a language I didn't recognize, some sort of Slavic or Eastern European language.

"Don't be afraid, Myrna. Come to me. I understand you. I'm a lot like you," the voice chittered at me in its odd language.

It was the deep voice of a woman. That I was sure of. Who was she? And what did she want?

Ducking back behind the wall, I kept trying to analyze it in the back of my mind that would not rest. A few more words were spoken, but I couldn't figure out what was being said, regardless of hard I tried.

Something else was odd. The place felt familiar to me, as if I had been there before.

As I stood there, collecting my thoughts, I remembered a time in my life. I imagined myself as a little girl again, came into my head just like a clear vision. I had been running down the exact hallways in the visitor's center building of some park holding a Raggedy Ann doll under my arm. The doll dropped from my arms. I kept running because at the age of five I had a lot of energy. Even I began spinning around in my yellow dress.

After searching in the corridors for my doll and not finding it, I was lost and began to get scared. All I could do was cry. My father must have heard me crying, because after a while he came from around the corner and scooped me up in his arms. He carried me to my mother, who took me in her arms to comfort me. After that, I didn't remember anything else.

What was I doing there, after all?

I almost cried in my sleep. But I didn't wake up.

The voice came again. Fear raced through my veins as I turned instinctively to face whoever was approaching, yet nothing but foggy air swirled.

The next thing I knew I was running again, trying to find a way out of this maze of a building, and found myself running in circles. It seemed there was no way out. Then, rounding a corner, I saw a stairwell and ran frenziedly toward it.

When I tried the door at the top of the stairs, it wouldn't budge. Growing more frustrated I tried again. I twisted the knob and used shoulder pressure. Moments later, I was banging my hands against the glass window of the door hoping someone would come and open it.

The door suddenly gave way. I pushed through it, not knowing what to expect and found only an empty corridor. With each and every step I took, the floor started to creak.

Then I stopped. Fear gripped me. My mind in turmoil, I dared not divert my eyes from what was coming toward me. A bat! I was so startled that I didn't have the sense to run away.

Its rustling black leathery wings made a whooshing sound as it flew toward the spot where I stood, scared stiff. It came closer and closer to me. There was nothing I could do but stare into its brown eyes.

When it got close to my face, I waved my arms to shoo it away and lost my footing. I slipped, fell to the floor and rolled over on my back. The bat flew down to me and bit into the right side of my neck, tearing through the skin and into a vein. The bite sent a wave of shock through my spine. I screamed and struggled until the creature got off. When the thing flew up, a few drops of blood fell from its mouth onto the black camisole and matching leggings that I had on.

Tension held me immobile. I stayed put on the floor, propped up on my elbows and tried to ignore the pain in my neck. With a squint, I looked, bringing everything into focus. The fairly large bat with black marks that streaked its brown fur and my blood pumping through its body, screeched and flew toward a castle I had seen before.

The bat flying in the distance had me locked in a trance until it finally disappeared and the corridor came into my sight again. I lay silently on the ground, as if waiting for something to happen, but nothing did. Shifting slightly, I wiggled around, looked, and saw that nothing was there. Except there was a pain in my neck that caused me to scream.

Chapter 28

I LITERALLY woke up screaming. At the same time, the sound of the tea kettle whistling in the kitchen muted the scream, which pushed me upwards. And I found myself sitting bolt upright in bed as I threw off my plaid blanket.

At first none of it made sense to me. Slowly, my tension eased out of the fuzziness. And I remembered I had been dreaming of a bat again.

The early morning light was in the room. I squinted my eyes and looked at the digital clock atop my nightstand. 8:37. It was earlier than I wanted to get up.

After rubbing the sleep from my eyes, I yawned and stretched my arms above my head. Getting off the bed, I dropped my bare feet on the fuzzy, colorful pink and purple rug at the foot of the bed. I stepped into my fuzzy slippers and went briefly to the window. After pulling back the curtain, I made sure the window was locked. It was. I noticed the sky was cloudy, but still no rain fell.

As I passed the mirror on my dresser en route to the door, I paused, took in the dishevelment of my hair, and the pallor of my face. I brushed my hair off my shoulders with my hand. A cold chill ran through me when I saw two small holes in my neck and three small drops of blood on the top right side of my gray, long-sleeved sleep shirt. Now I was worried.

The question ringing loudly in my head was — what exactly had transpired last night?

Momentarily frozen, I looked at the bite marks on my neck, thinking maybe they were there when I went to bed, but I just didn't notice them. Maybe, just maybe, the dream I had wasn't a figment of my imagination. It seemed more real, like something that had actually happened to me, but I just couldn't remember what it was.

I gazed at my necklace, a 24-karat gold chain with a locket containing a picture of my late parents. Safely around my neck, it was the only possession I cared about. Just then an ancient memory sprung into sharp focus. My parents had taken me to Jesmond Dene, a public park, many times as a child. Nostalgia took over, and I felt a desperate longing to see Jesmond Dene again. Instantly the castle I'd dreamt about flashed on my mind, like a picture before my eyes. Something jogged my memory of the castle being adjacent to Jesmond Dene.

Who lived in that castle? This was something I needed to investigate. But first I was going to the kitchen to tell Siobhan. Of course, there were some things I couldn't tell her. So, I quickly twisted my hair into a single fat braid and let it hang down in the front on the right side to cover up the two punctured holes in my neck and the drops of blood on my shirt.

Coming out of the bedroom, I rushed toward the kitchen, and noticed right away that the smell of the scrambled eggs made my stomach feel uneasy. Odd that I wasn't hungry, because I usually was around this time.

Almost out of breath, I stepped into the kitchen. Still in her pajamas, Siobhan was standing by the stove as she poured hot water from the kettle into a mug with a tea bag in it.

"I just had the weirdest dream ever," I hurriedly said with her back facing me.

Straightaway, she heard me, placed the stainless-steel kettle on a cold burner of the stove, and turned around. "What's going on, Myrna?"

"Hang on, just a second. I feel like it's fading away," I said, and felt my temples tighten as I remembered the dream.

Leaning her back against the sink counter, she nodded with a curious expression, and said, "I can't wait to hear."

I paused to gather my thoughts, sorting them out, then continued, "I was running, in foggy hallways, in some building, not knowing who was chasing me. I was so scared. And after slipping to the floor, I woke up screaming."

"That's some nightmare, Myrna."

"It was so weird. But it was so real. No matter what I could do, I just couldn't get away. And then I woke up."

"Wow! That's awful," Siobhan exclaimed.

"Yeah. It was so scary."

Siobhan handed me a mug of tea and said, "You need this more than I do."

I took it, and shrugged. "Thanks."

After taking a quick sip of tea, I realized I'd withheld some relevant details. Because there wasn't any way I was going to tell her everything. I just couldn't.

"Are you all right? You look shook," she asked with some concern in her voice.

"It was just like one of those dreams that was just so real."

With a shake of her head and a smile, she agreed. "How about some breakfast?"

"I'm good with the tea, thanks," I replied quickly, wondering if my face showed that my appetite just wasn't there.

"That's not like you, Myrna. You sure?"

"That dream has messed up my appetite. Really, I just want to hang out with you."

"Well, if you don't mind, I'm going to sit at the table and dig in," she went on, not seeming to notice my state of mind. "I'm really hungry."

The dream from last night was all I could think about. Thoughts like it really did happen were flowing in my mind and haunting me.

"Are you going anywhere today?" Siobhan asked, startling me from my thoughts.

It took me a moment to register what she had just asked as I joined her at the small, square oak table.

"I don't know what I'm doing today. I haven't decided yet," I said, setting my mug on the table and turning to her.

"It's Sunday, your day off. There's no need to make any plans."

Briefly, I sipped at my mug and watched her chowing down on scrambled eggs and wheat toast with jam with immense satisfaction. Then I closed my eyes, and sighed.

When I opened my eyes, I started feeling as if something was off between us. We didn't seem to be connecting as strongly. On top of the fact that she didn't take the dream I had seriously. But, in actuality, there was no reason for her to think of it as anything but a nightmare.

Immediately after she finished her breakfast, she stood up with her plate and took her mug from the table. She set the dishes in the sink, turned on the cold water and started washing them.

"Today is my day off, too. Why don't we head over to Clyde's tonight? We haven't been there in a while. We could both use some fun, right?" she suggested enthusiastically.

"Sure, let's do that," I said in a reluctant whisper, slightly choking on the words, though she failed to notice it.

I wasn't talking anymore. My head was just not into it. Instead, I sank deeper into my thoughts, acutely aware that something had happened — or was about to happen.

Chapter 29

WHEN I got up from the chair, my smartphone started ringing in my bedroom. The sudden ring caused me to back away, startled. The dream of the night before, if it was a dream, had thrown me a curve and made me jittery.

Siobhan looked at me and I looked at her. We were both wondering who was calling me and if I was going to answer it, or not. But neither of us said a word. We were waiting for the other to speak. Nothing came.

Finally, she asked, "Are you going to get that?"

"Yes, but," I said still in a haze.

Before I could decide or move, a thought occurred to me as to who might be calling. I realized in that instant, that I had made a commitment with my aunt and that it had just slipped my mind.

First I needed to ask her something, before I took off to answer the call. "What time is it?"

Siobhan was standing in front of the small clock on the counter by the sink, blocking my view.

She looked over and stated, "It's nearing ten o'clock. Why do you want to know, Myrna?"

There was no time to answer her. I sprinted across the hall to the bedroom and snatched up my phone from the dresser.

"Hello," I said, answering on the third ring.

As I had suspected it was my Aunt Eowyn, who wanted to know if I was coming over to her house today. She was worried because I hadn't call her to confirm.

"I told you last week that I have an appointment with the salon at eleven this morning. You didn't forget, did you?"

"No, Aunt Eowyn. I'm just getting ready now."

She needed someone to watch her dogs while she was away. I gave her my word and I couldn't renege on it now.

"I'm so glad to hear you say that, Myrna. I knew I could count on you!"

I quickly improvised and told her that I got caught up with housework and would be there soon.

"You sit tight."

"Myrna, you are such a dear," she said into the phone.

"Siobhan, I have to go out!" I spoke out loudly, just as I hung up the phone.

By the time the call was completed, I could swear that I had heard Siobhan in the hallway. Still, I needed to be certain she was out there. Before I went to change my clothes, I popped my head into the hall to make sure she heard me since I had cut her off before. Sure, enough she was walking down the hallway near the turn to her bedroom.

"Siobhan, that was Aunt Eowyn on the phone," I called out to her.

At the sound of my voice Siobhan's head turned toward the doorway.

"How is she?" she asked, stopping in her tracks.

"She's well, thanks. I promised her I would come over and take care of her dogs while she was at the hair salon. She wants to look her best because this Wednesday, she's going to a fundraiser for the Lord Mayor's Charity Fund on behalf of the Rotary Club."

I didn't give Siobhan time to respond. There was more I needed to say to her, so I kept going.

"She is very protective of those two dogs and doesn't like to leave them alone."

"Thanks for letting me know. You go on, and we'll catch up later," she said, starting to move again.

"Okay. I'll see you later," I said as she turned the corner.

After letting out a sigh, I pulled away from the doorway. There was no time for a shower, I decided as I went to the closet and ransacked it for something to wear. I was supposed to be at Aunt Eowyn's house at ten thirty this morning. That was thirty minutes from now. I couldn't keep my aunt waiting too long.

Eowyn Dymtrow was the only family I had left. I was her only family too, well, in the vicinity. Her only son, Andrew, recently married and moved to the United States a year ago. And three years ago, her husband Clark died in his early sixties of a heart attack.

Lately Aunt Eowyn was devoted to her pets and activities with the Rotary Club. A caring and community orientated woman, she had helped the Rotary Club of Newcastle upon Tyne for years. Even though it was September, she was already working with a committee on their Tree of Light event happening this Christmas.

Now that I was dressed, I covered up the holes in my neck with the scarf, imprinted with Fifi Lapin illustrated bunnies, that Aunt Eowyn had given me on my birthday. I slipped on my crossbody bag over my shoulder with my smartphone inside, grabbed the keys to my bike and hurried toward the front door.

Rushing out the door, I almost forgot to lock it behind me. I popped on my helmet and straddled my scooter. Turned the ignition. And zoomed off.

I didn't recall much of the ride there. Not so much because I was in a hurry, but my mind was still preoccupied with thoughts. I didn't know what I should or shouldn't say to aunt. Would it be prudent to tell her about my dream?

After thinking more about it, I came back with the answer. I wouldn't tell her anything. There wasn't time to explain it all to her. She needed to get to her appointment.

Plus, she was sensitive to such matters. I didn't want to alarm her.

Tearing down the streets, I was almost there, making good time. There wasn't much traffic on a Sunday. Thank God. And it wasn't as late as I had thought earlier. At the last red light, I checked the Seiko watch on my wrist, and the monogram read 10:26 a.m. Fingers crossed I would be a few minutes later than she expected.

Chapter 30

I PULLED MY SCOOTER into the driveway of Aunt Eowyn's detached house on Woodlea, parking in front of one of the garages next to her gold Volvo V40 T2 five-door hatchback. No sooner had I turned off the bike and took off my helmet, the front door opened, and she stepped into the doorway of her house. The instant I got off the scooter and headed directly toward her, I noticed a sign of relief on her face because it was 10:32 a.m.

"Thank you so much for coming, Myrna," she called out as I came closer.

"My pleasure. Glad to see you this morning," I said with a perky smile.

She held out her arms to me and I went in for a hug. Not a moment too soon, she released her embrace.

"I've got to dash if I'm going to get to my appointment on time," she said before turning to walk to her hatchback.

"Have a good time."

"If the dogs give you any trouble just give me a ring and let me know," she said as she unlocked the door of her Volvo.

"I've got it all under control."

"Don't worry about feeding them, because they just ate."

"Okay, got it."

"After the appointment, I may do some shopping. But don't worry because I'll be back before you know it."

"Oh, great," I said reluctantly, as I thought it would be hours before she returned.

She settled into the driver's seat, turned the ignition, and drove off. As the hatchback disappeared down Woodlea, I heard whining and barking coming my way. The noise of my scooter and the Volvo starting more than likely pulled the poodles out of their activities from somewhere in the house.

When I stepped through the doorway and closed the door behind me, Lindy and Trudy ran up to me. Her two poodles were so thrilled to see me. They looked adorable with pink ribbons attached to their ears, and very white fur as if they had recently been to the dog beauty parlor.

Aunt Eowyn certainly did invest in the care of these animals. It was rather sweet. I could understand her devotion to them. She got them six months after her husband died and they had become her constant companions since then. They were exceptionally good company and occupied a lot of her time.

"Okay, okay. Aunt Myrna is here," I said, unable to resist their charm.

I squatted down and gave the poodles a big hug. When Trudy stood up on her hind legs and put her front paws on my knees, begging for affection, I rubbed the top of her head.

"All right Trudy. You're full of affection."

A short bit later, I moved away from the dogs and moved into the living room. The dogs followed, rubbing against my legs and whining with excitement. They started to settle down when I sat down on the suede camel sofa, but they still followed me. I pet them as they poured out their excitement that I was here to play with them, of course. Why else would I be visiting?

Lindy made her way to the beveled glass French doors. She let out a low whine indicating her need to go out — right this instant. I got up from the sofa and opened the doors to the enclosed garden to let them out for a spell. In the interim, I walked through the house, from room to room, checking each one as I moved. Located in the residential village of Forest Hall, the four-bedroom house, where I had lived many years, had been barely modernized. My old bedroom was the same. Still, no memories surfaced.

Much sooner than I expected, I heard the dogs barking outside. I let them back in the house. They strolled over to a small oval rug on the wooden floor, in the corner of the living room, and sat down.

The little dogs were watching me with an amused look on their faces. I on the other hand wasn't as amused. Not intentionally of course. I liked them. It was just that, when I parked myself on the sofa, I kept flashing back to that castle. Perhaps I should do a little research.

After rummaging through my crossbody for my smartphone, I swiped the screen right to left. My finger clicked on the Google Chrome icon. On a whim, I put in the search words: CASTLE and JESMOND DENE. Like a mad woman, I began googling about the castle, not sure what I was looking for, but searching anyway.

The best I could find was a page with an article positioned next to a photograph of Wightwick Hall, the name of the castle. The article stated that the castle was designed by architect John Dobson. It was built in the early 1800s. In 1871, the castle with neoclassical architecture and a Gothic-style porch passed from William Cruddas to the family of Baron Glenkinglas. In 1929, the family put it up for sale. From what I read; I discovered the property had been sold to an undisclosed private party.

"What in God's name?" I asked aloud.

How could a place that had withstood many trying moments in history have anything to do with me? I came from a poor Irish family that had drifted from Dublin, thence to Newcastle upon Tyne.

Despite my Internet sleuthing, I felt I had come up empty handed. I didn't find out who lived in the castle. At this stage, it looked as if I wasn't going to find anything else. So, I didn't want to search the internet anymore.

Feeling a bit lightheaded, I couldn't think right. My eyes needed a break from the strain of staring at the smartphone's screen. I closed my eyes and rubbed them to clear my vision and get back on track.

Something just occurred to me. My eyes flew open as if lightning had struck right there in the living room.

In July, Siobhan and I arrived at the tail end of Aunt Eowyn's Friday afternoon Rotary Club meeting at the Best Western New Kent Hotel on Osborne Road. She introduced Siobhan and I to Lorraine Krag, a new member of the Rotary Club who had recently moved into a house on Jesmond Dene Road, in a mostly deserted neighborhood. It was near the castle. This I was certain of.

Aunt Eowyn said she thought that Lorraine Krag was asking a lot of questions about her personal life, later when we had lunch together at the hotel's restaurant. She was completely put off by Lorraine Krag's nosiness.

It was possible Lorraine Krag knew something, anything that would shed some light on some of the questions I had about that castle. And if she could tell me anything about the castle's resident, I wanted to find out. Sooner rather than later. Maybe it would be worth a visit to her home to pick her brain.

How could I approach her without drawing suspicion to myself? I thought about it for a little longer. There must be some story I could concoct that would explain why I was visiting her.

Eventually, I became too tired to think anymore.

Feeling like I needed a nap, I thought that a little rest would do me good.

The dogs were on the rug occupied playing with some toy. So, I didn't have to worry about them. Maybe now would be a good time to take a break. I sprawled out on the sofa and watched the two dogs playing. *They were just adorable*, I thought as I dozed off.

Chapter 31

THE TIME flew by quickly, passed just like that. It was close to four o'clock when I waved goodbye to Aunt Eowyn as I walked out of the door of her house. Despite the time of day, there was very little light as the clouds were covering the sun. The weather had been like that for two whole days.

As I walked toward my Honda scooter, I could hear the occasional bark from her dogs, which were happy she had returned. Despite all my worries, I must admit it was a joy to be around them.

After putting on my helmet, I straddled the bike, started the engine, and sped away from the house like a bat out of hell. In essence — and literally no pun intended — but that put a smile on my face. I still had the image of a bat practically tattooed on my brain, ever since the dream I had. And it was more than a dream, real in some way. The bite marks on my neck proved that something real had happened to me.

Once I left Aunt Eowyn's house, there was nothing to do except obsess about that castle. The image of that castle clawed at my mind. I wanted to know anything that might give me some insight into why it was in my so-called dream, and why this was happening to me. And I needed to know who was living there.

My mind was made up. I was going to visit Lorraine Krag. Was there any other option?

To get to the heart of the matter, I needed to see Wightwick Hall up close. I wondered if it was the castle in my dream, even though deep down I knew it was. There was so much I wanted to explore, so much I wanted to know.

The cool air on my body felt nice and refreshing as I tore down Front Street. My adrenaline surged, and somehow, I whooped with sheer fearlessness. I was feeling exhilarated — and that felt strange. What brought this sudden change in my mood? It seemed like I was starting to do things without a second thought. I didn't recognize myself — and I liked it very much.

At ten after four on a Sunday, I was glad traffic was practically non-existent. I rode the scooter faster than I needed to on the almost empty street and was thinking about my destination, rather than what was in front of me. For the most part, I was so distracted by my thoughts, which were running wildly from one thing to another, that I swerved to avoid the black Audi Q5 4X4 in front of me at the traffic light. I hit the brakes and skidded to a stop. My bike ended up sideways. The red light came so suddenly. I exhaled loudly in relief, thanking my lucky stars I was all right.

While stopped there, I allowed myself to think about something from that dream. All that was in my mind was that voice calling out to me in a strange language. I wish I knew what language it was so I could translate some of the words that I remembered hearing. But I didn't know what dialect it was. If I had to guess, I would say it was Eastern European.

I took off as soon as the light turned green. That was when I realized that in my haste, I had passed my turn-off and I was actually on Station Road. I was supposed to turn left when I got to Haddricks Mill Road. All I had to do was make a U-turn at the next light.

Just thank goodness I caught it in time. There was no time to get lost. I agreed to go with Siobhan to Clyde's later. It was one of our hang outs. I was already committed to it and I wasn't going to back out. It was the only way I could think to calm my nerves and so Siobhan wouldn't suspect anything was going on.

As I approached the traffic light at the intersection, I readied myself to make a U-turn. Waiting for the light to change to green, I noticed the clouds were thickening and getting darker, the darkness of an impending storm. The turbulent, cloudy sky blanketed the town, gave the streets a gloomy appearance, and added more mystery to the situation.

As soon as the light changed, I made the U-Turn and started back toward my destination. Picking up the pace, I tore down Station Road. I wanted to get to Lorraine Krag's house quickly, before dark and because it looked like it might rain.

Before taking a right turn onto Haddricks Mill Road, I saw a sight that almost startled me off my bike. I was completely caught off guard when I saw that street performer Viktor holding a leash, walking his monkey. Wearing his usual attire of a long black tuxedo jacket, white Oxford button down shirt, black trousers, and a black top hat, he stood out in a crowd. There was no way I could miss seeing him.

From what I could tell, from where I was positioned, I didn't think he spotted me. At the most unexpected moment, or maybe simply one of those serendipity times, there he was again. How bizarre was that?

For one last time, I looked at him. He was deep in thought, like I had seen him in Old Eldon Square.

While in the process of making the turn, the bike jammed and made a screeching sound. It was just a second's time, but it was deafening. The noise caused Viktor to look my way. I supposed he couldn't recognize me with my helmet on. But that didn't stop him from looking at me, staring at me oddly.

My scooter wasn't out of petrol, I knew that for sure. It just wouldn't budge. Not an inch. This was the first time it happened.

Just when I was starting to worry, the bike started to move forward again. As I was turning, I noticed the light was changing to red. I looked back briefly and could swear I heard Viktor shout something at me.

I didn't have time to analyze it, nor did I care. It was weird enough just seeing him. All that I was concerned about was that I was headed in the right direction. And I was.

As the street merged into Matthew Bank, I thought how soon I would be turning left onto Jesmond Dene Road. It made me nervous, butterflies welling up in my stomach just thinking about how close I was to the castle. In the short time Lorraine Krag lived on Jesmond Dene Road, I wondered if she had noticed anything strange about the castle.

But, ultimately, I knew I needed to be careful what I would say to Lorraine Krag.

The more I thought about this, the more I felt that I couldn't let on in any way that I was interested in the castle or its caretaker. It could work as long as I could convince her that I was getting information for someone else.

My plan was to get as much information as possible from her. But that was wishful thinking on my part. I wished myself luck.

Then I thought, perhaps I shouldn't ask too many questions.

It felt strange driving down Jesmond Dene Road. At first glimpse, the road was dusty, and gloomy like a cemetery. Still I rode on, feeling drawn to the area. It was as if I could feel the presence of something unusual. Something watching me. Yet, the castle wasn't in sight yet. It was a familiar feeling, like I was meant to be in this area. Was something calling me here? I couldn't understand why I felt this way.

Chapter 32

THE ECCENTRIC VIKTOR PAVLOVIC was smoking quietly and staring off into space, while leaning against the wall of a building on Haddricks Mill Road. A bit disconcerted, he was deep in his thoughts, thinking about the girl he had seen accelerating away from the traffic light on her scooter. It bothered him that he couldn't figure out why the girl had seemed familiar to him. He didn't believe in coincidences, nor did he like them.

Clearly the girl on the scooter was on his mind. Even though he couldn't see her face well because she was wearing a helmet, he felt sure that her eyes had been on him. She had looked at him with curiosity, though of course he could only assume. He was interested in knowing who she was, as he made a mental note to himself that the next time, he saw her, should he encounter her again, he would say something to her.

His trance was broken by Jasper, who placed his paws on his leg and looked up at him with his brown eyes. Viktor bent down and gave him a pat on his head. He couldn't resist the monkey, his companion and business partner.

"What is it, my little one?" he asked the creature.

Now eight years old, the monkey understood his master. Jasper raised his paws higher up his leg and released a screech in reply. That was how they communicated.

While bent over, he noticed the black leather shoes on his feet were unpolished and worn, reminding him of his financial woes.

"We'll head over to Allan's for dinner soon. How would you like that my old mate?" he asked as he raised himself up.

Viktor took a puff of his cigarette and thought about how the last six years he had lived in Newcastle upon Tyne, had been a hand-to-mouth existence, which scarcely kept him alive. More than ever before in his life he realized to himself that he had become dependent on the kindness of strangers, surviving on meager handouts.

Despite the fact that his clothes were sometimes worn, he had a taste for the finer things and fine food. He might be a street bum, but he maintained standards.

He was certainly fortunate to have struck up a relationship with Allan Palen. Being a regular customer of The Longbow Tavern, Allan gave him discounts on meals, and he was given complimentary servings of fruit like apples and bananas, which in turn he gave to Jasper. It was a big help to Viktor. And Allan allowed him to bring the animal into the restaurant as long as he sat at the farthest table from the kitchen.

Yet he knew that Allan viewed him as an outsider, a misfit of society. Odd character that he was, Viktor knew, too, that he stood out like a sore thumb.

Still smoking the cigarette, he took a quick look around the vicinity. The girl on the scooter was long gone now, and out of his thoughts. Instead, he reflected on his own life, his younger days, when he was fit and handsome man.

A long time ago Viktor Pavlovic was a young man of much promise. Early in life, he developed a love of acrobatics and magic. He grew up so tall and overshadowed other performers in the local circus, that his parents allowed him to participate in after school and weekends.

Coming from a poor family in Zagreb, Croatia, magic was his only opportunity. His mother was a grocery store clerk and his father worked as a welder at a local factory. With two brothers, there was never enough to go around. The extra money he brought in from the circus helped a lot. His parents were proud of him for his ability to earn a living.

Rather than go to college, he became the headline act for the circus. Three days each week, for fifteen minutes each show, he got to perform his favorite magic tricks which served as an introduction for the other performers. He had loved being in the spotlight and it stirred a passion deep inside him.

The circus traveled all over Eastern Europe as one of the leading big top shows. Among the many places he had visited, the one which pleased him more than any other was Medjugorje, a town in Bosnia and Herzegovina. He visited the Queen of Peace statue, the site of the appearance of the Virgin Mary to children in 1981. It was like a spiritual awakening for him.

But time went by so fast. He had carried on relationships with some of the women he encountered in his work, but never settled down with any of them. With the money he made in the circus, he could barely cover his own expenses, let alone support someone else.

His current financial problems had begun the day he had missed his train from London, six years earlier. He caught another train and arrived two hours late in Newcastle upon Tyne. The circus had left, and he was stranded in a city where he knew no one.

To say Viktor's life had fallen into misfortune would be an understatement. At the age of forty-six, he smoked incessantly, gambled on rugby matches, and had become a little more than a freak show. But he didn't care much. He drew sustenance from a life-enriching past, that he smiled about.

He would leave Newcastle upon Tyne soon, thought the cynical Viktor. It always troubled him that things had not gone the way he had hoped. Truth be told, he was tired of dreary old England and desperately wanted to get back to Croatia. Maybe even as early as next summer. There wasn't any doubt that he desired to see members of his family again.

His thoughts returned to the present. He gazed at the cigarette dangling from his mouth. It was burnt to the filter. He dropped it on the ground and crunched it underfoot. He reached into his jacket pocket, pulling out an empty pack. It was another disappointment, and something else he needed to buy.

In the air, rumbling came from the sky. Rain could be coming. Jasper wasn't into it. The little monkey's arms were clutched around Viktor's leg while his eyes stared up at the darkening sky.

Viktor looked up, displeased. The gloomy day hadn't been a prosperous one for him. Weather, as such, affected his collections from passersby and onlookers he attracted with his performance with Jasper. But thankfully, the little money he earned earlier would provide a much-needed dinner.

He looked left and right one more time. The streets were clear, but the sun moved in and out behind the clouds. He wanted to get under cover before the rain came.

"Come along my friend," he said affectionately as he pulled lightly on the leash.

Jasper let out a few screeches in response.

"Yes, we are going," he said and started walking.

As he passed a trash can, he dropped the empty cigarette pack into it. The wind kicked up a bit, sent a rush of air, and almost knocked off his top hat. He picked up his step. Jasper quickened his step too and huddled close to his legs. He turned right at the corner and disappeared from view.

Chapter 33

IT WAS exactly 4:21 p.m. when I pulled into the curb by the walkway leading up to the entrance of a small brown painted house with white-shuttered windows on Jesmond Dene Road. Near the streetlight was a red sign with white letters that read "Private Property" affixed to a low wrought iron fence on top of a stone wall. I knew it was the right place because the house looked lived in. Going by what Lorraine Krag had told me, she was living in the only house that was occupied for streets around. For reasons she couldn't fathom all the other houses had been deserted by their owners long ago and their doors and windows were boarded up.

After taking off my helmet, I sat there on my Honda scooter for a little bit preparing what I was going to say. The first thing I saw when I glanced toward the house was Lorraine Krag at her living room window peering at me from behind the curtain. In this quiet area, there was no doubt that she heard the sound of the bike's engine before I turned it off. I took that as a sign that she might be willing to talk to me.

After stepping off the scooter, I trotted to the front door of the house. Lorraine Krag left the window closing the curtains. Was she capable of pretending she wasn't there? I hoped not.

Perhaps I spoke too soon when I thought earlier that she would speak to me because when I rang the bell nothing happened. I rang the bell again and waited. As this brought no response, I reached for the doorbell a third time. Standing on the doorstep, I wasn't sure what to do next.

"Maybe she doesn't want to talk to me," I spoke out to myself and adjusted the scarf around my neck.

The most obvious thing came to mind. It was the most vulnerable point and was the reason I was there in the first place. I turned my head around so I could see the castle. The fading light in the sky cast an unearthly glow across the landscape. My focus returned, and I asked myself the most obvious question. Where was the caretaker? From the distance I was standing, it seemed vacant, a lonely place. One would think nobody lived there.

Still, I stood there looking at the castle, hoping it would trigger something in my mind. It didn't. Nothing appeared in my mind. It just looked like an old castle.

Glancing upward to the looming clouds in the sky, then back to Lorraine Krag's front door, I needed to act if I was going to get any answers. Instead of ringing the bell, I knocked on the door hard enough to rattle the frame. This was going to be my last attempt.

"Hello? I know you're there. I'm not leaving without talking to you," I called out in a loud voice.

"Yes. What can I help you with?" Lorraine Krag's voice called out from behind the door.

"It's Myrna Ivester. You know my aunt, Eowyn Dymtrow. She introduced me to you at your Rotary Club meeting last July. I know you don't know me well, but I thought you could give me some information. I have a couple of questions about Wightwick Hall. And I promise I won't take much of your time," I said, sounding desperate.

"The castle? Oh, for goodness sake! Why on earth would you be interested in that place?" she asked, with a hint of suspicion in her voice.

"A friend of mine wants to know, Lorraine. She's interested in buying it," I said with impatience.

Almost immediately she swung the door open wide, stood in the doorway and glanced at me with a displeased look. She didn't invite me inside her house. While she was looking at me from top to bottom, I looked at her the same way and noticed she was wearing a pink and white dress to her knees under a white cardigan sweater and a pair of white house slippers on her feet.

"I'm Mrs. Krag to you," she said sharply.

"Certainly, Mrs. Krag."

"Why are you here wasting my time?" she asked with a sneer on her face.

"My friend really wants to know if the castle is for sale. And who owns it exactly? Since you live nearby, I thought you might know."

She studied me for a moment, then said, "Very well, Myrna Ivester, if you must know, I think the castle is haunted. I've seen a strange woman dressed in black coming in and out of there all the time. And every so often, I hear the sound of animals screaming. It is the creepiest place. I tell my husband Arthur, all of the time."

As I took it all in, I sighed. Hearing the words that came from her mouth almost seemed unbelievable.

When she heard footsteps approaching her, she turned her head around, then back to me.

"Who are you talking to Lorraine?" came a man's voice.

It was her husband. I couldn't see him because she was in the doorway blocking my view.

"Is there anything else you can tell me?" I asked, pressing for more information.

Mrs. Krag cut me off with a wave of her hand, turned her head to her husband, and said, "Just a minute, dear."

Facing me again, she barked at me. "You don't want your friend to buy it. Don't go near the place!"

And with that Lorraine Krag turned on her heel and left, slamming the door behind her.

"Sure, Mrs. Krag," I said in a low grumble.

Her warning came too late. I was already hooked on that

castle. I knew I would have to come back to this neck of the woods. But next time it would be the castle I would be visiting. It was my only resort.

I could hear Mrs. Krag's cranky voice carrying on a conversation with her husband about me, telling him I was asking about Wightwick Hall. There was no need to bother her anymore. I didn't knock on her door again.

It was time to leave. I walked back to my scooter, grabbed my helmet out of the cargo hold, and strapped it on my head before getting on and starting it up.

While the bike was idling, I sat there a little while. Looking up briefly toward Mrs. Krag's house, I saw her at the window of her living room. She was looking at me in an eerie way. But her staring was short lived. Even though the helmet was on my head, the second she noticed me looking at her, she quickly moved out of sight of the window and shut the curtains.

The wind shifted and started to pick up just as the clouds made rumbling noises like that of an empty stomach. No rain fell, and I decided it was best I go. I pulled onto the road and headed toward home.

Walking into the house after a long day, I was thinking about Siobhan Mulcahy now. Lately, it felt like we were going in different directions, as if our friendship was drifting apart. Tired and feeling weak, I wasn't looking forward to going out. But I couldn't tell her no. If I didn't go with her, she would wonder and start to ask questions I couldn't answer. So, there I was, heading to my room to get ready for a night out.

As I was walking through the living room, Siobhan spotted me and asked, "Interested in an evening of wings, beer, and girl talk?"

I stopped walking and half-heartedly said, "Yes, I'm in."

"That sounds great. I'll go get dressed," Siobhan said, and left to her bedroom.

In contrast, I was too tired to change. My blue tie-dyed V-neck short sleeved T-shirt, black jeans, black leather sandals, and scarf around my neck, I had been wearing since this morning would have to suffice. After taking a quick shower, I threw it all back on.

Entering the living room, all I wanted was a place to rest, and think about what was happening to me. I simply slumped into the brown leather recliner next to the floor lamp by the sofa and waited for Siobhan.

Just when I was about to fall asleep, I heard keys jingling and footsteps entering the living room. Siobhan was wearing a pink tie-dyed V-neck short sleeved T-shirt, stonewashed jeans, and colorful flip-flops. We often dressed similar, but Siobhan looked better. Well, in my eyes, she did.

Chapter 34

SIOBHAN MULCAHY opened the door to enter Clyde's just as the rain started to fall. A bolt of lightning struck across the sky and lit up the area as I stepped inside behind her. We sat down in a booth by the window where I could see a full-scale downpour in progress. The dark sky was interrupted by the occasional strike of lightning. I did my best to get comfortable, knowing we might be here a while because of the storm.

The place on Mill Rise was one of the best bars in the city. It was dimly lit, with a hardwood floor and free-standing light maple-wood tables covered by brown gingham tablecloths and chairs with brown leather cushions piped in white in the middle of the room. There were brown vinyl booths lining the windowed walls except for one corner, where there was a small stage.

It was happy hour on a Sunday night and packed to the hilt. The music was as loud as the crowd. To top it off, the Newcastle Falcons winning rugby match against the Sale Sharks, played last Friday at AJ Bell Stadium, was being replayed on the widescreen television mounted above the bar. The noise in the place made it impossible to hear a conversation unless you were right next to the person with whom you were having it with. Siobhan and I could only shout and gesture with our hands.

Normally I would have loved it, but things didn't feel right. It couldn't be worse. I felt tired and just couldn't focus on what was happening.

A woman in her late thirties walked up to the table wearing a blue and white checkered apron over a white blouse and black skirt. She held up a small notepad and took out a black pen from the top pocket of her apron. The plump waitress with her blond hair in a bun stated that she would be taking care of us, and that the happy hour special was two for one on drinks and burgers.

She smiled and asked, "What can I get you girls?"

Siobhan jumped in immediately and said, "I want to order wings and two Fuller's beers."

There wasn't any time to intervene. I let Siobhan order for me. It was fine with me because I wasn't in the mood to talk.

Roughly twenty minutes later, the waitress appeared at our table with a large plate of chicken wings and put it down in front of us. Soon afterwards, she set two glasses of beer on the table.

Siobhan took a swig of beer and said, "These tasty wings are guaranteed to cure anything that ails you. I know they will put you in a glorious mood."

Her warm smile was contagious. So, surprised on that, I forced a smile. But I couldn't concentrate, let alone eat anything.

"Myrna, what's wrong?" Siobhan asked, interrupting my thoughts. "You hungry?"

My mind was on something else. I felt a million miles away from her, tonight, even though I was sitting across the table from her. It was like I was watching it all from a distance.

"Huh?" I asked, confused by what she said.

Siobhan tapped me on the shoulder and said, "I thought you might want to eat something."

After snapping out of it, I grabbed a wing and said, "Oh, yes."

Trying to appear interested, I picked at the wing. Eating wasn't something I wanted to do, even if I hadn't eaten a thing all day. Deep within I realized that I was craving something other than food or drink.

"Waitress!" Siobhan shouted, snapping me back to reality.

Seeing me almost jump out of my seat, Siobhan cracked up and burst out laughing. She laughed so hard that tears came to her eyes.

"Am I missing something?" I asked, a make-believe smile on my face. "What's so funny?"

"I remembered," she sputtered, trying not to collapse in laughter, "the way you looked this morning, when you told me about your dream about how you just couldn't get away."

The reason Siobhan Mulcahy was my best friend in the first place was that she could push my buttons like nobody else.

"I'll drink to that," I said and took a swallow of beer.

It was the best I could do. Because I tried to put on an act that I felt well, but that couldn't be farther from the truth.

"To us, down the hatch!" she said, and lifted her beer.

We touched our glasses across the table with a satisfying clink. Such was the excitement that we got caught up in the moment.

It didn't last. An annoying live performance was in progress. A lounge singer was belting out the tune of a 1970s song on the stage. And not a pleasant one either. His raspy voice flowed over and around us.

We both took a gander at him. His long-sleeved black button-down shirt was unbuttoned to mid-chest. Heavy gold chains mingled with his black chest hair. The man with thick dark hair and eyes as black as coal, appearing in his forties, was also wearing a pair of cream-colored bell-bottom pants.

"Feelings, nothing more than feelings. Trying to forget my feelings of love," he sang cornily and rather embarrassingly.

It was impossible to talk over the awful crooning because he was holding a microphone.

It got even worse when the people seated at the nearby tables joined in singing with him, "Feelings, wo-o-o feelings. Wo-o-o, feelings."

As far as I could hear, the singing did nothing for the Morris Albert song "Feelings." It was a shabby attempt of the classic.

Siobhan laughed careful not to seem like she was laughing at him. His singing had given her the giggles, which in turn affected me. For the first time that evening, I presented a smile, and an honest-to-goodness, genuine smile at that. I even laughed a little.

After gaining her composure, Siobhan said, "I feel sorry for him."

"Yeah, he's clearing the place out," I said, and we laughed again.

After wiping her mouth with a napkin, Siobhan brought the subject back to food, "There's one wing left."

"You're welcome to it."

"Sure, Myrna. How about a sweet treat?"

"I'm done for the night," I said politely.

After the plates were cleared, Siobhan ordered her favorite dessert, Yorkshire pudding. The waitress returned with the dessert and placed it on the table. She picked up a pitcher to pour some more beer and noticed that my glass was more than half full. I placed my hand over my glass to signal that I didn't want anymore.

Suddenly, I felt the urge to get up. I began sliding out of the booth.

"Please, excuse me for a moment, Siobhan. I'm going to the bathroom."

"Sure, go on ahead."

Her face wore a gloomy expression, as she watched me walk toward the women's room. It wasn't difficult to tell that she was aware that most of the evening it seemed as though I was someplace else. She knew it was time to call it a night.

Chapter 35

IT WAS HALF PAST TEN when Siobhan and I left Clyde's and arrived home at a quarter to eleven. I went to my room, locked the door, and headed for the bathroom. Closing the door behind me, I took a good look at myself in the mirror above the sink. Looking tired and very pale, I took off my clothes. I filled the bathtub with cool water and lay down in it with my eyes shut for about an hour without moving. After that, I changed into my pajamas and got into bed.

A good night's sleep would help a lot. And maybe I might feel better tomorrow and everything would be back to normal again. It was wishful thinking on my part.

That night in bed, I was feeling restless. My mind was reeling, a confusion of thoughts flitting through it. It was beginning to frighten me. After tossing and turning in bed for what seemed like an eternity, I fell into a deep sleep.

When I woke up in the morning something strange had happened, something beyond any experience my twenty-four years had shown me. My body was floating in the air and I was really scared. Now I knew something was up because this time I wasn't dreaming. I was suspended above the bed a full four inches, with my arms held tightly in place at my sides.

Somehow — like magic — my body gently fell back into bed. Instinctively I buried myself under the blanket, laying there quivering. There was no doubt that I was terrified by what had happened.

Something inside wouldn't let me tell Siobhan. In retrospect I couldn't tell her or anyone else what had happened to me. I needed to sort this out by myself.

There was no way I could go to work.

I rolled over to my right side and looked at the clock on my nightstand. It said 8:24. I got out of bed and grabbed my smartphone off my dresser. I calmly dialed my work number and spoke to the receptionist who transferred me to Joyce Gunn's voicemail. She must be away from her desk because she reported for work at 8:00 a.m. on Mondays. I left her a message telling her I would not be coming in today.

After I hung up, I turned around and went right back to bed. There were chills running up and down my body. But I found that I wasn't craving anything to eat.

There came footsteps outside in the hallway. It was Siobhan, who was coming from the kitchen. Not much later, a soft knock came on the door.

Like lightning I sprang from the bed and it felt like I flew in the air. My fingernails were clenched in the wood of the door. I was clinging to the door.

My senses were heightened so much that I could feel Siobhan standing on the other side of the door. What was more unusual was that I sensed the blood running through her veins. I was attracted to it. And I was longing for it. Well, not specifically hers, just any blood.

"Myrna, are you going to work today?" she asked loudly.

For a long moment I didn't answer. I was stalling for time to get my thoughts in order. Additionally, I was pretending to be in bed, not wanting her to know that I was behind the door, smelling her blood. I could even taste it. There was an urge inside me that I couldn't understand. It was something I couldn't control.

"No, I'm not going to work. I'm feeling really tired. I'm sure I'll be all right by tonight," I said, finally, hoping it was enough to ease her worries.

Considering the way, I was feeling last night, she would probably believe it.

"Do you need anything?"

"No, thanks. I'm just going to stay in bed and rest."

This wasn't a conversation I wanted to continue. I was worried that my desire for her blood could cause me to hurt her.

"I'm leaving for work now. Call me on my cell phone if you need anything."

Thankfully, she didn't pry any further. I had the sense that she didn't have a clue what was happening to me.

I responded with the first thing that came to my mind. "Okay. We'll talk later."

"I hope you feel better," she said as I heard her walking away from the door.

My emotions and thoughts were running faster than I could keep up with them. Major changes were happening to me. It felt like I was in the process of becoming someone new. But, who, and what, I didn't know yet?

One thing I did know was that Siobhan Mulcahy was drifting further and further away from the world I was living in.

The revelation hit me like a ton of bricks. I slowly turned around in agony, leaning my back against the door. My hands were trembling, and tears formed in my eyes. I couldn't stay here anymore. With things the way they were, I didn't see any other choice. I didn't know what I might be capable of.

It had been sometime since I heard Siobhan's car drive off. I went to the window, pulled back the curtain not knowing what I was looking for, or maybe I did. Thoughts of that woman, I had caught staring at me in the library, resurfaced. The images of her were still fresh in my mind. I thought, with a sigh that perhaps I expected her to be outside somewhere. She wasn't out there, just in my mind.

I couldn't analyze it because I was feeling oddly emotional. Hurrying from the window, I got back into bed to sleep. Again. I felt weak and faint, as if I would pass out. There was a need to plan something out, but it would have to wait a little longer, maybe even another day. With that last thought, I was asleep shortly after.

Chapter 36

THE NEXT DAY, TUESDAY MORNING, I woke up a
little after eight o'clock. I got out of bed and stretched my
arms high into the air. Standing before the dresser mirror,
I found I looked awfully pale, with eyes glowing red. A
little wary by this further evidence of my transformation, I
sat down on the bed.

What would Siobhan say if she saw me in this state?

In a time of uncertainty, faith had something on which
to stand, but I was sitting down. In the recent years, I was
less interested in spirituality. Coming from an Irish
Catholic family, I wasn't exactly devout. The last time I
went to church was when my parents were alive. So, other
than myself, there was nobody I could turn to for advice or
guidance.

This was a turning point in my life. I knew it was time to take a risk and didn't dress for work.

I came off the bed, grabbed my smartphone from the dresser, and called my job. The phone rang a few times, and in the interim I thought about not going back. Finally, the receptionist picked up.

"Can you hold?" the voice answered on the other end.

"Sure, I'll wait."

There was a pause, but the voice returned quickly, "Longwood Nursing and Rehabilitation Center, how can I help you?"

"Hi, it's Myrna Ivester. Can I speak to Joyce Gunn?"

She came on the line at once. "Myrna, how are you feeling?"

"I'm all right, thanks for asking Joyce. I'm actually calling you this morning for another reason."

"What is it that you want to tell me?"

"I'm sorry, but I won't be returning to work."

Joyce asked me if I was sure about my decision. All I could think to tell her was that I had other job prospects lined up after I return from a long sabbatical. Lying didn't sit right with me. But I couldn't exactly tell her the truth. She said that she was going to miss me and that she hoped that I would come visit her some time. After that I told her that it was nice knowing her. Then I hung up and sat back on the bed.

Since, I quit my job, I felt relieved, not sad by any means. I had wanted to quit for a long time.

Utterly alone with my thoughts, my gut was telling me something about myself that my head wasn't ready to hear but needed to confront. I had a notion, a theory of the metamorphosis that was happening to me. I had ascertained that I was undergoing a transformation into a vampire. Me a vampire? It felt plausible. Actually, it made all the sense in the world. I had seen movies about it but didn't think it was possible. And it was so much like a movie, I had a hard time believing it was real.

I couldn't talk about this with anybody. Not my Aunt Eowyn, not even Siobhan.

Was I bitten by a bat? Maybe it didn't happen that way. My assumption was that it was a vampire disguised as a bat. Somewhere in my mind, there was something swirling like a drop of indigo ink in a clear glass of water. And I couldn't grasp what had taken place.

Looking back on recent events, I thought about the dream I had the night of my birthday. There was a bat flying around the cemetery. My body was in a coffin for burial. Then I came to life from the grave. It was like I was being reborn. It was as if I saw my future self through a window in my present. I wholeheartedly believe that it was a premonition of things to come. That I would be living a new life as a vampire.

Was this the life I had longed for? I asked myself that very question, because now I was faced with the imminent possibility that the very thing, I had been waiting for all my life was here at last. As an afterthought, I hoped it was.

Right here and now I decided that it was a path I wanted to pursue.

My mind started flashing back to that woman from the library. There was just something about her. I was still thinking about the way she had looked at me and what it had made me remember. I still feel her eyes upon me, nailing me to the spot. Her eyes were so fascinating that I couldn't look away from them. As if in a trance, I kept seeing her eyes, seeing her soul.

What interested me the most was the conclusion I reached about her. Intuitively, I knew she was a vampire. I was sure she was.

Was she the reason this was happening to me? Had she somehow made this happen? The questions resonated but yielded no definite answers.

Another burning question in my mind was whether or not she was the caretaker of Wightwick Hall. Something inside me told me she was. It fit with what Lorraine Krag had said concerning a strange woman in a supposedly haunted castle.

Vampires had a sixth sense, and paranormal abilities. I sensed all of this because I was changing. I was going to transform into a supernatural being. That being the case, what should I do next?

Not that I needed time, I knew what I wanted to do. I would go to Wightwick Hall. The best thing to do was to go now. Assuming that woman lived there, I hoped she would assist me. Surely, she could provide me some answers.

Since I was dead set on leaving, I looked around thinking if there was anything I wanted to take with me. Nothing in the room meant anything to me. I grabbed the locket hanging from the gold chain around my neck and gazed at the picture of my late parents. I would keep this with me. But what else?

After a few minutes, I went to my closet. Rummaging through my clothes, I pulled out a couple of outfits. After placing them on the bed, I searched the closet again and found my large brown canvas backpack. I threw the backpack on the bed and put the clothes in it. Then I emptied the contents of my crossbody bag into the backpack and threw in my cell phone.

Nothing else was coming with me. Starting a new life, I didn't want to take anything that would remind me of the past. And I didn't want to hold onto a bunch of things I didn't really need. A lot of things were going to be different now. And I was prepared for that difference.

After getting dressed, I realized that I was leaving so much behind. It also hit me that I was heading into a future filled with equal parts excitement and uncertainty.

I grimaced at myself in the mirror on the dresser. The holes in my neck really stood out. I grabbed the white silk scarf imprinted with Fifi Lapin illustrated bunnies from the top dresser drawer and tied it around my neck.

As the daylight crept into the room, my body shrieked out against it. I had developed a sensitivity to light. It was another sign of my changes. I took the sunglasses from the dresser and placed them over my eyes.

There was only one thing left to do. I needed to talk with Siobhan Mulcahy. There was no more procrastinating.

Chapter 37

AS SOFTLY AS I could, I opened my bedroom door and stepped out into the hallway. As I was turning away from the door, Siobhan appeared in the hallway and began to approach. It was her day off because she was still wearing her pajamas. When she was about five feet away, she stopped, and looked at me closely.

"Myrna, are you all right? You're not going into work today, are you?" she asked with a worried look on her face — and then some.

"I'm not going into work, but I'm feeling better," I told her.

"What's with the sunglasses?"

"I had a headache earlier and the light was bothering me. And I just forgot to take them off."

I took off the sunglasses and put them in the front pocket of my black jeans.

"Since I'm off today, how about I make you some herbal tea?" Siobhan asked with her gentle smile.

"Okay, if you insist," I said, giving in.

I knew she was concerned about me, so I let her help as much as she wanted. She reached over and took my hand and led me to the kitchen. Her hand tightened on mine and I could feel the blood pulsing through her veins. I suddenly felt euphoric. My thirst for blood was growing.

She let go of my hand and went to the cabinet and took out two tea bags. I sat down at the square oak table, trying to sort out my emotions and settle down my nerves. All the while Siobhan filled the kettle with cold water and set it on the burner of the stove.

When the tea was ready, Siobhan took a seat across from me at the table. We were mostly quiet.

She took a sip of her tea before asking, "Better?"

"Yeah, it's fine."

Siobhan swallowed the last mouthful of her tea, and then went to the sink and rinsed out her mug.

"We have to talk," I said and stood up from the table.

This conversation was going to be painful for both of us, I thought. But it was time I got it off my chest. She wasn't going to like what I was about to say. At this stage of my transformation, I couldn't postpone the conversation any longer.

"What is it? Something bothering you, Myrna?" she asked, and quickly put the mug in the cabinet.

As far as I could make out, she was nervous and unsure of what would happen next. She knew something heavy was on my mind. By the look on her face you could tell she felt she was about to hear something she wasn't going to like.

After careful consideration, I prepared in my mind what I was going to say and how I was going to say it, because I was about to drop a bombshell.

I hesitated for a moment before I said, "Siobhan, please don't be mad."

"It's okay, Myrna. I could never be mad at you."

"I wish there was an easy way to tell you this, but I'm leaving. I can't live here anymore," I said, laying it all out there.

Not once did she look away from me. This wasn't what she was expecting to hear. It was like a punch to the stomach. I was bracing myself for whatever it was she was going to say.

There was a long pause before she asked, "What's happened? Why did you wait till now to tell me?"

"I didn't want to say anything until I was sure. I wasn't ready. Now I am."

"Are you certain about your decision?" she asked, fighting back her emotions.

Siobhan was waiting for me to say something more. I could see from her face she wanted to know what was happening to me.

"Too many things have changed for me. Please don't try to talk me out of it or try and stop me," I said with some emotion in my voice.

She wanted to argue, but didn't. Not even did she beg me to reconsider. So much had changed between us since first meeting at Northumbria University. I think she saw that I was changing and decided to let me go.

We stared at each other for another minute. Not a word was spoken. A trace of sadness lingered in her gaze as silence embraced us both.

"I'm your friend in this," Siobhan said softly.

There was hurt in her voice.

"I know you are. And I will always be your friend. But I need to do this for me," I said meaning every word of it and hoped she noticed.

A little lump started to form in her throat as she fought back the tears. I came closer to her and hugged her. The emotions inside of us were running so deep that I didn't once think about her blood, while I held her in my arms. Our embrace lasted long enough for tears to fill her eyes and stream down. Never had I seen her cry before.

"What's your plan?" she asked, wiping the tears off her face.

I considered my response. "It's not something I can talk about. For your reassurance, know that I will be fine."

She took a deep breath before she asked her next question. "Will I hear from you again, Myrna?"

"Probably not," I said and shook my head for emphasis.

And there, she knew it was the end for good. She took a step backwards. It was clear that she was hating every second of this conversation. Nothing she'd heard had left any room for hope.

"Don't worry, I'm not going to stand in your way when...,"

There was a stiffness in her voice. She was trying to say more but couldn't get the words out. There was so much sadness in her eyes.

Even after all this time, Siobhan adored me and would do anything for me. Even if it meant stepping aside and watching me leave. In all the time she had known me, this was the first time I had acted indifferent to her. But it wasn't on purpose.

She looked down into my mug on the table and noticed it was almost full. I barely drank any of it, only took a few sips. I didn't have the appetite for tea or any food.

"I have to go, Siobhan."

"Don't you want to finish your tea?"

As the words hung in the air, she waited for an answer. Looking into my eyes, she was searching for something, but not finding it. Instead she sensed I didn't want to keep talking to her.

I felt I should say something, but I didn't. There was nothing left to say. There were no words for what I was feeling.

Siobhan lowered her head and tried to contain her emotions. She was the one who couldn't speak now.

In that moment, I walked out and wanted to keep going until I was in my bedroom. I couldn't even say goodbye. As I hurried away from her, I was crying inside. All I could do was run, away from her. There was nothing I could have done differently.

Chapter 38

CLOSING MY BEDROOM door behind me, my heart
was in agony as if it were being torn apart. It hit me, all
at once, all the feelings I had been suppressing. I
sagged back against the door balling my eyes out. Muffling
my crying, all that came out was a pathetic, whimpering
sound.

Siobhan couldn't see me like this. She would think I
was confused. And there was no doubt about my decision.
I knew exactly what I was doing.

It felt like I was lying to her, which I had not done
before. A part of me wanted to tell her what was going on
with me. She had kept many of my secrets in the past, but
this secret couldn't be shared with her.

Well I cried so hard that at some point I felt a little
relief in my heart. I went over to the nightstand and

grabbed a pen and pad of paper out of the drawer. There were things I couldn't say to Siobhan and could only put on paper. Above all, I needed to thank her for her friendship.

My hands were trembling, and I could barely keep my grip on the pen. It was hard to say goodbye to her.

My own tears blurring my vision, I paused, inhaled deeply, released my breath slowly, searching for the proper words to end the letter. Then I put my endearing thoughts down on paper. I hoped that when she read this very emotional letter, it would speak directly to her soul. And I wanted her to understand I meant every word written.

After finishing the letter and leaving it on my dresser, I couldn't dwell on it anymore. I put on a long red wool cape, that made me look like Red Riding Hood, for the walk ahead of me. The weather outside was cool. I estimated it was a twenty-five-minute walk, but I welcomed it, wanting to be close to nature. Since I had been undergoing changes, I was craving nature.

As hard as it was for me to believe it, I didn't feel the same way about my scooter. It didn't thrill me anymore.

Another thing I noticed was that my hair was loose, wilder looking than before, and a lighter shade of blonde. It was darker before. All my life I had had dirty-blonde hair. Not anymore. The new hair color complimented my skin, which was paler.

All these changes kept me in a state of anticipation. And more changes were likely to come.

There was an overbearing sense of the unreality of all this that was happening to me. I was anxious to move forward, curious about what would come next. My instincts urged me forward. I took the sunglasses out of my pocket and put them on. Then I did a quick look over of the room, threw my backpack over my right shoulder, and made my way toward the door.

Exiting the bedroom, I headed toward the living room. I looked around the house one last time, believing it would leave a lasting impression on my mind.

Siobhan wasn't around. I thought maybe she was in her room or in the kitchen. There was no time to look for her. She would find out soon enough, I had left. Although it would take time to get used to it, she was emotionally stronger than me. *She would be all right*, I thought.

It made me feel pretty strange thinking about never coming back. A memory that crept into my thoughts was when I first moved into the house. How Siobhan and I loved it and were excited and nervous. Now I was practically running out the door. It didn't feel like my home anymore.

Here it was, the moment of truth. I took a deep breath as I dropped the keys to my Honda scooter on the small round oak table in the hallway. It was the last thing I did before I opened the front door and stepped outside. I didn't even look back for Siobhan, who I was certain would make good use of the scooter.

As I started to walk away, I looked at the scooter parked by the house and frowned. There was no desire in me for it.

As I headed southwest on Lilburn Gardens toward Freeman Road, I thought there was a chance that Siobhan could follow me, but there wasn't anything I could do about that except hope that she wouldn't try. Just in case, I looked about to make sure that she had not followed me, because I couldn't ever go back. She hadn't, from what I could see, and I was relieved.

It scared me to think what might happen if Siobhan found out. If there were any, I wasn't sure what the consequences would be if she discovered the true reason why I left. What would she have said if I told her that I was turning into a vampire? I was afraid she wouldn't accept it and could cause trouble down the line.

I walked on, buoyed up on the excitement of it all. Being a vampire was my calling. The feeling inside of me was though it had always been a part of me. There were still many things I didn't know. But I was ready to learn.

When I got to Freeman Road, I made a left, heading toward Castles Farm Road where I would make a right. I wondered what would happen when I got to Wightwick Hall. Should I just knock on the door and wait for a response? It seemed the most logical thing to do. Would this woman, who holds the key to my future, let me into her home? A woman whose name I didn't know. Would she answer my questions? There was so much I wanted to know.

I strongly sensed that the resident of Wightwick Hall was the same woman that had been gawking at me at the Newcastle City Library. Was she a vampire or not? I was hoping to soon find out. Last but not least, I felt an attraction to her spirit. It was deep and intense. I had never felt this way for anyone before. Most of all I didn't expect to have feelings for a woman.

Suddenly nothing made sense to me — and then everything made sense. Now, I understood why I was naturally attracted to her. It was as if our souls were connected in which I was part of her, and she was part of me. The vampire connection. All my thoughts led to the same conclusion — this bond was real.

Chapter 39

"IT WASN'T LIKE MYRNA TO DO THAT," Siobhan Mulcahy whispered to herself.

Her arms were folded across her chest, and her face that was set in a worried frown, as she leaned with her back against the kitchen counter. By the obvious grief on her face, it was clear she was utterly heartbroken. She noticed that Myrna had been withdrawn lately like she was a completely different person.

Siobhan's mind swirled with thoughts as she realized Myrna Ivester was no longer in the house. Some time had passed since hearing the front door slam shut from Myrna's waltzing out the door — which left her in a state of shock, after being taken completely by surprise. Slowly the message was sinking in, and she was doing her best not to cry anymore.

What had inspired her to leave? So many questions were running in her mind. It was too late to ask Myrna now. And she was powerless to do a thing about it because things had changed quickly between them.

Thinking about all that had transpired, she considered talking to someone about it. The only person who came to mind was Myrna's aunt, Eowyn Dymtrow. She nixed the idea because she didn't want to go behind Myrna's back and meddle in her life. Her aunt might not know anything anyway.

As she stood pondering, something suddenly occurred to her. Myrna couldn't have carried all her stuff. She decided to go to Myrna's room to see what she left behind. Maybe there were some clues to be found there. Or maybe not. But either way, she wanted to see what was there.

Curiosity got the better of her and she walked out of the kitchen into the hallway heading to Myrna's bedroom. Upon entering the room, she was slightly astonished to see that Myrna had left a bunch of clothes, decorative items, and furnishings. Why did she leave all this stuff? She was standing by the closet, not knowing what to think, only that something felt wrong. The sight sent her mind into a spin.

"What is going on?" she asked aloud.

There was an uneasiness in her gut, and she didn't like what she was feeling. It was taking her time to accept that Myrna wasn't coming back either. Missing her badly! As she looked through her favorite Juicy Couture clothes in the closet, she couldn't believe she'd left them behind.

She came out of the closet and saw the Precious Moments figurine she had given her last Christmas on the dresser. Myrna had said she loved it. Yet, there it was. On the dresser. It irked her seeing many of Myrna's favorite things around, which meant only one thing. They meant nothing to her anymore. And she wondered if their friendship mattered to Myrna at all.

Until Siobhan found a personal handwritten note on the dresser. It was addressed to her from Myrna. She quickly grabbed it up. Now she hoped it would shed light on why Myrna had left so abruptly. Dear Siobhan, it said. Her hands were trembling as she read it.

I can't seem to find the words to tell you to your face what I want you to know, so I am writing them in a letter. I'm hoping it will be enough for you.

Thank you for your friendship these past six years. I will never forget you. I hope this letter helps you to realize the depths of my feelings for you.

You may keep or dispose of leftover belongings in my old bedroom. I won't be coming back for them.

Do not be upset if you never hear from me again. And please don't be mad at me. The reason I left isn't because of you. But instead, because of me.

After I lost both of my parents in a car crash at the age of five, I spent the rest of my life longing for something. Something I can't describe. Not sure of finding it either. Until now. I can't tell you what it is, only that I want it. It is not a man, nor is it religion, but something else I can't explain, not even to you, my best friend of many years.

Please don't go looking for me. The life I am living now is for me, but not for you. In any case, I will be grateful if you look in on my Aunt Eowyn every so often. This way we will always be connected.

I remember you mentioning a nurse at work, I think her name is Alysa, the one who is looking for a place to stay. Why don't you ask her to move in with you? The timing can't be any better. It will help to have someone around for support during this time of transition for you.

Just know that I adore you, and I want you to know how much you mean to me. You are the best person I have ever come to know. I cherish our moments together. And love you dearly.

Always your friend,
Myrna

There were tears in Siobhan's eyes now. The flood of tears was distressing to say the least. She took a deep sigh and put the letter down on the dresser. It had brought some comfort reading it, but it didn't answer all of the questions inside her mind other than the fact that it was exactly as she suspected. Myrna wasn't returning.

The letter proved that Myrna did care about her. But something had torn them apart. Myrna was just caught up in something she didn't fully understand.

It was a hard thing for her to understand. This new life Myrna was now leading. It was such a sudden decision, in leaving her home and going to God knows where. Was she in danger? Should she inform the police? She didn't want to cause Myrna any trouble. But she didn't want any trouble for herself either.

The more she thought about it, the more she fretted. What was she going to tell people if they asked her where Myrna was? Was she considered a missing person? People might think she killed her and buried her in the backyard. She assumed that people always thought the worst.

She didn't want to think along those lines. But she needed to consider all the possibilities. Nevertheless, just in case, she would keep the letter from Myrna in a safe place.

Mere moments after stepping into the office, she put the letter inside a folder in a file cabinet where she kept important papers. It was something she would always have to look back on, a memory of one of her best friends in life.

Thoughts about the incident in the hematology unit of the hospital where she had seen a woman disappear, fluttered through her brain. She meant to tell Myrna about it, but it skipped her mind. She believed Myrna would have gotten a kick out of knowing about it because of the kind of dreams that she sometimes had. Her face lit up with a smile, and a tear burned a trail down her cheek. And for a moment, she wished she could go back in time to when their friendship began.

She closed the file cabinet drawer, left the office, and headed to the bathroom in her bedroom. After stepping inside the bathroom, she switched the light on. She leaned on the sink, then ran cold water, splashing it on her face, and washing the tears away. Then she grabbed a towel from the rack and dried her face off. After gaining her composure, she inhaled a deep breath.

Chapter 40

WALKING ALONE BENEATH THE vast shimmering blue sky with only a few clouds, I was almost at Wightwick Hall. At ten thirty in the morning, the air was seasonably cool with a temperature in the high fifties. This was real, not a dream, I told myself as I drew nearer.

High over the castle I could see the golden orb of the sun. Its rays cascaded over my body. It made my hair look fiery. The bright sun was warming my face and the wind soothed me. The combination of warm and cool felt nice.

A bit breathless, I hesitated, stopping approximately six yards from the castle because I was having the jitters. My eyes went up and down the front of the building, then around the grounds. The shadow from the sun was halfway across the right side and made the castle hauntingly beautiful.

I needed to ask myself, "Are you sure this is the right move?"

Staring at Wightwick Hall, I wondered, would anyone look back? But no one did. I didn't see anyone inside. All I could see was a darkness as if the place was empty. How could that lonely looking place be the key to my future?

"Myrna, what are you doing?" I asked myself.

Could that woman see me? I was disappointed that she didn't come out and invite me in.

My inner voice responded immediately: *Maybe she wants to talk to me as much as I want to talk to her.*

Fear of the unknown was driving me. My questions needed to be answered, I reminded myself. In order to embrace the woman, I was becoming, I needed to find the woman who could help me through it.

Contemplating my next move, I paced a little bit along the grass. My body was shaking nervously. Excitement jitters were building inside me. You'd think I was getting married. Was this how you felt on your wedding day?

Did I have the courage to step into an uncertain future? The newness of it all excited me to the bone. Did I really have it in me to start anew? The danger enticed me, like falling in love with a stranger.

"Well, this is it! I was hooked," I said encouragingly.

Just a bit light-headed, I stopped walking around in a circle. As I looked around, I saw a curtain move at the window of Lorraine Krag's house. Staring intently toward the window, I wondered why Mrs. Krag, or her husband had been staring at me because I was sure someone had been watching me from the window. The second I looked that way, the curtain closed. I stared a little longer at the window to see if whoever looked before, would look again, but the curtain didn't budge an inch. Well, I didn't care.

Just then, it occurred to me that when I had gone to Mrs. Krag's house asking about the castle, she told me not to go there. She tried to ward me off, claiming the place was haunted. What if she was right? Should I be scared? From where I was standing, the castle looked quite beautiful. I didn't sense anything strange, other than Mrs. Krag herself.

So, what if Lorraine Krag, rather than her husband, saw me from the window? All I could do was hope she wouldn't come out and tell me to go away. In pondering this, a thought came to mind that Mrs. Krag could make a scene. She seemed to be a crabby old lady. However, some more minutes passed and not a sound or movement came from her house. And I felt relieved.

Turning my attention back to the castle, I was startled when three black carrion crows flew overhead cawing loudly. Was that a sign? For one fleeting second, I wondered if that was a warning not to go. I looked up, only to see them circle around and fly off into the woods. The whole incident was over so quickly. Perhaps, after all, it was nothing to be worried about.

Right when I was about to make my move, my thoughts scattered in my head. Beneath my sunglasses, I squinted into the sunshine, scanning the castle for a glimpse, any sign of the tenant. It was like no one was there at all. What if that was the case? What if the trip over here was for nothing?

My skepticism quickly faded. I couldn't let myself believe that all of this could come to nothing. Despite the empty look of the place, I sensed I would find something there.

It was time to make my debut. The closer I got to the castle, the harder it was to turn back, not that I wanted to anyway. I wasn't going to turn around and leave at this stage.

Now only a few steps away, here I was on the stone path about to enter the place without a clue as to what would happen next. A little voice inside my head was telling me to keep going. The worst that could happen was that she would tell me to leave.

My big moment was at hand. I took off my sunglasses and slipped them in my backpack. Standing close to the front door, which was slightly ajar, I listened, taking it all in. What waited for me in there? Although I couldn't see any person, I felt a presence of some sort. I could hear a faint moan of a soft wind. It was peculiar, to say the least. But something, sheer curiosity, propelled me forward with a sense of underlying excitement. It was as if my life and my whole future was depending on this visit of mine.

"Here goes nothing. Or possibly everything," I said softly to myself.

Chapter 41

AS CRAZY AS IT would have seemed to Lorraine Krag a brief moment ago, she felt the way Myrna Ivester had looked at her was frightening. She could tell something wasn't right with Myrna's facial expression, despite the sunglasses covering her eyes. That was precisely why she had quickly closed the curtain when Myrna had glanced her way.

Standing near the living room window, she was feeling so rattled by it all that her mind spontaneously remembered that she had suggested to Myrna that she stay away from the castle, and yet, there she was. Why didn't Myrna heed the warning? In the first place, she still didn't understand why Myrna had visited her last Sunday, asking her questions about Wightwick Hall, of all things. Now that she had seen Myrna near the castle, her suspicions that something was amiss were confirmed, and then some.

Lorraine Krag's suspicious eyes darted around the living room. Her thoughts were spinning wildly, like clothes in a dryer. Myrna didn't look the same at all, and she wondered how it was possible. Her complexion was pale, and her hair was wildly loose and a lighter shade of blonde. Seeing Myrna in such a state, she was on the verge of some sort of revelation. She thought for certain she was onto something, though she couldn't put her finger on it.

Should she go out and ask Myrna if she was all right? Was it wise to confront her? Her eyes narrowed as she couldn't shake the thoughts from her head. But then again, perhaps she shouldn't do anything. And so that was settled.

Naturally, she wanted to tell Arthur, but he had stepped out earlier that morning to buy some groceries at Tesco. If only he could have been here to see Myrna. Then it crossed her mind that if Arthur had been home, he would have kept her from looking out the window, and she would have missed seeing Myrna, which of all things was an act of destiny.

It had been some time since she saw Myrna. More than likely, she wasn't there anymore. Was Myrna inside Wightwick Hall? How could she know for sure? In spite of her curiosity, she couldn't bring herself to look out the window again, at least not at the present time. Just thinking about the look Myrna had shot in her direction gave her the willies. Something just didn't feel right.

"Yes, that's it!" she exclaimed, as an idea sprang into her head.

Excitement overtook her and she ran to the telephone to call Siobhan Mulcahy, Myrna Ivester's roommate and friend. Stopping halfway, she remembered that she didn't have Siobhan's cell phone number, nor Myrna's.

Or did she? With her recently acquired Rotary Club Membership Directory, she could locate Eowyn Dymtrow's phone number. She would have to telephone her first.

She opened the drawer of the mahogany end table and took out the small book. In searching through the pages of the alphabetical list of members, she turned to the D section and found Eowyn Dymtrow's telephone number.

Quickly, she grabbed the telephone on the end table and dialed, putting it to her ear. After two rings Eowyn Dymtrow answered, to her delight. Her face got all twisted, contorted with a dark mood, listening to dogs barking in the background.

She spoke straight away. "Hello, Eowyn. It's Lorraine Krag. How are you?"

"Hello, Lorraine. What a nice surprise to hear from you," Eowyn responded.

"Let me not waste any of your time," Lorraine said in a crotchety voice. "I'll get right to the point. I know how busy you are."

"Actually, I'm not busy at all."

"Yeah, yeah," Lorraine said, talking right over her. "Would you have Siobhan Mulcahy's cell phone number? My garden needs some work. She and only she can do it."

"Work in your garden?"

"Myrna Ivester came over to my house on Sunday and told me Siobhan could do it. But Myrna didn't give me Siobhan's phone number."

Lorraine Krag told the little white lie with a devilish expression on her face. She had an itch she needed to scratch. More than anything, she needed to get to the bottom of the goings-on in Wightwick Hall.

"Well, if Myrna thinks it's alright."

"Yes, she does," Lorraine insisted.

"Okay, let me go find Siobhan's number. Can you hold a moment, Lorraine?"

"Certainly, dear."

In the time she was on hold, she thought about how those pesky dogs, who were babbling, annoyed her. She didn't know how Eowyn could deal with it. Still, she maintained her composure. There was no other choice for her but to carry on this sham of a conversation.

Just as she had hoped, Eowyn returned to the phone and gave her Siobhan's cell phone number. Lorraine felt on top of the world that she had pried it out of her. As she ended the call, she poured on a little charm.

"Give a big hug to those cute little dogs of yours. See you at the next Rotary Club meeting," she ended the call before Eowyn could get in another word.

Next, she dialed Siobhan. As soon as the phone began to ring, she smiled with anticipation. This could be the break she was looking for.

Chapter 42

THE TELEPHONE RANG. Siobhan Mulcahy got excited thinking it could be Myrna. But she squashed that thought as soon as it appeared in her mind. It would take her some time to come to terms with the fact that she shall never see, nor hear from Myrna again. She pulled herself together enough to come out of the bathroom and slowly trudged over to her Apple iPhone ringing on the nightstand next to the bed.

After putting the phone to her ear without checking the caller ID, she answered, "Hello?"

The woman's voice on the other end asked, "Is this Siobhan?"

"Yes. Who is this?" Siobhan asked suspiciously.

Siobhan couldn't even begin to speculate who this might be.

"It's Lorraine Krag. Eowyn Dymtrow introduced me to you at the Best Western New Kent Hotel after a Rotary Club meeting in July. Don't you recognize my voice?"

How did Lorraine Krag get her phone number? She didn't care to ask. In her current state, she wasn't in the mood to deal with this woman whom Eowyn Dymtrow had mentioned was more than a touch nosy, the little that she knew about her.

"No, not really."

"You're probably wondering why I'm calling. I saw…"

"This is not a good time, Lorraine. Could I call you back later?" Siobhan interrupted, cutting her off in a moment of frustration.

Siobhan wasn't into it. She just wanted to hang up the phone and deal with the sadness that had come over her since Myrna left.

"Actually it's Mrs. Krag. And I think you may want to hear this," she sang into the phone.

From what Siobhan could tell, Lorraine Krag wasn't the type to back down, obviously needing to tell her something of some urgency. It could be worth her while to hear what she was going to say.

"All right. Go ahead and tell me," Siobhan said, caving in.

"I just saw Myrna Ivester outside the castle, across from my house here on Jesmond Dene Road. Who is the woman living there? I didn't know Myrna knew her. A woman can't live in Newcastle upon Tyne without knowing something about her neighbor."

There was a stunned silence. This news took Siobhan completely by surprise. She sat down at the edge of the bed.

"Myrna is at the castle across from you?" she asked, sounding about to cry.

Lorraine Krag came back with, "Didn't you hear a word I said?"

Not a word was spoken by either of them for almost a minute.

Another moment, before Lorraine pressed on. "Who is the tenant of Wightwick Hall? Do you know?"

Siobhan tried to speak, but in her emotional state, only a sigh left her lips. Still not a word came from her, as she was quiet for a long time, thinking and not ready to speak. Then most involuntarily there came another sigh.

"Of course, I know who she is," Siobhan said with a tremble in her voice.

Rather convincingly, Siobhan was trying to act like everything was all right, buying some time to come up with an explanation as to who the woman was. The fact was, she didn't know.

Lorraine's impatient voice rumbled, "I'm waiting."

"Myrna's half-sister from her late father's first marriage lives in that castle," Siobhan finally blurted out.

"Myrna has a half-sister? I didn't know that," Lorraine exclaimed.

"Well now you do. Anything else, Mrs. Krag?"

"No. I have to run. Bye for now!" Lorraine said and quickly hung up.

Siobhan stood up and put the phone down on her nightstand. Already her mind was racing in all the wrong directions. Lorraine Krag was right to ask. Who was that woman in the castle? Wightwick Hall? That was how out of the loop she was.

She was standing by the bed taking it all in. It was getting to her. She wasn't the type to speculate on many things, but in this instance, she couldn't help herself. An uneasy feeling gnawed at the pit of her stomach as she flashed back to the night of Myrna's birthday party at the Cinema 'N' Drafthouse. Myrna had insinuated her invited guest Casey wasn't a man. That could have been the case, Siobhan supposed, assuming Myrna hadn't made Casey up.

In light of this revelation, there was no other alternative but to believe that Myrna was on the other bus. Maybe the signs had been there all along, and she just didn't want to see them.

"I guess I subconsciously ignored it. Sometimes you just don't know people like you think you do," she said to herself.

It all made sense to her, but at the same time it didn't make sense. She hadn't paid close enough attention to notice. Come to think of it, she'd never actually seen Myrna on a date with a man. Although Myrna had claimed to have been on a double date once when she was attending Northumbria University.

This was a rude awakening for her. She was surprised that Myrna had a relationship of some sorts with the woman of Wightwick Hall. Although she wouldn't have cared that Myrna was interested in girls. For whatever reasons, Myrna couldn't bring herself to tell her the truth. As hard as it was to accept, she was determined that she wasn't going to pry into that part of Myrna's life.

On the brighter side of things, she knew what to tell people if they asked her where Myrna was.

Emotionally despondent, she couldn't take a shower, nor change her clothes. She walked into the living room, threw herself down on the brown leather sofa, and laid her body across it. Her legs curled underneath her, she rested her head on the small black throw pillow.

The emptiness of the house was getting to her. A wave of sadness filled her heart and soul. All of a sudden, the impact of it all was too much. It wasn't going to be the same without her longtime friend.

A rush of tears came into her eyes as she asked the silent room, "Oh, Myrna, what am I going to do without you?"

She could think of nothing but Myrna's angelic face, her sweet smile, and her enthusiasm about things. How she ached to hear her voice one more time. Just the thought hurt her heart more than she'd ever thought possible. How she wished she was with Myrna now.

Quite recently, she had told Myrna that she didn't take enough risks in life and had played it safe for too long. So, she understood that Myrna needed to follow her heart, which made her proud of her for taking a chance. Still, she missed her so much.

As much as she tried to keep the emotion suppressed, the tears fell down her cheeks, anyway. Her eyes were so wet, she could hardly see, and her breathing turned into sobs.

She grabbed the crocheted black and burgundy afghan from the end of the sofa and used it to wipe the tears off her face. Next, she wrapped it around her. She curled into a ball, facing the back of the sofa, and closed her eyes. Why did it have to be that way? She wondered to herself as she cried herself to sleep.

Chapter 43

THE CALL didn't go the way Lorraine Krag had hoped and she was left with questions instead of answers. She felt that she had been lied to, and that infuriated her.

As she placed the Rotary Club book of members back in the drawer of the mahogany end table, she thought about what she had not said to Siobhan Mulcahy. Myrna Ivester had visited her and had shown such great interest in the castle and its tenant. Myrna didn't know who lived there. This was certainly at odds with what she had been told by Siobhan.

She closed the drawer thinking that Eowyn Dymtrow had told her that she was the only family Myrna had left. That Myrna "had no other family except her because her parents had died in a car accident" — those were the exact words Eowyn had used on one of the occasions she had spoken with her at their Rotary Club meetings.

Was she supposed to believe what Siobhan had told her about the woman in Wightwick Hall? No way! She knew better. That woman could not be Myrna's half-sister. Her reeling mind knew it wasn't and she rejected that explanation swiftly.

As she stood by the end table, she came to one conclusion. This meant Siobhan was fibbing. But why would she lie? Lorraine found this very odd, indeed, since she hadn't sounded like she was lying.

"No, that's not possible. Myrna has to be lying, not Siobhan," she thought out loud.

The call was still on her mind. She remembered that Siobhan had answered quickly and sounded as if she was expecting someone else on the line — probably Myrna. She could hear the disappointment in Siobhan's voice, which was low and shaky. When Siobhan discovered who she was talking to, she was reluctant to talk to her. But when she told her that she had seen Myrna outside the castle, Siobhan was all ears. Was it possible Siobhan didn't know anything? Something was amiss and she didn't like not knowing what it was.

One thing particularly puzzled her: Siobhan seemed convinced of what she had said. It was likely that Myrna told her she had a half-sister living in that castle. It was possible Myrna had lied about that and about other things. With the way she'd been acting lately, she wouldn't put it past Myrna to do something like that.

There must be a reason why Myrna had lied to her friend. Why would she lie to me? She shook her head and started thinking about how Myrna said she was asking about Wightwick Hall because her friend was interested in buying it. What friend? Another lie.

Something was definitely wrong between Myrna and Siobhan. How could she believe either of them?

Lorraine walked around the cream-colored Victorian sofa and was about to pick up the newspaper from the coffee table and toss it in the trash when she realized that she was still wearing her white apron embroidered with gillyflowers over her peach linen dress, cut above her knees, with a high neck and short sleeves. She tugged at the ties on the back of her apron and yanked it off.

She went to the kitchen, holding the apron in her right hand. After hanging the apron on a hook near the kitchen door, she felt there was something queer about it all. Something didn't gel. It struck her that Siobhan would have known that Myrna didn't have any other family. After all, she was her roommate. And she appeared to have a particularly close relationship with Myrna.

This led to more questions: Could Siobhan be lying? What would she want to hide? Had she failed to grasp the whole of the truth about the relationship between Myrna and the woman of that castle? What kind of relationship? What was the real story with Myrna Ivester?

"Wait a second," she said as she entered the living room.

Lorraine Krag started seeing things in a different way than she had seen before. She remembered when Eowyn Dymtrow had introduced her to Myrna and she had questioned her as to why she didn't have a boyfriend. Eowyn had told her that it was nothing to worry about. After a little more snooping she found out that Siobhan also didn't have a boyfriend, which was odd in itself.

"Myrna must be on the other bus," Lorraine murmured to herself.

Lorraine could definitely see it and raised an eyebrow. She understood the secrecy. Searching for a reason for all the lies, that made more sense to her.

It was alarming to think that she had never seen any men at the castle. There was only that strange woman, who was always alone. How Myrna got entangled with that woman was beyond her comprehension.

She scooped up the newspaper off the coffee table and headed toward the kitchen. After placing the paper in the trash can in the corner of the room, she glimpsed the clock on the wall. It was ten to 11 a.m.

Returning to the living room, she wanted to take a gander at Wightwick Hall. Curious in her own right, she walked over to the living room window and pulled back the curtain. At first glimpse, Myrna, nor anyone else, was out there. Not that she was disappointed. She sensed Myrna was inside the castle. That she knew for sure.

To her surprise, she heard footsteps enter the room. Then the footsteps stopped. There was a hint of panic stirring inside her as she knew who it was. It could only be Arthur. It had completely escaped her mind that he would be home soon. Her mind was so engrossed with the events of the day, that she failed to hear him enter through the front door. She didn't know how long he had been in the house, but it couldn't have been more than a minute.

There she was looking out the window. She knew it was the last place he wanted her to be and he was going to chastise her about it. There was no way around it.

Chapter 44

AS LORRAINE KRAG TURNED AWAY from the window, she saw Arthur standing in the living room. He was holding two full, plastic, Tesco shopping bags in his hands. The look on his face was not one of amusement.

The sour expression on her face gave it away. Caught in the act, she knew what was coming. She let out a gasp as she stood by the window, waiting for him to speak.

Arthur stood still, staring, but saying nothing. It didn't take him long to figure out what was going on. It was clear to him she had been spying again. Maybe it wasn't the smartest thing to do, but he needed to ask why.

"Lorraine, please tell me you're not spying on Wightwick Hall again?" he asked, louder than he meant to.

"Myrna Ivester is out there," she said, rolling off her tongue as if she couldn't wait to tell him.

"What was Myrna doing here again?" he asked in a softer voice.

"Not here. She was at Wightwick Hall," she said, all huffy.

"What's she doing…"

His voice trailed off in confusion, so she finished the sentence for him.

"At the castle? That is precisely what I want to know."

Dumping the shopping bags on the coffee table, he pushed past her.

"Let me have a look," he demanded. "I have to see her for myself."

"But, she's…" Lorraine stopped herself from saying anymore.

He pulled back the curtain of the window and looked out. His head moved left and right. Then he closed the curtain quickly and turned to her with suspicion in his eyes.

"She's nowhere that I can see."

"That's because Myrna's in the castle."

"Are you certain you saw her?" he asked as he picked up the shopping bags from the coffee table and headed toward the kitchen.

"Of course, I did," she said following him to the kitchen. "I told her to stay away from there."

Pressing the matter further, he asked over his shoulder, "What are you trying to say?"

After setting the bags on the kitchen counter, he opened a cabinet and began to put away cans of soup.

"She didn't listen to me," she said, standing with her hands on her hips in front of the white wood kitchen table.

Before he could say anything, she kept talking, "Aren't you in the least bit suspicious?"

"I'm sure it's all innocent. Your old husband knows not to waste time on insignificant matters."

To wish that she would give it a rest is to ask her to change her nature, he thought wishfully. After closing the cabinet, he removed vegetables and a carton of eggs from a grocery bag and placed them on the counter. Gathering them up, he walked to the refrigerator to store them.

"I had thought something was fishy with the tenant of Wightwick Hall, and now with Myrna there, my gut instincts are confirmed. I just..."

She stopped herself before she could say anything else. Her arms dropped to her sides in pathetic surrender so fast, her wrists bounced on her hips.

Arthur closed the refrigerator door, thinking how she hadn't uttered a word worth listening to.

"Lorraine don't put your nose in other people's business. You're going to have to find another way to distract yourself."

"Actually, there's," she said, but that was as far as she got.

He interrupted her in mid-sentence. "Why are we even having this conversation?"

Grabbing the empty plastic bags, he opened the cabinet under the sink, and tossed them in a metal bin. After shutting the cabinet, he proceeded to wash his hands in the sink.

After more careful thought, Lorraine Krag seemed determined to get something off her chest.

"But there's more, Arthur."

"There is?" he asked a bit nervously and accidentally spilled some water on the green and black argyle sweater and forest green corduroy pants he was wearing.

"Yes, I've been trying to tell you," she snapped back at him.

"I can't imagine what else there is."

She wasn't going to let up until she finished saying what she needed to say.

"Are you going to let me talk or are you going to keep interrupting me?"

He grabbed the dark brown hand towel from its hook, and said, "Just go ahead. I'm ready for it."

"I telephoned Siobhan Mulcahy, Myrna's roommate and friend."

"Why on earth did you do that?" he asked after drying his hands and hung the hand towel back on its hook on the wall above the counter.

"I wanted to know why Myrna was at Wightwick Hall."

"Did she give an explanation?"

"Yes! According to Siobhan, the woman that lives there is Myrna's half-sister."

"This is getting more ridiculous by the minute. What's the big deal if Myrna has a half-sister?"

"Don't you get it?" she asked him.

He turned away with her words ringing in his ears and headed out of the kitchen toward the living room, with her following behind. Once in the living room, he sat down on his comfy beige suede chair. If only he could ignore her. But she wasn't going away.

"Last Sunday, Myrna didn't know anything about Wightwick Hall. She was here asking all kinds of questions. Now, the tenant, that woman is her half-sister. I'm not buying into it," she said, standing in front of him.

"This is getting odder and odder," he said and folded his arms across his chest.

"My point exactly."

Arthur shook his head but didn't argue her point. This time she was right. Instead, he attributed the circumstance to the misunderstood youth of today's generation.

"You know how young people can be. I just don't understand them. And neither do you apparently. Next time you see Myrna you can ask her all about it. I'm sure she'll tell you the same thing Siobhan told you. That she has a half-sister," he said as he unfolded his arms.

She sighed in exasperation, threw up her arms and said, "I don't know why I bother."

At this point and place, she headed over to the cream-colored Victorian sofa to sit for a spell hoping her frustration would dissipate itself.

"Yes, it's best not to," he added to irritate her.

He wasn't going to cater to her whims primarily because he felt that she was meddling again.

"Easy for you to say," she jabbed back.

"Best you forget all about it."

"Whatever you say, dear," she whispered sarcastically and gave him a scowl.

After a deep breath, she tried to force all the frustrating thoughts from her mind. That was when it dawned on her that if she continued the conversation, she would lose her temper with him. In her current state, she'd likely say something she'd regret later.

Lorraine Krag didn't know who frustrated her more — her husband or herself. That was hard to decipher.

Chapter 45

IT SEEMED LIKE TEN MINUTES had passed since I'd knocked, and the door opened a crack on its own. I had pushed it open just wide enough to stick my head in for a peek.

All I had gotten out was, "Hello?"

Another couple of minutes went by, and nobody had come to the door. I had mustered up the courage to walk inside, not waiting any longer for a response. Is there anything more brazen than someone entering without being invited?

During my wait, I stood in the middle of the impressive, chandelier-hung foyer and had appraised everything in the room. There were a couple of things I couldn't help noticing. First was the twenty-two-foot ceiling, and a spiral staircase that wound upward, round and round, stopping at the third level as far as I could see.

The breathtakingly beautiful, enormous, ornate Venetian glass chandelier hanging from the plasterwork ceiling reminded me of the chandelier in Andrew Lloyd Weber's "The Phantom of the Opera" musical, Aunt Eowyn had taken me to see for my sixteenth birthday.

Now it was probably around eleven o'clock. Was she even here at all? In my boredom, I glanced over at an old painting. The landscape canvas mounted on the wall was embellished in an ornate gold-leaf frame. Nearby it I saw something that caught my eye. On the narrow shelf below the painting sat a small figurine of a bat. I picked it up for a better look.

There was no doubt I was in the right place.

While I held it in my hand, I felt a presence in the room that I knew was her. A shadow fell across me and a way-too-familiar cool breeze came from behind me. I could feel her stare even though my back was turned. She had probably been watching me all this time.

My eyes darted around to see her gliding across the floor like a ghost, closing in on me until she stopped very close to me and said, "It's carved, jade porcelain."

Up close, I found that she was even more beautiful than I remembered, given her striking European features. She was dressed in black — just as Lorraine Krag had told me she'd seen her wearing. The loose black, short-sleeved top, black leggings and black leather sandals complimented her pale complexion.

Speechless, I merely stood there, riveted to the spot. Whatever I'd planned to say was lost.

After putting the figurine back on the shelf, I took a quick breath, trying to remain calm and not to let her see how nervous I was.

Recollecting my thoughts, I bounced back and said, "Excuse me for intruding, but I didn't think anyone was here."

She stole a sideways glance at me and introduced herself. "I am Ileana Vladislava. Welcome."

"I'm Myrna Ivester. But I guess you knew that already."

From what I was able to make out, she wasn't surprised by my appearance. Maybe she wanted this visit.

"Now then, Myrna, to what do I owe the pleasure of your visit?" she asked with a smile that hinted at amusement, and deep brown mesmerizing eyes that sparkled with delight.

"I want to talk to you," I said with a sincere look on my face.

After I said that, Ileana's eyes came up and met mine. Her gaze bored into my soul like she could read my thoughts. I carried on the conversation even though I was doing most of the talking.

"I know what you are," I said, and I lowered my voice to her, "I came here to see you because I need help trying to understand."

Her face lit up with interest, but she had nothing to say, didn't even blink. Based on this reaction, I could tell she knew exactly what I was talking about.

My right hand fluttered nervously around the knot in the white silk scarf around my neck. It covered the bite marks. That was the key reason I was here.

"You know what I've been dealing with," I said, untied the scarf around my neck and let it float down to the floor.

There would be no more covering it up. It was a pivotal moment. The marks were from a vampire's bite. It was all out in the open now.

"Are you responsible for this?" I asked, pointing to my neck.

"Yes, I am," she said with a calm collectedness.

"It was you I saw at the Newcastle City Library, wasn't it?"

"It was me."

I knew the moment I put my eyes on Ileana that she was the woman I had seen at the library. But I asked anyway.

Not sure how I wanted to ask my next question, I paused for several seconds. I felt light-headed with the thought of what I was about to ask her.

"Am I like you? A vampire?" I asked, before I'd even realized the words had left my mouth.

Not only did I know the answer, I answered my own question. And the look on Ileana's face told me I was right.

Ileana quickly broke eye contact with me, looking down. She didn't reply right away, and I wondered if she was thinking. I was staring at her with anticipation, wondering what she would say.

"We are one and the same," Ileana said, nodding.

Hearing her say that, gave me such relief. She didn't say the actual word vampire, but that was what she meant. And that was that.

Suddenly her eyes fell upon me. She looked like she thought I would run away. It was possible that she thought the truth would scare me away. But it wasn't fear I was feeling. It was curiosity. And she appeared as curious about me as I was about her.

"I want to know more," I demanded softly.

Ileana stared straight ahead and didn't say anything.

Using the direct approach again, I decided to press her a little more. So, I launched into some questions about the vampire's life that I'd been saving up for her.

"How do you satisfy your taste for blood? How old were you when you became a vampire? Are there more vampires? How long have you lived here?"

She paused a second before speaking. "I feed on the blood of wild animals. Thirty-one years old. To my knowledge I am the only one. For eighty-eight years, I have lived at Wightwick Hall."

"Thanks for answering my questions."

Her eyes locked on mine, but she fell silent. I looked into her eyes and saw uncertainty. It appeared as if she was overwhelmed by what she had said.

Suddenly she broke eye contact with me and she immediately averted her gaze elsewhere, giving me the back of her head.

Suffice to say, Ileana was done. She wasn't

talking anymore. The silence that engulfed us was overpowering. I was longing to speak to her, but I was out of questions to ask. And I was tired of thinking too much, analyzing too much.

Chapter 46

AS SHE SAT ON THE SOFA Lorraine Krag decided it was best to keep her temper in check. And that she was determined to do. She wasn't giving up and would only convince Arthur that she was.

Without saying another word, she stood up, straightened out her peach linen dress with her hands and regained her composure. She forced herself not to argue with him, biting her bottom lip as she smiled.

"You have a point, dear," she said, conceding.

"That's the spirit," Arthur said, which made her feel resentful.

When she crossed the living room, she tried to be coy, and smiled at him, facetiously.

As she headed toward the kitchen, she looked at him and stated with that smile, "It's got to be after eleven o'clock. How about I fix us some lunch?"

Arthur didn't respond. Rather, he was shocked when she smiled at him that way, her eyes shining with devilry. He wasn't sure exactly what she was up to, and he didn't care to find out either.

"I will tell you something else, too," she said loudly as she stepped into the kitchen. "I think I'll accept your suggestion. As soon as I see Myrna Ivester, I will ask her about her half-sister."

"That's a wise thing to do," he called out from the living room.

"I figured I might as well get acquainted with the woman, being our neighbor and all. Don't you agree?" she called out.

"Dear, let's just take it one step at a time. Baby steps, my dear," he called back to her.

"Baby steps, indeed," she mumbled under her breath, as she grabbed her apron from a hook on the wall by the kitchen door and began wrapping it around herself.

After closing his eyes, Arthur slid down a little in his chair with his legs thrust out in front of him, leaned his head back and got comfortable. His mood seemed a little perturbed because of the earlier conversation. A little nap was looking like a really good idea right about now.

Lorraine took out two plates from the cabinet and placed them on the counter. After she shut the doors of the cabinet, she turned around and grabbed the wheat bread out of the refrigerator along with the mayonnaise, lettuce, scallions, and other fixings for lunch.

For the time being, she was going to act this way,

playing all nicey-nice, but only as a means to an end. And she pretended the situation with Myrna Ivester and the castle was long gone from her mind, determined to convince him she wasn't interested in the matter. She wouldn't bring it up anymore.

But in reality, she was secretly planning to go out and spy on Wightwick Hall. She thought she could find out how Myrna was mixed up with that woman. Maybe there was something more to their relationship. Whether instinct or intuition, it was something she couldn't ignore.

After setting the plates of chicken salad sandwiches and cheese and crackers on the table, she said in a singsong voice, "Lunch is served."

Lunch was precisely what she needed to calm her thoughts. And entertaining Arthur with polite conversation would surely convince him that she was off the subject of Wightwick Hall for good.

"Coming, dear," Arthur said and got up from his chair.

"I made your favorite chicken salad," she said with the best smile she could muster.

"How gracious of you! I'm looking forward to it," he said with a hesitant smile as he sat at the table.

Setting two glasses of fresh lemonade on the table, she winked at him and sat down on the opposite side from him.

His eyebrows raised as he took a swig of the lemonade. He was pleased to see her in such a good mood. Perhaps it was wishful thinking on his part, but she resembled the woman he'd married so many years ago.

They sat quietly eating for several minutes. Arthur tore into his lunch, while Lorraine casually took bites of her sandwich, occasionally glancing and smiling at him.

Not wanting to draw any suspicions, she thought it was a good time to begin a simple conversation.

"Anything of note happening at Tesco today? she asked with a twinkle in her eye.

"Nothing of interest. It was just a quick shopping trip."

"I'm just curious," she said with a smile across her face.

"Well, dear, thanks for asking."

"It's my pleasure," she said with another smile and a wink.

Arthur was warming to the conversation. But he was in no mood for any hanky-panky, not now, or even later tonight. He hoped she wasn't, either. So, he simply smiled back, and began eating the cheese and crackers.

After he thought about it some more, he decided to test her. He put down the lemonade he had been drinking and leaned toward her.

"You know what, I like the way you're talking to me," he said, eyeing her mischievously.

Lorraine got the hint, realizing he had misunderstood her. Clearly, she needed to scale back her attempts to pretend she had forgotten all about their earlier conversation.

Noticing his plate was empty, she asked, "All done?"

"Why yes," he replied.

"Allow me," she said as she stood up.

He watched her as she took his empty plate off the table without looking at him. As she turned away from him, he sat back in his chair and picked up his glass of lemonade. Of course, just as he thought, she was teasing him, for reasons he didn't question.

Lorraine dropped the plate in the sink and asked, "Was it cool outside?"

"Yes. It was a bit nippy this morning."

"I've decided I would like to go shopping with you next time," she said with a wicked flash in her eyes. "That is, if you don't mind?"

Surprised by what she had said, he didn't say a word right away.

While waiting for him to respond, she took her empty plate and glass to the sink and began rinsing it under the tap. A wicked smile spread across her lips while her back was turned to him. She didn't say anything either and kept herself busy washing up the dishes.

Now that he thought it over, he finally answered her, "Of course, dear. We need to go out together. However, I told Allan that I would stop by the restaurant later in the week. Maybe we can go out next time. You're not disappointed, are you?"

"By no means. Another time is fine with me," she said compliantly and grinned sinisterly.

She knew he would say something to that effect. It was typical of him to do that, postpone their activities. Little did he know that that was exactly what she wanted. She wanted him out of the way so she could go spying.

Arthur drank the last of his lemonade, wiped his mouth with a napkin from the table, and said, "I'm glad. The last thing I want to do is upset you."

Still with her back turned, she grabbed the peach towel hanging on a hook next to the sink and began drying the plates that she had washed.

"No need to worry yourself. I wouldn't be upset with you at all," she responded slyly.

Chapter 47

EOWYN DYMTROW was standing at the counter in the kitchen. She had just put some food in two bowls for her two little dogs. After wiping her hands with a paper towel, she tossed the empty cans of dog food and paper towel into the garbage pail in the cabinet underneath the sink.

"Trudy, dear," Eowyn said, holding up a bowl.

Trudy looked up at her with her soft, sparkling black eyes.

After placing the bowl on the floor, she said, "There you go, cutie pie."

Her soft whine made her grin as she put the bowl down for Lindy.

"That means you, too, Lindy," she added, not wanting to leave out the other poodle in her affections.

Now that both dogs were elated, she quickly washed her hands in the sink. After drying her hands with a pink towel that had been hanging on a hook above the sink, she pulled the sleeves down on her thin white knit sweater and stood there watching the dogs eat their meal as she thought. Something in the back of her mind told her not to be a woolhead. Why did Lorraine Krag really want to call Siobhan Mulcahy? She had a growing feeling that her story couldn't to be trusted. Was something going on that she didn't know about? The whole thing seemed fishy to her. She didn't want to pry, but at the same time she desperately wanted to know.

That was the first time Lorraine had ever called her. She had been suspicious, hesitant to provide her with Siobhan's cell phone number. But the urgency in Lorraine's voice gave her the feeling that there could be some truth to the story she had told her. She had thought hard on the matter. What harm could possibly come from giving her the number she was desperately trying to wring from her? Eventually she had given in.

Now, more than ever, she wanted to call Myrna.

"A fool of a woman like Lorraine Krag is not going to get the better of me!" she murmured to herself as she came into the living room.

She picked up her iPhone from the small, dark oak side table by the suede camel sofa and dialed up Myrna. After four rings she was directed to her voicemail.

"Hello, Myrna. It's Aunt Eowyn. Can you call me when you get a chance? There is no rush. I just want to chat with you about something."

Eowyn hung up and put her iPhone back on the side

table. She was sure that Myrna would call her back very soon, which she usually did. In the meantime, she went to her bedroom, took her dirty clothes out of the hamper and carried them to the laundry room in the basement.

After starting the washing machine, she realized the phone hadn't rang. Still no call from Myrna? She wasn't worried, though, not a bit. Not much time had passed since she'd phoned her. Likely, she was at work and not available for personal conversations.

The thought arose that she should call Siobhan Mulcahy. This way she could explain why she had given Lorraine Krag her phone number. So, she quickly headed upstairs.

Back in the living room, she was dialing her number on the phone. Three rings later, Siobhan answered, sounding like she just woke up.

"Hello?"

"Hello, Siobhan. It's Eowyn. I'm sorry, did I wake you up?"

"It's fine. I was just catnapping, being lazy on my day off from work. It's so nice to hear your voice. Is Myrna with you?"

Why would she think Myrna was here? Now Eowyn was a little worried.

"No, she isn't with me. I called to tell you that I gave Lorraine Krag your phone number. She said that Myrna had come over to her house last Sunday and told her you could work in her garden."

"I already spoke to Mrs. Krag. She didn't mention anything about her garden," Siobhan told her precisely.

"Is Myrna working today?" Eowyn asked for curiosity.

There was a long silence on the other end of the line that Eowyn almost thought she had hung up.

"I asked you earlier if Myrna was with you because today is her day off."

"Do you know where Myrna is?" Eowyn asked, eagerly wanting to know every detail.

"Mrs. Krag told me that she had seen Myrna across from her house at Wightwick Hall. She wanted to know what Myrna was doing there. That was the reason she called me."

"You don't say. That Lorraine Krag sure is nosy."

"I remember you telling me she was nosy during lunch at the restaurant inside the Best Western New Kent Hotel last July," Siobhan said.

"So, I did. Now that you mentioned Wightwick Hall, I've seen it a few times when I was visiting Jesmond Dene. But I didn't know that Myrna knew the owner."

"All I know is that she met the owner on her job at Longwood Nursing and Rehabilitation Center."

"Well, that makes sense. She's met people at her job before," said Eowyn.

"There's more I need to tell you," Siobhan said in a serious tone of voice.

"Okay? Please tell me."

"You may as well know that Myrna is no longer my roommate. She's living at Wightwick Hall now."

"This comes as a complete surprise to me," Eowyn said. "What happened?"

"Don't be alarmed. Nothing happened. It's just what she wants. I'm sure she'll explain it to you when she gets around to it."

"I gave a call to Myrna and left a message on her cell phone to call me."

"I'm sure Myrna will call you soon," Siobhan reassured her.

"I hope you're not upset with me for giving Lorraine Krag your phone number."

"I completely understand."

"You go back to your nap. And I hope we talk again soon."

"Don't hesitate to call me anytime, for anything," Siobhan said before she hung up.

Eowyn hung up the phone feeling much better. However, she was up in arms about Lorraine Krag pilfering Siobhan's phone number from her for the purpose of gossiping about Myrna, no less. It didn't surprise her, though. She had noticed in the few months Lorraine had lived in the area, that she was asking many questions about things that she has nothing to do with.

What was Myrna doing living in that castle? That was something she couldn't imagine.

The dogs barking attracted her attention. Up till then they had been quietly resting on a small oval rug on the floor. She looked in the corner of the room to see that

Trudy was spinning around chasing her tail. And Lindy was pawing at Trudy with swipes of her paws.

"What is it, my little sweethearts?" she called out to them.

The dogs whimpered and sat down. She knew how to calm them down quickly.

Chapter 48

ILEANA VLADISLAVA CAME CLOSER and looked at me in a way that made me feel as if she was trying to read my thoughts, but I didn't have anything in my head. My mind was devoid of thoughts. Whatever she was looking for, she wasn't going to find it.

"A moment ago, I heard a noise coming from your bag. The sharp ringing of a phone broke into my thoughts," she said, catching me off guard.

"It was probably my smartphone."

"You didn't answer it."

"No, I didn't."

In a flash she turned her face in another direction. It was as if she was gathering her thoughts with difficulty. While I could only guess she was trying to think of something to say next, she moved her head in a semi-circle to the ceiling, then to me. It looked like she was about to say something except she only stood there.

What I felt looking at her face was loneliness. I could sense she found herself not wanting to look at me because of how she felt when she did. It seemed to me that Ileana had been alone for a very long time.

"You look tired. You can stay the night," Ileana said, with a coolness in her tone, showing no emotion.

I was so caught up in my own thoughts that I failed to notice how tired I looked.

Stretching my arms up over my head, I nodded and said, "Yes. Actually, I am tired."

She smiled at my answer. "I'll take you to the room."

Ileana was in front of me as we walked up the staircase. She kept her head and eyes forward. Not a word was spoken by either of us. All you could hear were the stairs creaking.

For a short moment it felt as if the stairs would never end, as if I would never reach the next level. I looked up the spiraling staircase and felt faint. Perhaps I was more tired than I realized. I put my fingertips on the railing to steady myself as I took the last few steps to the second level.

At the top of the stairs, I turned left, following her down a hallway. I studied her as she walked ahead of me. Her raven, shoulder-length hair was striking, definitely her most valuable asset. She was about five foot four and weighed maybe one hundred and twenty. And while she was in good shape for a woman of her age, she was still a woman of her age in vampire years.

Ileana glanced over her shoulder to find me studying her. On some level, she had probably sensed it too. I merely smiled and kept following her. Turning her head forward again, she turned right into another hallway. After a few steps, she stopped in front of a door.

Still keeping her back to me, she opened the door to reveal a lovely bedroom. "You can stay in here."

It was as lavish as everything else in the castle. It looked like a guest room, impersonal, lacking any personality, as though it had never received any guests before. I wondered why that was.

"I trust you'll find it comfortable. It has a private bath attached with anything you may require," Ileana said, as she stood near the doorway.

"This is really lovely," I said looking around the room.

In the middle of the room, against the wall, stood a large four-poster bed, covered in a burgundy counterpane that matched the draperies. The dark wood gleamed as if it had just been polished. Gold-tasseled red velvet pillows were piled high on the bed. At the end of the bed was a curved burgundy settee. A 5' X 8' Persian rug was positioned just in front of the settee. To the left of the bed was a large, chestnut armoire polished to a blinding gleam. There was a kerosene lamp sitting on the bedside table. And in the corner of the room, opposite of the armoire, was a bathroom door next to a small window.

"I am pleased you like it."

Ileana's eyes lit up as she saw a smile form on my face. Her beautiful eyes bore directly into mine, and in that instant I felt it. I wondered if she noticed, and if so, what did she think of that?

There was no denying to myself that there were sparks between us. My mind raced with thoughts of my being powerfully drawn to her, something I hadn't felt before with a woman.

We were quiet for the next minute or so. Then she walked a few steps forward and cast a quick look in my direction.

Not a second sooner, she looked away, as if in thought, then turned back and looked at me in an odd way, and then looked away again. She had been acting this way since my arrival. I could only assume that she was awkwardly, again searching for something to say.

There were so many things I wanted to ask her. I looked at her about to say something, but changed my mind. It didn't feel like the right time. Not now, at least.

When she saw me yawn and rub my eyes, she took a couple of steps backward toward the door. It looked like she was getting ready to leave.

"I will come to check on you later."

"What if I need to find you?"

"Don't worry, I will find you," was the last thing she said to me.

Ileana glided out of the room, gently shutting the door behind her.

"All right, thank you," I said, watching her go.

After putting my backpack and red wool cape in the armoire, I sat on the edge of the bed, taking in the room. It was strange because I felt Ileana's presence. For all I knew she could possibly be standing on the other side of the door, listening to me. I thought that because of the way she looked at me when she left. It was as if she thought I would leave the minute she turned her back. Smiling to myself, I knew I wasn't going anywhere. I came here with the intention of staying. And even stranger was the fact that I didn't miss my old life. Didn't even cross my mind.

The sound of lightning striking a tree, ripped through the air. I was surprised that the weather had changed so fast. The sound of pouring rain startled and soothed me.

I quickly went to the window to take a look. Pulling back the curtain, I could see dark clouds in the sky and drops of rain streaking down the glass.

All the sudden the sound of the rain made me even more tired. The air in the room felt cool against my body, which felt weak. Unable to concentrate, I closed the curtain and turned toward the bed.

After stripping off my black boots and jeans, I laid down on the bed and wondered what would happen next. Whatever it was, I was ready to accept all of it. The unexplained and the unexpected was exciting to me. I knew I was undergoing the most profound and the most overwhelming transformation. It was hard to put into words the feelings running through me. It seemed as if somehow, I was metamorphosizing like a butterfly emerging from a worm and I was loving it. I fell asleep with that thought in my mind.

Chapter 49

"AT LAST, SHE IS HERE!" Ileana said to herself.

Myrna had suspected right. Ileana was standing in the hallway, outside the bedroom door. Concerned about her new friend, she listened to the movement on the other side, and felt responsibility toward her.

Now that she was sure Myrna was resting in bed, she stood there not sure what to do next. So, she started pacing the length of the hallway.

It had been so long since she had felt a sense of belonging, to anyone, that she'd forgotten what it was like and even forgotten that she craved it. A part of her was fearful of Myrna changing her mind and leaving. By all accounts, Myrna's visit had gone off well. What intrigued her the most was her intuition was correct, for Myrna to want the life of a vampire.

Now, she wanted to go to her study and reflect on the matter some more with soft music in the background. She breezed down the hallway, and into the room.

Flipping through a stack of albums next to the turntable on top of the square oak cabinet, she selected one and put it on. "La Lisonjera" by Cecile Chaminade started playing as she sat down on the Victorian armchair to the right of the cabinet. Closing her eyes, she let the music engulf her.

The charming tunes of the music brought memories flooding back over her. Just like that, she was remembering things she hadn't thought about in years. The time when she had become a vampire. Images rolled through her mind like a movie.

On a cold and rainy evening in December 1539, a week after her thirty-first birthday, that she remembered well from her days in Toplita, a commune in Hunedoara County, in the southwest corner of Transylvania, she sat in a wooden chair in front of the fireplace in the living room. She was lonely and tired of working on the farm.

She hadn't married and lived at home taking care of her father until his death of cirrhosis of the liver. It had been six years since her father had died. Still she hadn't met anyone significant. Working on the farm, she had no time to forge close relationships with anyone.

A knock on the door had surprised her and disrupted her train of thought. It was odd considering the horrible weather.

"Ms. Amanar, it's Simona Bellu. Open the door," the girl said in Romanian.

She opened the door to find the fifteen-year-old girl whom she had tutored in reading and writing skills some years earlier, solely as a favor to the girl's father who had been a friend of her late father. Three years had passed since she had last seen Simona, and she barely recognized her. Simona had on a long hooded black cloak over a white dress with a short ruff collar that was wet from the rain. Quite unusually, there were no grass or soil stains on her shoeless feet.

After letting her inside, Ileana closed the door and led her near the fireplace to dry off. Simona immediately moved away from the fireplace and stared at her in a peculiar way.

"What brings you out in this weather?" Ileana asked her in Romanian.

Simona told her that she could offer her a better life than the one she was living.

"A life that didn't involve hard work and loneliness," Simona specifically had said in Romanian.

Ileana's defenses were weak from years of a solitary existence, and she had caved. For the heck of it she told Simona that she did want a better life for herself but didn't know how to go about finding it. Simona came close to her and sunk her teeth into her neck.

The next thing she remembered was waking up in her bed the next day. She had lost her appetite and was physically changing. Her desperation for blood drove her to attack the pigs on her farm and consume their blood.

Four days passed before Simona Bellu came back and explained to her that she was a vampire. That she had to go with her to be with the others and live in a castle near Brasov, Romania, for which she did. She never returned to the farm.

The record was no longer playing music, and she just noticed that it had stopped. Her thoughts returned to Myrna Ivester. She wanted to know how Myrna was doing. Should she assist assist in Myrna's transition? Would she need another neck bite?

After much thinking on the subject, she decided that one more bite would help, though she wouldn't take much blood. It would speed up her transformation.

With that in mind she got up, went to the turntable, turned it off, put the record back in its cardboard and put it back with the other records on top of the cabinet.

She briskly left the study and stopped in front of the door of the room where Myrna was asleep. The only sound she could hear was the rain falling hard on the castle.

Quietly entering the room, she floated around contemplating how she was going to seduce her. She hadn't worked out this part yet. Stopping by the window she studied her sleeping form where Myrna lay under the beige wool blanket and burgundy counterpane with gold-tasseled red velvet pillows all around her.

The soundtrack of heavy rain beating against the window took her out of her concentration. After briefly looking at the window, she pulled the curtain and peered outside. She took in a deep breath while watching the downpour, which was soothing her nerves. The spot by the window was ideal for what she planned next.

She turned around to face Myrna with a look of desire. As she gazed on Myrna, her thoughts turned to the blood coursing through her veins. Now Ileana's brown eyes glowed reddish.

Chapter 50

 of lightning some time after its flash, I rose to a sitting position in bed, looked all around. Hazy tendrils of light fell into the room and drifted around me. The curtain on the window was drawn aside, but I didn't remember leaving it that way.

I turned my head away from the window. That was when I saw a figure in the shadows and realized it was Ileana. There she was in the room.

Was I awake or asleep? Or somewhere in between? It felt as if I was in a hypnotic state. It was as though I was looking at myself from the outside. Like a dream within a dream.

As I looked up to find Ileana's eyes focused with hypnotic penetration on my face, there came a flash of lightning. Unable to turn away, her hypnotic stare was all I could see. And I was looking at her just as intensely.

Her beautiful, sparkling reddish-brown, enticing eyes burned into my skull. I had never seen eyes like hers — so filled with feeling. Right now, in this moment, those feelings were good.

With her gaze fixed on me, I left the bed and went toward her. As I came closer to her, I began to feel a sense of exhilaration inside of me. My emotions intensified and sent me into a spiral of delight.

Standing in my long-sleeved white button-front, cotton blouse and underwear, not able to contain my excitement, I looked directly into her eyes. Face to face with me, I saw how magnificent she was. She looked beautiful in the dim light, with her wonderful eyes, shining down on me.

We moved closer together, and grinned, mirroring each other's delight. It seemed important to make something as beautiful as possible out of each moment, to live it to the full, as I gazed, enraptured.

Sensing what was coming, I took a quick breath. The agony and ecstasy of it was beyond anything I could have imagined. I was giving in, without a single protest. No words needed to be spoken. She knew I needed the same thing as badly as she did. The vampire's life was very desirable to me. Ileana sensed this in me; after all, she was a vampire.

The rain continued to beat against the window without letup. The sound added to the alluring atmosphere. Another vivid flash of lightning illuminated the room, which highlighted Ileana's features and made her more attractive.

My mind was a jumble of thoughts and emotions. What should I do, and what shouldn't I do? Something unique was happening. This moment seemed to mark a turning point in my thoughts, my concepts and all the familiar notions of what women should want. Nothing like this had ever happened to me before with a woman, my every move something unimaginable till now. Our connection was deep-rooted. The absolute nature of the bond between myself and my vampire maker, and the certainty which it was intimately close. We might be the only two vampires in the world, which made us even closer.

From this close proximity, what I saw in Ileana's eyes was genuine. I looked forward to her next move.

Ileana spoke, her voice just a soft whisper. "You are so beautiful."

Whatever she had said in the vampire language, I knew it was something nice. She didn't have to try because I was eating out of the palm of her hand. Nothing could stop her.

I tilted my face toward her, closed my eyes, listening to the sound of the falling rain. Her fingers lightly caressed my cheek. I actually liked that she touched me, as if I was something precious. A chill ran up my spine just as she brushed my hair off my neck with the back of her hand.

A shuddering moan escaped from my lips as her sweet lips were on my neck. Her lips glided down my neck, forming delicate kisses as she explored the carotid artery pulsating beneath my skin.

Her tongue found the little holes she had made. She kissed them and then softly licked them. It was a sensational feeling, causing me to tremble.

My eyes opened slightly to see her eyes had gone fully red. Her upper lip pulled back, exposing her elongated incisors. The bloodthirst took over, she nuzzled into my neck then inserted her fangs in the holes. My eyes closed again as I felt her sucking the blood out of me. It didn't hurt. I fluttered so needful. It was stimulation overload. I was filled with ecstasy.

Ileana pulled her teeth out. I felt her tongue brushing against the bleeding holes in my neck. It seemed as if it was over in a flash.

When she slowly released her mouth from my neck, I slowly opened my eyes and attempted to steady my emotions.

A bolt of lightning broke across the sky and light penetrated the room, briefly illuminating her. Ileana tilted her head back and sighed with contentment. A trickle of blood seeped out from the corner of her mouth as she lowered her head to my level.

She put her right arm around my shoulders and ran her fingers over the side of my neck.

Ileana whispered up close to my ear, "Sleep well, Myrna."

Ileana licked the blood off her lips as she watched me walk back to the bed. She didn't take her eyes off me for a second. I laid down on the bed and immediately fell sound asleep.

Chapter 51

I SLEPT, awoke and slept again. My body was changing, and I was tossing and turning. I was in an altered state of consciousness. At times I wanted to scream out loud between shuddering breaths as my body shook uncontrollably. Finally, I awoke in a cold sweat, sometime in the evening, because I was looking at darkness through the window.

As I watched the rising moon in the distance, I found myself levitating a few inches off the bed. Just coming out of the hypnopompic state of consciousness, passing through from sleeping to wakefulness. As my body fell to the bed, it felt like my body weighed less. I was certain I'd lost some pounds, ten perhaps.

Lying in bed, I wondered how long I had been asleep. I'd lost track of time. I didn't even know which day it was.

As I was preparing to get up, my mind drifted to Ileana. I remembered the softness of her lips on my neck. And the gentle touch of her soft hands made me shiver. The more I thought about it, the more I was getting turned on just thinking about it.

I put my fingers on the holes on the right side of my neck, to make sure it wasn't a dream. The way that they felt, I could tell they had been tampered with.

It struck me that Ileana was a lonely vampire. Initiating me into her secret society, biting me, changing me into an immortal, seemed like an act of desperation on her part. This was her way of reaching out, the only way she could, as a vampire.

My mind started wandering again, I got up from the bed. In doing so, I discovered there was no mirror anywhere in the room. How odd! I thought to myself. And though I couldn't see myself, I knew that my body had undergone more changes.

"I'm a vampire. I know it," I whispered to myself.

There was only one person who knew for sure. I needed to find Ileana.

After slipping on my black jeans, I started to walk toward the door. On the way there, I started feeling very weak. There was another thing, too: My body ached excruciatingly for blood.

Quickly leaving the bedroom, I went in search of Ileana. At every turn in the hallway, something told me I would get lost if I wasn't careful. I breathed a sigh of relief when I saw the entrance to the spiral staircase coming up on the right.

I made my way down the staircase to the floor below. Crossing through the foyer, my eyes turned toward the hallway where I saw an open door to a brightly lit room. I could sense Ileana was there.

When I came into the room, I saw her there, sitting in a Venetian chair of ebony and mother-of-pearl, turned away from me reading under a purple laced Victorian lamp next to a large ornate vase on a dark brown cherrywood end table. She was dressed in a simple, long-sleeved, gray tunic with draping sleeves and matching leggings, with thin-soled dark brown sandals on her feet.

The room was a very fancy library of sorts. Most impressively, the marble floored room was filled with books on four dark oak bookshelves on the east wall. From what I could tell they were classical literature, opera, art, and music.

A pair of large ornate vases sat on two dark brown cherrywood end tables at either end of the bookshelves. At the far end of the room, there was a small window next to an Edgar Degas painting on the wall anyone could raise an eyebrow at. I took a glance at the portrait of ballerinas, staring at it briefly, then looked at Ileana.

"What are you reading?" I asked, startling her into looking up at me.

"It's a rare edition of the Grimm's fairy tale *Little Red Riding Hood*, and it is my joy," she said.

"I've read it. I recently saw a movie version of it," I said and managed a weak smile.

The corners of my mouth turned up before I could hold back the smile. Besides, I didn't want to. Feeling a little embarrassed, I hoped she didn't mind me walking around the place in my bare feet.

"Interesting," she said, thinking, "How did you sleep?"

"Very well thank you."

"What time is it?"

Ileana pointed to the clock on the wall, which read a quarter past eleven o'clock. "You will eventually get used to being awake in the night and asleep in the day."

"The vampire schedule," I responded automatically, jokingly to lighten the mood a bit.

Without stopping to think, I had said the first words that came into my head. Judging by her lack of reaction, she didn't get it. Or maybe she couldn't relate to my sense of humor.

Ileana put the book on the shelf, took me by the arm, and began to walk me around the mahogany wood-paneled walled room, pointing out the leather-bound volumes and the first editions by well-known authors.

"I'm glad you are still here," she said after her tour.

"I'm not planning to leave."

"That's good to know."

She released my arm and sat down in the Venetian chair again.

"How long have I been sleeping?"

"Today is Thursday, September 14. You've been in bed for two days."

"I would never have guessed."

A sudden weakness swept over me. Feeling I was going to faint, I staggered as I reached for the other Venetian chair and gripped it so hard that the knuckles of my thin hands went white, as if holding on for my life. I hadn't had nourishment in four days. My body was about a pint low on blood, on an empty stomach. I became painfully aware of my hunger for blood.

When I looked back, I saw that Ileana was already standing by my side. With one glance at me, she had seemed to intuit what was happening to me without me saying anything. She kindly helped me sit in the chair.

Very quickly the conversation got serious.

"My body is cold all over and I feel very weak," I said in a near whisper.

"I'll get you something," she said too quickly.

Ileana left the room for a few minutes and returned with a smoked-glass goblet, filled to the rim with blood and a straw. She handed it to me. I pushed myself up straight in the chair, held the goblet of blood with two hands and sucked half of it down through the straw. Then I slowly sipped through the straw, for the last of it.

"Feel better?" Ileana asked as I handed the empty goblet to her.

"That does make me feel a lot better," I said, relaxing back in the chair, smiling a bloody smile at her.

There was a dizzying effect of the blood rushing through my body. It did wonders for my insides. And I felt the urge to say something more. Instead of words, a yawn came out of me as the sensation of oxygen-enriched cells tingled through my body. Tiredness had fallen upon me. Perhaps I drank too much, too fast.

"Why don't you have a short nap, Myrna? I'll check on you in a while."

The last thing I remembered was I thought I saw her leave the room. As I closed my eyes, I faded off into sleep, hoping it wouldn't be a long nap, just a two- or three-hour power nap. I didn't want to be sitting in this chair for another couple of days.

Chapter 52

AFTER TAKING THE GOBLET to the kitchen, carefully washing it, and putting it back in the cabinet, Ileana came back into the library. She seemed to be very relaxed, standing there watching Myrna sleep in the chair, but in reality, her mind was occupied with many things: the fear she'd felt again, and worrying for Myrna.

Little did Myrna know why she had been looking over *Little Red Riding Hood*. She knew what it was like to fear a wolf, specifically a werewolf. For years she had tortured herself about it. The lesson she had learned from *Little Red Riding Hood* was that no matter how the wolf might have attempted to kill her, she discovered her courage and forced herself to overcome her fears.

Naturally, she couldn't share these feelings with Myrna. All she could do was try to stay cool and hope that the werewolf would never find them.

Knowing that Myrna could be asleep for hours, she thought she should bring her to the guest room. She carefully lifted Myrna into her arms — and managed without much exertion of strength. Ileana carried her up the spiral staircase to the next level and into the hall that leads to one of the six large bedrooms.

Upon reaching the room, she pushed the door open with her shoulder. She laid her gently down on the bed and arranged the pillows comfortably behind her back.

"Rest well, Myrna," Ileana whispered softly near her ear.

With a sigh and a sideways glance out the window, she pulled the curtain shut. She left the room closing the door behind her and headed for her greenhouse, knowing that working with her plants was a way to get lost in her thoughts. In 1940 she had taken up horticulture — a rather unusual pastime for a vampire, but it suited the environment of her home within the leafy valley and public park of Jesmond Dene.

Ileana made her way up the spiral staircase to the room and headed right for the section of geraniums. They had grown significantly because they absorb a lot of light coming through the skylights which also opened and closed automatically allowing much needed fresh air to circulate in the room.

After trimming the geraniums with scissors, she made her way around a section of marigolds, to the sink in the corner of the room. She picked up a watering can from the floor, filled it, and went to water the geraniums.

Two pretty butterflies flew past her head, fluttering in all directions, as she walked to the far side of the greenhouse, where pansies and orchids grew. It looked like a jungle because of the scores of shelves of white and orange orchids, about half of them in bloom. After watering the orchids, her next task was to repot the azaleas.

With so much to occupy her time, her hands worked on their own and her mind was free to wander. The first thought that entered her mind was the day she had arrived at the stone castle with reddish-brown roofs, sixteen miles southwest of Brasov in Transylvania.

The first vampire Simona Bellu had introduced her to was Ruxandra Tepes, who served as the right hand of Morsus the Elder. At first sight, Ileana thought she looked like an angel. She had long, sandy blonde hair, and hazel eyes and had on a light green flowing dress that fell to the ground and brown sandals on her feet. As she walked, her flowy long sleeves billowed out like bat wings, and the fabric was so bright.

Ruxandra caressed her face with her hand and said with a smile, in Romanian, "It is with pleasure I welcome you, Ileana Amanar. From now on you will be called Ileana Vladislava. You deserve a new name for your new life."

While Ruxandra entertained her by giving her a tour of the lavishly decorated castle, Simona wandered down a vaulted hall and disappeared through some doorway. Ruxandra went on to explain how in the early 1200's, Turcu Castle was built as a wooden fortress of the

Teutonic Knights, to protect Transylvania from the Turks. In the late 1300's it had been reconstructed with stone by Saxons to guard a mountain pass between Transylvania and Wallachia, the south part of Romania. In the early 1400's the castle and adjoining territory passed into the hands of the House of Basarab. Thus, the Draculesti family, a splinter branch of the House of Basarab, and the city of Brasov had invested interest in the castle.

"Now it is the home to nearly fifty vampires, who come and go as they please," Ruxandra had said proudly in Romanian.

After the tour she was given a new set of clothes. After changing into them, she was taken down a narrow staircase carved in the stone that snaked to the bottom of the castle. Not unlike a large cellar in appearance, the dark vaulted chamber was referred to as a "sanctuary." This was where the vampires were sleeping, hanging upside down.

For the next thirty-eight years, she rarely left Turcu Castle. There had been plenty of blood on hand. It was served in silver goblets any time you needed it. She had assumed the blood came from animals, or maybe even from people. She didn't ask.

She had spent her time learning the vampire language and listened to stories told by other vampires. At night there was music and dancing, but, more often she sat listless on the steep cliff, looking down on the plains.

The next time she saw Simona Bellu was in 1561, for a special ceremony celebrating one hundred years of vampires in Transylvania. Everyone had dressed up for the occasion. At the time she had believed Simona spent all of her time traveling around Transylvania, possibly creating more vampires. That evening was the first time she had ever seen Morsus the Elder. He had shoulder-length black hair, dark brown eyes, a slightly crooked nose, thin lips and had on a white dress shirt beneath a black velvet jacket, black pants, and knee-high black boots. He made a powerful speech to the vampires gathered in the dining hall.

From what she had learned about Morsus the Elder, he was the oldest vampire in existence as far as anyone knew. He had become a vampire during the time of Vlad III, ruler of Wallachia and a member of the Draculesti. Morsus the Elder made the important decisions for the different vampire clans who sought to control their own territories in Europe. He kept sacred scrolls of the vampire language, culture and the genealogies and records of the clans.

Ileana was the happiest at Turcu Castle. She had received nothing but kindness from the vampires. So, in July 1578, when the people rose up against the vampires, she was completely shocked. She knew there was fierce rivalry among the vampire clans but had no idea they were killing and torturing people.

All of the vampires had to leave Turcu Castle. They scattered themselves to towns in Transylvania. That was when she fled to Gheorgheni.

Even after all these years in England, she missed her past life. A tear slipped from her eye as she stood up holding pots of different sizes. Despite her emotional remembrances, she was immensely pleased with her work. The azaleas looked bright and fresh.

After the pots were stored, she headed toward the sink to wash her hands. Then she left the room, thinking, it must be five in the morning, which meant it was time for a nap. She worked her way down the spiral staircase heading for the cellar.

Chapter 53

EITHER THAT NIGHT, or the next day into the night — not sure which exactly — I found myself in bed in the guest room again. Tossing and turning throughout my sleeping hours, I didn't remember how I got into the bed. I could only assume that Ileana whisked me away from her library and put me into the bed.

I was lying here thinking about all the strange images in the dream I just had. It was spectacular enough to feel real and chilling at that. Strange dreams were part of the baggage I had carried with me way before Ileana bit into me.

How it started wasn't clear. No matter. The first thing I remembered was that I was breathing hard and running as fast as my feet could carry me in a forest I didn't recognize. My speedy steps rustled the leaves on the ground. Tree branches scraped my dress that I held with both hands to keep myself from tripping over it.

It struck me odd that I was wearing a dress from a time in history that could be something my ancestors had worn. The European-style floor-length, long-sleeved, white dress with ruffles across the bust was absolutely stunning and could pass for something from the Renaissance era. My hair, in one long braid hanging down my back and tied at the end with a yellow-and-white bow, contributed to the fairy-tale look.

When I glanced over my shoulder, I saw my stalker trailing about ten yards behind. It was a dark-haired werewolf. His black eyes had fallen on me the instant I looked at him. The beast reacted by growling more deeply than before. His mouth was wide open with razor-sharp teeth on full display and blood dripping from them. He looked vicious and determined to grasp me with its claws and tear off my head.

I turned my eyes forward and ran faster. As I heard the cry of the werewolf linger in the misty air, my fear kept me from looking back again.

Despite my efforts not to look, I took a quick peek over my shoulder to see how close that wretched wolf was to me. That was when I tripped over something and went down, ending up on my hands and knees.

Tired from the chase, I slowly started to raise myself up. I didn't look behind me, but I could hear the growling of the werewolf in the distance.

As I stood up, I could see my dress was soiled. I took a look at my surroundings, realizing that I didn't even know where I was. When I looked down, I saw a very gruesome sight. In the midst of all my fear, I just found out that I had fallen over a dead body.

The dead woman had been wearing layered Renaissance period clothing that was a dark-blue dress under a short red cloak. Her head was lying a few feet away from her body. The woman's red eyes were wide open in terror, two razor-sharp fangs hanging from her mouth. To my horror and astonishment, I discovered by the light of the moon that it was the body of a dead vampire.

My brows furrowed and I wondered how it could have happened, and what it might mean. And my mind was consumed with worry about the approaching werewolf. So, running was something I should do.

Panting heavily, I was running faster than before. I could hear the howls of the werewolf, but I wasn't going to look behind me. This time I was looking fiercely around for dead bodies on the ground to avoid tripping over them, or worse, stepping on them.

That was when I ran into Ileana. She caught my upper arms to steady me, her face showing worry. The way she was dressed made her look pure and attractive. She had on a low-cut, long-sleeved embroidered gold dress and a sheer silk veil draped over her shoulders. Complimenting the outfit was a simple white flower in her raven hair that was pinned up loosely at the back of her head.

I spoke to her, but she didn't answer me. Instead she released her hold on my arms, lifted her arm, and pointed toward the approaching werewolf.

"Beware of the werewolf. He knows what you are, Simona," she said in the vampire language.

The only word I understood was Simona, the name she had called me. Who was that?

"Ileana, it's Myrna. Please, let's go…from…here," I said, desperately trying to catch my breath.

"He is coming for you," she said again in the vampire language.

"Hurry, we must leave now," I said, unable to keep the fear from my voice.

Pulling her arm, I pleaded with her to run away with me. She wouldn't budge at all. I grabbed her by her shoulders and looked at her with desperation in my eyes. Still, she wouldn't move. Why wouldn't she come with me?

Frantically, I looked back and saw the werewolf moving closer to us. I looked back at Ileana, then on the werewolf not knowing what I could do. I looked again at the werewolf and saw him leap to pounce on us. It was a terrifying image.

At that point, I woke up. The dream was still vivid in my mind. I might call it a vision from a past life, though I didn't believe in reincarnation. It was as if I was seeing someone's life through their eyes.

Still, with no idea why I dreamt that, I remembered the dream that I had the night of my birthday about the

German Shepherd chasing me. Was there a link between the two dreams? Now I could chalk up to a coincidence, except it happened to me a second time. But this was something I should talk to Ileana about to make sure. I thought she might have some insight which might be beneficial.

I rose from the bed feeling stronger than I had in days. Perhaps I was returning to my former self, or rather adjusting to the changes that my body had undergone. Overall, it felt as though my whole body had been rearranged as if old pieces had been removed by some unseen hand and new pieces had been inserted.

Though I wasn't sleepy, I stood beside the bed, lifted my arms above my head, and yawned a couple of times. It was an automatic reaction. I guess it was from being in bed so long.

Meanwhile, I was liking my new-found energy. So, what if I was a bloodsucker? I must face the facts. That was what I was. And I really liked it.

Entering the bathroom, I ran the cold water in the sink, washed my hands, and splashed some water onto my face. Although I couldn't see myself straight-on, I felt refreshed. I braided my hair in one long braid as I found it comfortable that way.

Retrieving my backpack from the armoire, I dug out a change of clothes. I removed my white button-front, cotton blouse and black jeans and threw it in the backpack. Then I put on a pair of faded blue jeans and a light-blue long-sleeved crepe blouse.

Still wearing no shoes, I ran out the door to find Ileana and tell her about the dream. I hoped she would help me understand because I felt I wasn't out of the woods yet.

Chapter 54

I OPENED THE DOOR to the roof and deeply inhaled the cool fresh air as I stepped outside. Something in my gut told me Ileana would be here — and that she was. There, alone, she stood with arms outstretched on the ledge of the roof, sixty feet above the ground. She looked light enough to fly. With the crescent moon in the background, it was an impressive sight. I wondered what she might be thinking as she stared across the wooded valley of Jesmond Dene.

I decided to join her on the ledge. As I came closer, she said nothing, but watched me out of the corner of her eye.

"Sure, is chilly out here," I said rather casually.

She remained silent, tilted her head at an angle and looked back over her shoulder with her dreamy eyes into mine. It was just something she did every now and then.

The air whooshed around me as I jumped up next to her. The cold night air blew on my face and clothes. Startled by my appearance at her side, her eyes widened, and her body jerked briefly. Maybe she needed some time to get used to having someone to lean on. Once she adjusted to my presence in her life, I hoped, she might feel more comfortable confiding in me.

"So, this is the life of a vampire?" I asked.

"How do you like it?" she asked with a mischievous glare on her face.

"Would it surprise you if I told you that I like it very much?"

"I am not surprised at all. It's exciting at times."

A smile formed on her mouth, which then curled into a devious grin. What could she be thinking now?

"What's on your mind, Ileana?"

"My dear, you look divine in the moonlight."

"Why, thank you dear. It's so kind of you to say that. The vampire life suits me after all."

Standing so high above the ground, it was almost as if I was breathing in the stars, like a wind goddess, from a time before the modern era when the most extraordinary creatures walked this earth. Maybe I was overly dramatic. But it felt good to overcome one of my biggest fears. You'd never have believed that all my life I had a fear of heights.

"It's a breathtaking view and I'm experiencing a feeling of euphoria up here," I said.

"It is very soothing."

"Do you ever worry about falling off?"

"If I slip, I can just float back up onto the ledge. Vampires can absorb, transform, and manipulate life force energy. As you practice, you will be able to do that too."

Her saying that made me think of all the things I could and couldn't do. Without any doubt, I was starting to get hooked on this supernatural stuff.

"What are you thinking about now?" I asked, focusing on her again.

"You are a vampire. Do you have to ask?"

"I like to hear you talk," I said, a little playful.

Her expression told me she was taken back by my answer. I tapped into her vulnerability, which could be a turn-on for a vampire. On the surface, she was very attentive and caring. Still, I was sure there was a dark side in her, being a vampire and all. If I wasn't already a vampire, I was sure she would have stuck her fangs in me.

"Many times, I have been up here alone. The thought of you being next to me makes me so excited. I need the comfort that you provide," she said with a slight smile revealing her sharp fangs.

Just as I thought, she had been aroused by our conversation at such heights. I also felt beguiled from the close conversation.

"That's such a sweet thing to say," I said gazing at her with my newbie vampire eyes of wonderment.

Abruptly changing the conversation, she said, "In case you were wondering, it is Saturday, September 16 approximately half past one o'clock in the morning. And we are very low on blood."

"How low?" I asked, rather worried.

"There is one half full blood bag left out of the six whole blood bags I took from Freeman Hospital a week ago."

"Freeman Hospital? That's where Siobhan Mulcahy works."

"Is that so?"

"Yes, it is so."

"Right! Going back there is not an option. There are some deer out there. Now is a good time to strike."

"There is something else I want to share with you. But I guess it can wait till later."

Ileana gave me a good hard look, and said, "It will have to."

Getting into position, she walked a few steps to her right with her back to me. She slowly turned her head to look at me. Her lust for blood was present in her reddish-brown eyes.

"We must hurry up if we want to catch one of those deer," she said in an urgent tone.

There was something really dreadful about killing an animal. On the other hand, a girl needed to eat, right? I didn't want to do it, but there wasn't any other way.

"So, are you ready?" she asked impatiently.

As Ileana looked expectantly at me, waiting for my answer, I couldn't help but notice how lovely she looked in the moonlight that bathed her face with its soft silver.

"No time like the present," I said wittingly.

Before she could respond, I said taking off fast, "I'll race you to the bottom."

Here goes another 'first' for me, I thought as I plunged forward. I moved straight down the side of the castle wall toward the ground below. Ileana followed behind me with her long-nailed feet gliding down the wall. She caught up with me and we were moving side by side a bare two feet apart.

"Remind me later to tell you about my strange dream," I said, before our feet touched the ground.

Chapter 55

WE WERE PERCHED on a large rock watching two deer in the woods twenty feet away. I wouldn't allow myself to think how cute they were. It was bad enough knowing that I was about to kill one of them. It goes without saying, this creeped me out in a big way. But I tried not to let it show.

Before I knew what was happening, Ileana was on the move.

"Stay near me," she said as she took off running.

Suddenly, and taking me completely by surprise, my head wasn't in it. My legs were shaking from nerves. I took a moment getting my bearings, to study my surroundings. It was so dark where we were, that I almost couldn't see her. But I forced myself to run after her.

As I was running at top speed, this was uncanny and dream-like in nature. I had done this before — in my dreams. The only difference was that I was chasing an animal rather than the animal chasing me.

When I saw her wrestling with the deer, I stopped running, walked a short distance and stood near her. Hoof-stomping and snorts, the deer lay on its side, struggling on the ground. In front of us stood two tall trees acting as pillars below, the moonlit sky wrapping around. The grass swayed back and forth in the breeze. The trees waved their branches, and leaves fell all around us landing on the grass before rolling to a standstill.

Ileana straddled the deer and bit into its neck, and it let out a whine. A handful of minutes after, she raised her head up and glanced in my direction, looking straight at me with her red eyes, blood trailing down her mouth, pale as the moon. The look on her face indicated that it was my turn.

Was I ready for this? My desire for blood was so strong I cared for nothing else — which had me in disbelief. But I couldn't stop myself.

Without thinking I slowly kneeled on the ground. My eyes were glowing red. I could feel it. The smell of the blood of the deer overpowered me. My fangs were beginning to show in my mouth. I approached the deer's neck and closed my eyes as my teeth came out and sank into its jugular vein.

The blood of the animal electrified me. I felt revived. Apparently, I needed the blood more than I cared to admit to myself. I liked the taste so much that I kept feeding.

"Uh-hum," Ileana cleared her throat to get my attention.

Seemingly, I had gotten carried away in the moment. I lifted my head up and turned toward Ileana. There was a look of shock on her face. So, with as innocent a face as I could muster, I gave her a simple smile with blood on my fangs and lips. Her expression was now indifferent to me.

Shifting around I had settled with my butt on the ground. I felt icky all over. Blood dripped and stained my blouse. I noticed too that my blouse had grass and soil stains on the elbows. There was no other option for me but to rub the blood off my hands onto my jeans.

Ileana was about to drain the remaining blood from the deer's circulatory system for our use later. Reaching into her crossbody, she pulled out a plastic bag attached to a needle attached to tubing that resembled an IV infusion set. After inserting the needle into a vein in its neck, the bag began filling up with its blood. Quickly the deer lost strength and then went limp as its life dwindled away.

After putting the plastic bag of blood in her crossbody, she looked at me and asked, "How do you feel?"

"If you want to know the truth, I feel like I just killed Bambi," I said as I brushed the dirt off my jeans.

"Who?" she asked and threw her crossbody bag over her shoulder.

With a funny expression on my face, I suddenly realized that she really didn't know. Her childhood was so long ago that there hadn't been Walt Disney movies in those days. With that, I decided to rephrase my previous statement.

"What I meant to say was that I feel bad about killing that deer. I'm not completely comfortable with it yet. It's kind of depressing."

"You will adjust in time. We must obtain blood from animals from time to time. Blood is a source of life force energy we need to survive."

"I know, Ileana. I understand it goes with the territory. Nonetheless, I think it's frustrating being a vampire."

"Is it?" Ileana asked with a perplexed expression.

"Please don't try to humor me. I am just a mess. I just want to get out of these clothes."

"You look just precious," she said, and looked around her, but nothing moved.

"I am quite sure you mean well in saying that. Just bear with me because I'm not used to this the way you are."

Preparing to leave, she stood up. After brushing some of the dirt off of her beige colored, long-sleeved tunic, she came over to where I was sitting on the ground and extended her arm.

"Let me help you up," she offered.

Wordlessly, I took her hand and she pulled me up to my feet. Unable to contain my emotions, I surprised both of us by grabbing her into a hug. I just needed to be comforted feeling that I had acted a little irritable. That she had seen a side of me, she had not recognized before.

For what seemed like the longest time, the two of us stood holding each other. We felt like we both needed it badly. Then I suddenly remembered how dirty I was and thought about all the mess I might have transferred onto her.

"Oh my!" I said, releasing our embrace.

I'd gotten some dirt on her long-sleeved tunic. Ileana looked where my eyes had gone. Then she dusted it off quickly as if it were unimportant to her.

"It's fine. I am a mess myself," she said lifting her arms.

There were drops of blood on the back of her shirt cuff. I also noticed that there were soil stains on her beige colored leggings. Though I was the messiest of all.

The pit in my stomach told me to look down. I saw the deer lying dead on the ground. It died with its eyes wide open. It stared at me in its eternal silence, which was creepy and sad at the same time.

"This will take some getting used to," I said, with my eyes still on the deer.

"You've done very well for your first time," she said in a reassuring voice.

"I think I missed the vein when I bit into its neck. Did I do it wrong?"

"I have always believed it's automatic for a vampire to strike correctly. Though I can't say for certain. No need to trouble yourself about it. You'll get another chance to do it again."

After saying that, she looked at me with a gleam of something like humor in her eyes.

"Thanks for reminding me," I said in a depressing tone.

"You're very welcome. Shall we turn in?"

"I thought you would never ask," I said excitedly as I started walking to the castle.

Peering over my shoulder to see her trailing behind me, I felt a sense of peace wash over me. All my tension faded away. There was no other place in the world I'd rather be than right here, with her.

Chapter 56

HUNTING was a dirty business. It was the yuckiest thing in the vampire's world. I reflected on this as I stripped off my dirty clothes and stuffed them into a drawer of the armoire in the guest room.

Once inside the bathroom, I washed the dried blood off my hands in the sink and ran a cold bath to wash the soil from my feet. As I bathed, the cold water soothed my body.

When I came out of the tub, I wrapped myself in a pink towel and released my hair from the braid I'd tied it in some hours earlier. Then I changed into an above the knee gray, tunic-camisole combo, lacy black capri leggings, and short black boots and let myself out of the room.

I followed the music down the hallway to a room that was her study. After a few steps inside, the music had suddenly stopped, and I found Ileana removing a record from the turntable.

Dressed in an olive-green long-sleeved tunic, trimmed at the neck with embroidery and matching capri leggings with black sandals, her raven hair accented her attire. She had polished herself up very well.

Before I said anything, I checked out the clock on the wall above the inglenook fireplace. Almost four in the morning. I frowned and moved closer to Ileana.

"You look lovely," I said to her as she placed the album on top of the cabinet.

She threw me a quick glance and said in a soothing voice, "How very kind of you. You're not so bad-looking yourself."

I liked her wittiness and laughed a bit. Then she laughed a little, surprising herself, so she stifled her amusement.

"Did you have a dream that you wanted to share with me?" she asked, surprisingly looking towards my face.

Good thing she mentioned it. The truth was that I was actually building up to telling her.

"I'm so glad you remembered."

"Be my guest. Tell me, Myrna."

Ileana stepped over to a Victorian turquoise velvet buttoned back armchair and sat down. I walked over and stood next to the chair she had deposited herself on.

"I've had dreams like this off and on since I was a child, so I don't know what to make of it."

"Tell me everything you remember."

"In the dream, I had on a Renaissance period dress. I was running from a werewolf. I ran into you in the forest.

You just stood there and warned me of the werewolf. I told you to come with me. You didn't budge."

"A werewolf. How interesting," she said, as if reflecting, then asked, "Is there more?"

"Yes, there is more. I had tripped over a dead vampire's body and fell to the ground. Her head, separated from her body a few feet away on the ground, happened to face me. What do you make of this?"

"It may be a vision into the future," she said, looking up at me. "On second thought, it feels a bit like my past. I believe you have tapped into my memories. Your abilities have increased tenfold. You are more intuitive, you feel, see, and know more."

After a beat or two, I asked, "How so, Ileana?"

She took a more serious tone. "It feels like forever ago that I fled Romania. At that time, all throughout Transylvania, the misfortune fell on the vampires, disdained by Romanians and Hungarians alike, hunted down and destroyed with the assistance of the werewolf."

"It sounds terrifying. I'm glad you escaped," I said, hoping it would make her feel better.

"I sense magic in you. You have the gift of sight like Karelyna the Seer," Ileana said, and took my hand in hers.

"It seems my dreams are clearer, bigger now that I have these new abilities. Tell me more about this Karelyna."

Taking a deep breath to calm herself, she released my hand. She sat forward in the chair and clasped her hands in front of her.

She attempted a smile and continued, "For nearly forty years I lived in a castle with vampires near Brasov, Romania. Karelyna the Seer had long red hair and dark eyes, and the sweetest face in the world. No more than your age when she became a vampire, Karelyna could see things no one else could see. She was a close confident of Ruxandra Tepes, a high-ranking vampire, and may well have had a hand in her decisions. Karelyna shared her premonitions with Ruxandra who determined whether they were important enough to bring to the attention of our leader, Morsus the Elder."

"I find this all so fascinating. Oops, I didn't mean to interrupt. Please continue."

"Her premonitions were never wrong, even if at times they were vague. Tensions and conflicts with the Ottoman Empire and Moldavia spilled into Transylvania with an invasion in 1541, ending with a raid on Szekely Land. During that time, many claimed Karelyna's visions had saved the lives of many vampires."

"If I have this gift, what do I do with it?"

"Take note of your dreams. Interpret them and make the best decisions concerning them."

"There's something I almost forgot to tell you. In my dream, you called me Simona. Is that name familiar to you?"

Ileana wasn't quick to answer. Her expression went somber.

"Must we go on about it anymore? They are all dead!" she declared, her voice rising with annoyance.

She got up from the chair, went to the window, shoved the curtain aside and peered out. Her back faced me, as if what I'd said had struck a nerve. Now I saw a side of her, I had not seen before.

"I didn't mean to dig up unpleasant memories of your past," I said, as I sat down on the armrest of the Victorian armchair.

Ileana stood, quiet and still, with her back to me and halfheartedly waved her hand in the air at me.

"You're sure you're the only one who escaped?"

Closing the curtain, she turned around to face me, and enthusiastically asked me, "Have you dreamed about others?"

"Not that I remember. But if anyone comes to mind, I will tell you."

"In all these years, I have never come across any vampires, though I have never left England," she said stiffly.

"I've never left England either."

Seemingly calmer now, she appeared interested in the conversation, even though she was still standing by the window.

"For all we know, somewhere out there, there are more vampires," I said enthusiastically.

Her eyebrows raised on that one.

"The castle is still there southwest of Brasov. It has a different name now. And it's a museum. Some years ago, I used the computer at the Newcastle City Library and searched for it on the Internet."

"I can search it on my smartphone."

"I will be happy to show it to you."

"Which reminds me that I should call my aunt before she starts to worry. I'll call her first thing tomorrow afternoon."

"That's a good idea. So, your friends won't become suspicious," Ileana added.

"Nobody knows where I am except Mrs. Krag or her husband who I believe saw me from the window of their house last Tuesday."

"It must be Lorraine Krag. Why didn't you tell me before?"

"I don't know," I said and shrugged my shoulders.

"She has been nosing around Wightwick Hall ever since she moved next door to me."

"Let's not worry about Mrs. Krag now. We both need to rest," I said and stood up.

"I'm inclined to agree with you. Let's shelve the conversation for now and pick it up again later," she said, then asked with a sparkle in her eye, "Shall we walk to the cellar?"

"We shall," I said agreeing with her.

We silently left the room arm in arm and walked that way all the way to the cellar. Ileana glided right up and hung upside down from the ceiling. I climbed up and hung upside down beside her. Roosted on the ceiling, I actually felt comfortable in this position. The two of us were more alike than I'd first thought. My eyes closed and I fell into a peaceful sleep.

Chapter 57

"YOU CAN LEAVE ANYTIME you like. You can go back home right now," Ileana said in a rather strange tone of voice.

Back in the study, I had just got through telling Ileana that I had spoken on the phone with my aunt. She seemed relieved to hear from me. Lorraine Krag had seen me and told Siobhan Mulcahy who told Aunt Eowyn that I was staying with a friend at Wightwick Hall. I appreciated Siobhan covering for me and I had corroborated the equivalent to my aunt. It was very believable because I often met people at my former job. Rather than being upset about Lorraine Krag's spying and telling Siobhan, Ileana thought I was homesick.

"What is there to go back to?" I asked her.

She explained, "Your friends, your job, your home…"

I interrupted with, "It's not the same anymore. I'm immortal like you now. I can't go back anywhere."

We stood there in front of her desk and regarded one another silently for a moment. She gave me a smile. This was when I knew she was playing with me, but I felt a little slighted.

"Well, I'm just saying, that's all."

"Has something happened, Ileana? Do you not want me here?" I asked with hurt eyes.

"All I am saying is that one day you may want to leave. And if you do, I'll understand," she said, not wanting me to feel obligated to her.

I firmly said, "I'm not going to run away from you."

Her eyes brightened at my words. And I meant it too.

"If you say so," she said and looked at me with her soft eyes.

The fear was understandable. There was a chance she could lose someone she cared about. Because she had lost people she cared about before. I, too, had lost people I'd cared about in my past. My parents. Now, suddenly, here I was. And she was apprehensive.

The clock on the wall read 11:17. As vampires we had so much time on our hands. I hoped she could drum up something for us to do.

"The night is still young. Any plans?"

After a moment's thought, she said, "Myrna, there is something I want to share with you."

"Is that so?" I asked, coming closer to her.

"I have never shown it to anyone before."

"That makes it even more special," I said and came to stand closer to her.

Lifting my hand, I brushed her hair off to the side. I was making her feel comfortable around me. She needed reassurance, I realized. I wanted her to feel like she could trust me because I was her friend. And then I did something I hadn't planned. Something inside me said for me to lean in close. She understood. I took her hand into mine.

Ileana looked at me, dumbly, her eyes beseeching. "I think you will love it."

"I can't wait to see it," I said as we walked out the door.

Holding hands, arms swinging gently back and forth, we sauntered down the hallway. It felt good to be together like this, enjoying a carefree moment. She kept her hand firmly clasped in mine as we made our way up the spiral staircase to the third level.

She stopped in front of a door in the hall. A moment's hesitation and she released her hand from mine. After opening the door, she walked into the room, stopping a few steps ahead of me and looking back in my direction.

In order to satisfy my curiosity, I stepped inside. Moonlight filtered in through skylights in the ceiling, and my eyes focused on a marvelous sight. I was standing in the most impressive greenhouse, which resembled a small paradise. I could feel the humid air and smell the various aromas of the plants.

"Everything about it is simply spectacular," I said in awe.

"Feel free to take your time looking around," she insisted, then turned away to busy herself with something.

By the time I turned around, Ileana was already at work. She was snipping yellow roses with pruning shears on the other side of the room. I think it was therapeutic for her.

My concentration fell on the colorful tulips. They were the loveliest I had ever seen. I walked over to them and gently felt the texture of the petals. They smelled like a fresh spring rain.

Wandering slowly about the room, I took everything in sight. I was attracted by the fantastic forms and brightly colored flowers. The blooms were so alive, it.

Nearly two hours later, I was worn out after covering every nook and cranny of the room. Ileana was already standing by the door waiting to go. She wore a quizzical expression as I approached with a smile on my face.

"There is something else we have in common. Besides a love of reading." I said, bursting with enthusiasm.

"I am fascinated to know."

"We had both spent too many years afraid to take any risks. Lately, we've been taking more and more chances, and everything is better now. Don't you agree?"

"I do agree."

"I have a theory about us. Care to hear it?"

"Myrna, please continue," she said with interest, and added a smile as I came to stand next to her.

"We're both really afraid to get close to anyone for fear of losing someone we care deeply about."

She came back with a thoughtful comment. "I like it that we're friends."

I said quite endearingly, "I like it, too."

My feelings were genuine. We'd both taken a chance on each other, and here we were as happy as could be. And that thought reminded me of something else.

Maybe this was the time to bring up something I had been meaning to ask her. I opened my mouth to ask her, but then I stopped myself from speaking. I was hesitant to say what was on my mind. I was sure Ileana caught it because she looked at me, waiting for me to speak.

When I didn't say anything, she asked, "Is there something troubling you, Myrna?"

"How did you know? That I was meant for this kind of life."

Her response wasn't immediate. She looked at me in a curious sort of way. Her eyes met with mine, and she seemed to be searching for the right answer. Perhaps she wasn't used to all this talking. In my case, I wasn't used to her not talking much.

"You know us vampires, we just know things," she said earnestly, then asked, "Are you ready to go?"

That was all she could say, which summed it all up. Far too perceptive for her own good, she knew I was the one that day she had seen me at the Newcastle City Library. It was that simple.

"Lead the way," I said cheerfully.

"I will gladly do so."

"So, where are we off to now?" I asked as I followed her out the door.

Once again, she was at a loss for words.

Chapter 58

IT WAS HALF PAST SEVEN O'CLOCK in the
evening, on Thursday, September 21. Claymor Elgany sat
at a table in The Longbow Tavern on Stepney Bank. While
there, he kept his head down low, not making eye contact
with any of the customers, doing his best not to draw any
attention to himself. The fewer people who saw his face, the
better he liked it.

His attire was plain, consisting of a pair of black boots
and black slacks worn under a loosely hanging blue and
black flannel shirt with a turned-up collar like a vampire.
That he was not. A short, well-set fellow, with dark brown
bushy hair, he seemed to be in his late twenties, He was
unshaven and there was stubble on his face, but it suited
him.

"Your steak, sir," the server said with a smile,
setting the plate in front of him.

He looked intently at the food in front of him. With a knife, he cut off a slice of the rare filet mignon. He tore into his steak with gusto, displaying his closely set pronounced teeth. Blood seeped onto the plate, spreading out into a dark pool. Eating in such a way, without so much as a thought as a tiger or wolf would eat. Needless to say, he was a hungry man.

The server, wearing a light gray shirt and matching pants under a black apron, approached his table and said politely, "I don't mean to disturb your dinner. Forgive me for not introducing myself earlier. I'm Allan Palen the owner of The Longbow Tavern. I hope the food is to your satisfaction."

Barely giving him a glance, and after a few more chews, he said, "It is very tasty, thank you."

"May I interest you in some dessert and coffee?"

"Just the check, please."

"I will bring it right over," Allan happily said.

All that was left on the plate was a little blood. His glass of water was empty. After reviewing the check, he took out his wallet, and left twenty pounds on the table.

As he stood up to leave, Allan Palen started coming his way, holding a pitcher of water. Claymor did not look at him but turned the other direction. He didn't want anyone to be remembered by anyone along his path. People were not to know he'd been in their midst.

When he approached the door to make his exit, the door suddenly flung open and a man entered and bumped right into him. The man was wearing a long black tuxedo jacket over a white dress shirt and black dress slacks. Claymor didn't like this one bit.

"Please forgive me, sir," the man said with a startled look on his face.

"It's no bother," Claymor said, keeping his head down.

"It's good to see you here, Viktor," Allan called out from across the room. "Will that be two for dinner?"

"Yes, Allan, you are right," Viktor answered cheerfully.

Allan lastly added, "Your table awaits you."

While they had talked, Viktor remained standing, blocking the door and Claymor was forced to wait. That was when he had noticed that Viktor was holding a wire leash to a little brown monkey. The monkey had looked at him with fear in his eyes. It moved quickly to hide behind Viktor's leg and buried his face in his knee.

Finally, Viktor began walking forward. Claymor quickly maneuvered around him and made a quick move toward the door. He flung open the door and the monkey screeched at him.

"Don't be afraid, Jasper," Viktor said to his pet, as the door slammed shut.

Claymor walked with a purpose, heading east on Ouseburn Road for about one hundred and twenty-five feet. He then turned left and walked about one hundred and fifty feet before making a right turn. After walking about one hundred feet, he went under Byker Bridge.

With his back against the brick wall under the bridge, he waited for the moon to come up. There were still a few minutes of sunlight left, but he was eager. He had been waiting for this moment for over four hundred years.

As patient as it was possible for him to be, he took in the scenery around him. It was a peaceful environment. Though it should have calmed him. But it did not. His thoughts were erratic and in contrast to his surroundings.

Tonight, he was a long way from his home in Sofia, Bulgaria. Clearly, he wasn't in Newcastle upon Tyne for a social visit. Unbeknownst to him, there had been a vampire living in this quaint city in Tyne and Wear. With old-fashioned churches, old style buildings, where sheep graze among the shrubbery, and a gateway to the Farne Islands that was a home to a colony of puffins, turned out to be the perfect hiding place.

For reasons he couldn't explain, he had discovered the whereabouts of the vampire. It had come to him in a dream. Or at least he thought that was what it was. Last Friday night he had dreamed about chasing a vampire in a forest with the Tyne Bridge in the background. And it was an encouraging sign to see. At long last, it had been the vision he'd sought.

Just this afternoon, he had arrived on a British Airways flight out of Sofia and came straight to The Longbow Tavern. He didn't want to delay his planned attack. It wasn't that long ago many people considered him to be the most fearsome vampire hunter in all of Transylvania.

When he glanced down at the Ouseburn River, a tributary of the River Tyne that ran under the bridge, a rag doll floated gently and drifted past him. His thoughts began to drift. The moment he saw the doll, he knew that some child might be missing their toy. For that short instant, the desire for revenge faded away from his troubled mind.

Chapter 59

A SHADOW fell upon the small Ouseburn River in front
of Claymor. The sun was fading fast and the mist rising,
making the air cool and hazy. Anxiously he watched the
sun disappear out of sight. It wouldn't be long now before
his transformation would take place.

In the distance a full moon gradually rose in the night
sky. The gray fog settled around him, and his body was
changing — slowly, and painfully. He fell to his knees as
gurgling animal sounds came from his throat. If anyone
heard them, they would believe it was a bear or a coyote.
They'd never imagined what it actually was.

Behold the man had changed into a werewolf.

It was not long until the beast emerged from under the
bridge. And he looked like something that crawled out
from under a bridge. Lurking in the shadows, he descended

by the Ouseburn River on the outskirts of town. In walking along the side of the river, he considered that he was the last of his kind. At least that was what he believed. Over time, he learned how to control his animal urges and turned his aggression on vampires instead of humans. As a result, he had not touched another human being in years. Not a bite nor a scratch. Therefore, he hadn't created new werewolves. Although he had heard tales of werewolves in Norway, he had yet to confirm it.

Luckily for him, as far as he could see, nobody seemed to have noticed him. And why would they? No one could possibly expect a werewolf to be in their vicinity, and neither would expect a vampire to be in their town. It was the stuff that fairy tales were made of, and people didn't believe in fairy tales. Rest assured, he had hundreds of years of experience in this matter.

He followed the vampire's scent toward City Stadium. Concealed in the dark woods, he blended in with the other animals. He looked like a bear. Nobody would get the chance to scrutinize him up close to tell the difference.

This was the day he had planned to show no mercy to this bloodsucker. The very one who had managed to elude him so thoroughly. Consequently, he still held a grudge against the clans of vampires who had killed many werewolves in Transylvania before the people's uprising in 1578. As he passed through Heaton Park, that was what crossed his mind.

By the time he reached the edge of the woods of Jesmond Dene Road, he was tired and stopped for a short break. He hung his head, closed his eyes, and breathed in and out heavily a couple of times. Claymor wasn't the same, vigorous werewolf he had once been. Still he was confident he would succeed in defeating this vampire. The element of surprise was on his side. The vampire couldn't possibly know he was here.

Once he had his breath back, he walked a little further. Glancing around, he spotted the castle. After a few grunts, he stood there, motionless. The wind blew through the trees, scattering leaves all around him. Leaves fell on his body and disrupted his thoughts. In a fit of rage, he swatted at the leaves with both arms swinging forward. A flock of goldfinches took flight from the trees, soaring up into the sky. Seemingly, they were in fear of this beast.

The night crept on. The grounds of the castle were empty but for the werewolf heading directly toward it. Continuing on with determination, each step drew the malevolent werewolf closer to the vampire he wanted to eliminate.

Without hesitation, he walked to a corner-edge of the castle. All around him was thin fog. He bent down and rose again wanting to howl at the moon which was glowing above him, but refrained with some effort. It wasn't the right moment to bring attention to himself. Low-sounding grunts came from the depths of his throat, whispered in the lowest tone, so that not even a bird could hear him.

Claymor absorbed the moonlight like an energy source. The heat within him increased tenfold. He let out a soft moan of pleasure, feeling his adrenaline rush through him.

Still a bit breathless after walking a little over two miles, he stayed under the moonlight for a little while longer to build more strength. He took in a breath of air, shaking his head. Then his fierce eyes glared mistrustfully around. Nothing moved in the vicinity, or anywhere around for that matter. The only thing he heard was the wind, rustling the trees that was producing melodious music in the otherwise still of the night.

The castle was very quiet, as if no one was there. But he knew that wasn't the case. The feeling of isolation and loneliness was a façade. It was the dwelling of a vampire.

Moving his head from side to side he sniffed the air, scrunching his face and growling. The smell hit him, certainly vampire in origin. Knowing that the vampire was close within his grasp, gave him a feeling of peace and strength.

He circled the castle, looking for the best point of entry. Hidden behind the bushes where no one would see him, he searched frantically for a window big enough for him to jump through. Soon, after looking around, he stopped under a good-sized window at the second level.

The moment was at hand. At last he was about to fulfill his destiny.

Claymor broke into a full sprint toward the castle. He threw his arms up in front of his face as he jumped through the large window on the second level.

Chapter 60

AT A LITTLE PAST TEN on a Thursday evening, I stood at the guest bedroom window with the curtain drawn back gazing at the glowing moon on this dark night. I had just changed into a pale-yellow chiffon sweater with a V-shaped collar, dark gray capri leggings and black sandals before I pulled my hair into one long braid down my back.

The sound of breaking glass startled me. Where from? Needing to know what happened, I tore away from the window and left the room.

My mind was in turmoil as I hurried down the hallway. Suddenly the noise came again, but it sounded different this time. I stopped near the entrance of the spiral staircase. Listening quietly to the sound of footsteps on broken glass, I tried to figure out where it was coming from, but all of a sudden, the noise stopped.

There came this nagging feeling something wasn't right. Then came the unpleasant odor of a wet dog. What in the world could it be?

Before taking another step forward, I needed to know that Ileana was all right, so I called out to her and asked, "Is that you?"

I looked around for Ileana and found myself gazing upon two red eyes in the darkness, on the other side of the hall. I think I just found the culprit of the smell. The eyes were moving closer. And the stink of a wet dog was getting stronger.

"Who is there?" I asked with dread in my voice.

The shadow was materializing into an animal. If this was some kind of beast, why was it here? Why was it coming toward me?

It came out of the darkness and into the light. The stinking beast was illuminated by the light of the moon from the window across the staircase. It was a werewolf, the same one from my dream. Not believing what I was seeing, I shook my head and blinked my eyes. To my shock, there it was.

A feeling of fear ran through me. I stood there, frozen, watching him approach me.

Without another moment's thought or hesitation, I ran for the staircase. As I descended the steps, I looked over my shoulder to see the werewolf coming after me.

Before I could take another step, my left arm was seized in a tight grasp, and I barely missed falling on my face.

Somehow, I managed to grab hold of the handrail with my right hand to maintain my balance.

Not even giving me a chance to catch my breath, the werewolf tugged hard on my arm and I slipped onto the stairs. I shuffled around to put my back against the wall near the top of the staircase.

He growled loudly and moved to stand over me. His eyes glared down at me. My eyes were wide with terror. He was standing. The leverage was on his side.

Any sort of escape was impossible. He was preventing me from getting up and blocking me from getting away. I lay immobile, an easy target for this beast.

He swung his arms towards me, trying to grab me. I put my arms out to block him and forcibly knocked his arms back. Although, he outweighed me by over one hundred pounds, I wasn't going to give up and kept embers of hope alive. I kept pushing his arms away, fighting back tooth and nail with everything I had.

"Stop! Why are you doing this?" I screamed at him.

I knew I hadn't done anything to deserve this. But the werewolf didn't care. And I could see the hatred in his eyes.

Luckily, the werewolf had tired himself out; and then he ceased throwing his arms around. Now he was taking a break. He raised up higher and howled at the full moon shining through the second level window across the staircase.

The bright moonlight illuminated some of his features. Standing more than six feet tall, looked rather ... intense, and towered over me. He emitted a low growl as he turned his head to face me. His eyes were bulging with fury. He showed his teeth and looked like he was about to bite my head off.

Of anything after that point, I was unsure, for my eyes were clouded with distress. I thought this was it. My life was going to end right here. This monster was going to kill me, because I didn't know how much longer I could hold him off. He was much stronger than I was. As the grief became too much to bear, I almost started to cry.

My mind was also consumed by Ileana. I didn't know where she was, hoping he hadn't harmed her. My senses were out of whack. I couldn't detect any sign she was around.

"Ileana, where are you?" I called out for her.

She didn't answer. Terrible thoughts battered my mind. I was in such despair about it. It was a horrible feeling, but I tried to focus on the immediate situation.

The werewolf looked around for Ileana. It looked like he didn't know who I called out to. That gave me a lot of hope. It was possible he hadn't seen her at all, or if he had he might have missed where she went. This meant she was alright. So, where was she?

His attention came back to me. He opened his mouth, growled, showing rows of sharp teeth. His eyes pierced through mine, giving me a chilling look. There was so much hate inside him. He was determined to finish me off. It was the most terrifying moment of my life.

How could it end this way for me? It wasn't so much that I was afraid of dying, but I was terrified by the thought of dying this way. It was impossible to comprehend it.

Chapter 61

IT WAS LIKE ONE SECOND LATER that I could feel
Ileana's presence. The werewolf, engrossed in attacking
me, still had not detected her presence by the time she
appeared at the bottom of the staircase where I could see
her from the corner of my eye. For a flash, my spirits were
lifted again. I knew she wanted to protect me. But I didn't
know how she was going to do it.

"Ileana, be careful!" I shouted, tension in my voice.

Hearing the fear in my voice, she yelled, "Stay down!"

That was when I saw it. In the span of seconds, the
silver .357 Magnum Smith & Wesson revolver held in
both her hands moved to the werewolf. As I had
suspected, he hadn't anticipated, that there were two of us.
He was completely taken by surprise and had just started
to turn his body toward her.

One fraction of a second to pull the trigger. A lot could happen in that amount of time. The sound of a gunshot rang, and he froze. To the werewolf's misfortune, the bullet hit him in the shoulder, and he grunted.

Growling, the werewolf turned to face Ileana. She held the .357 Magnum pistol pointed toward the werewolf's face, ready to blow his head off. He opened his mouth wide, showing his sharp teeth, and she pressed the trigger and another bullet flew from the chamber while smoke oozed out of the barrel of the weapon. The bullet slammed into his upper chest over the place where his heart would be.

Even though the werewolf was weak from the impact, he was determined not to die. To this end he turned toward me with what strength was left in him. I saw him raising his right arm to strike me with his paw at the same instant Ileana pulled the trigger for the third time, and shot him with a bullet through his back and into his heart.

I shrieked in horror when I saw the hole in his chest. On impact, all the air left the werewolf's lungs in a painful jolt. He heaved in a full breath before he fell back and tumbled down the staircase, landing with a heavy thud on the floor. Long story short: he was dead as a doornail.

His body slowly transformed into a human man. Without the piercing gaze and without that aggravating will of his, he was lying in a pool of blood, naked at the foot of the stairs. If I didn't know better, I would say he looked like a harmless young man. Though he still smelled like a wet dog.

Ileana dropped the revolver on the floor and stepped forward a couple of steps. The sight of her standing over him victorious would always stay in my mind.

I slowly rose from the steps. Once I was back on my feet, I hurried down the flight of stairs. I couldn't wait to embrace her. She saved me. She saved us both.

"Is he dead?" I asked, trying to catch my breath as I arrived at the bottom of the stairs.

She nodded yes, unable to speak. Right then all I wanted to do was hold her. I threw my arms around her and clasped her close to me. Then I kissed her softly on the cheek, then her ear, and her cheek, again. A sense of peace overwhelmed me.

"I was so worried about you," I whispered softly into her hair.

"Silver bullets work every time," said Ileana.

"This stays between us, okay?"

"Don't worry," she said in a promising way, "I won't say a word!"

"I'm so glad you weren't harmed, Ileana."

"I'm glad that you were not harmed," she said and broke our embrace.

Before I knew it, Ileana had gone upstairs into a bedroom and returned with a brown blanket. I was sitting on the bottom step of the staircase, watching her as she covered the body of the dead man with the blanket. She kneeled on the floor and rolled the body up in it. Then she tucked in the corners of the blanket tightly. It was obvious where she was going with this.

Her past had come back into her life like a whirlwind. Was there any way to escape it? Would another werewolf come? I refused to even think about that likelihood, since most of the time the things I worried about never happened. Still, I couldn't help but wonder: Would we ever be safe?

"How did he find us?" I asked, desperately wanting to know.

"There is only one possible explanation. Your gift of sight opened a realm between you and him and it helped him find you."

"How is that so, Ileana?"

"You somehow tapped into his thoughts. The dream you had of a werewolf chasing you may have been his dream too. From the dream, he discovered your location. He thought you were me. The vampire who had long ago escaped from Transylvania."

"So, it's my fault?"

She came up to me and put her hands on my shoulders. "You can't blame yourself. Your vision helped me. I already had the gun loaded with silver bullets. I'm sorry I didn't come faster."

"Oh, Ileana, I don't know. It's all just so awful."

"Forget your worrying. I need your help. We're not out of this yet. We've got to dispose of the body," Ileana said as she stepped near the body on the floor.

So much for the old days, I thought. I never imagined in all my life that I would be drinking the blood of animals and burying a dead body. Such were the many ironies of my existence as a vampire. It was just one thrill after another.

"Is it wise to do this under the light of the moon?" I asked, showing concern.

"What do you say we wait till tomorrow, in the light of the day?" Ileana answered sarcastically.

"Fine. Let's do it. We better hurry, in case someone calls the police about the gunshots."

"Who would call the police?" she asked, her dark brown eyebrows furrowing with worry.

I gave her a funny look, wondering if maybe it would jog her memory. In light of the evening's events, it took a minute for her to comprehend what I was suggesting.

"Lorraine Krag," we both said at the same time.

"Clean the blood stains from the floor and the stairs, and I'll check the windows to make sure no one is around," I said and stood up.

"Good plan."

After looking outside through the windows in the kitchen and the library, I was certain that no one was around. I came back into the foyer and found her wiping the drops of blood off the floor and the stairs. Then she put the rag on top of the blanketed body.

Ileana grabbed the end of the blanket covering the man's head, lifting him by the shoulders. At the other end, I lifted his feet. We carried the corpse down into the cellar, and there we gently set the body down on the floor. Ileana walked to the closet near the door of the room and pulled out a shovel. Then we carried the body out a wooden door, up a flight of stone steps, and into the darkness.

Deep in a secluded area of the woods of Jesmond Dene, we took turns digging until the hole was about three feet deep. After covering the body with dirt, I scattered leaves over the grave. That was when I noticed that there were streaks of dirt on Ileana's face. Her long-sleeved dusty rose-colored tunic that reached to her knees and matching leggings were covered in soil. I imagined I looked about the same.

A serious look came on Ileana's face. She was brooding about something and I wanted to know what it was. I suspected it was something more than what we'd just done.

"Tell me what's on your mind," I implored earnestly.

After some serious thought, she said, "Come to the study after you clean up. We need to make a decision together."

None of us said anything else for our walk back to the castle.

Chapter 62

SHORTLY AFTER ELEVEN O'CLOCK in the evening Lorraine Krag was at her living room window, peeking out between the curtains. Usually, at this time, she would have been preparing for bed. Instead she was in her pink chiffon nightgown and matching slippers, looking for signs of anything out of place.

"What on earth could be going on in that castle?" she whispered out loud.

Her eyes moved up and down and side to side. The faint moonlight revealed the surroundings, but she didn't see any movement outside the castle. It had been almost forty-five minutes since hearing gunshots echo outside, and it had thrown her into a panic. She had just argued about this with Arthur, who claimed he heard nothing.

"I know it was gunshots," she said, closed the curtains and began to pace the floor.

In the midst of her pacing to and fro, she looked over just as Arthur came into the room in his light blue pajamas. She was still worked up, ignored him, and continued her agitated pacing.

When he dashed a hand through his hair and cleared his throat to get her attention, she turned her haughty gaze on him and stopped in her feverish pacing. Standing close to the window, she shook her head slightly and faced him as if she had been running the script of what to say in her head.

Standing near the sofa, he placed his hands on his hips, and asked, "Well, what did you see?"

They were staring each other down as though they were playing high-stakes poker. Thus far, neither of them had blinked.

Finally, she spoke, saying, "Nothing! There's nothing out there."

"I knew you were making a fuss about nothing," he said, dropping his arms to his sides.

"They were gunshots!" she said with fire in her voice.

"These days it's difficult to tell the difference between gunshots and the sound of a car backfiring. But if those were gunshots, it was probably some hunter shooting a deer or testing his range."

"Now you are saying you heard it as well as I?"

"Don't try to twist my words, Lorraine. When you said you heard gunshots outside the house, I was in the bathroom brushing my teeth with the faucet on. I don't remember hearing anything of the kind."

"So, you say. I beg to differ," she said, her voice laced with scorn.

The hard look she gave him told him that she wasn't going to accept an evasive or flippant answer. She glared at him, waiting for him to confess. When nothing came from him, her heart fell a little bit. She clenched and unclenched her hands.

All she could say was, "Hear me now and listen well because I'm going to tell you again: I heard three gunshots."

"What do you want me to do about it?"

"First I will tell you something else. The gunshots came from Wightwick Hall where that woman and Myrna Ivester are."

"There you go again with Myrna. I'm going to bed. See you tomorrow," he said, starting to turn to leave.

"Wait a minute. Aren't you going to call the police?" she asked, and he stopped, looking back at her.

There was a look of shock on his face, and his eyes seemed ready to pop from their sockets. Adding to that, a corner of his mouth twitched.

Arthur's veins exploded in his eyes as he said, "I will do no such thing!"

"But, Arthur, you must!"

He continued, talking over the top of her protests. "There are no buts about it. There is no reason to call the police. If I call them, they will come here and ask questions. I will never get any sleep tonight. And for what? For nothing but a hunter in the woods."

"The police will visit the castle. They will check on Myrna to make sure she is all right."

"You realize when the police find out Myrna is all right, you'll look like a meddling old woman, which isn't far from the truth. The last thing I want to do is cause any trouble, which is the first thing you want to do," he said as if he was scolding a child.

"Then I'll call the police myself," she said carefully, her high-pitched tone revealing her frustration.

"Aw, come on, Lorraine, you'll make yourself batty if you go on like that. I know what you are up to. You want to know who that woman is and how Myrna is connected."

"Arthur, that just isn't so," she said, and unlocked her arms in front of her chest.

"It is so," he insisted, then asked casually, "You haven't heard any more gunshots, have you?"

"No, I haven't."

"If you hear any more gunshots, and I hear them too, I promise you, I will call the police," he said, trying to appease her.

Lorraine let out a deep sigh and released her arms and let them fall to her sides. She was very upset, but fed up with debating the matter with him.

"Whatever you think is best, dear. I'll go and make some tea to calm my nerves," she said throwing up her arms and heading toward the kitchen.

"Now that that's settled, I'm going to sleep now. Good night, dear."

"Don't let the bed bugs bite."

It was her habit of making comments under her breath when she didn't get her way. Arthur didn't react, didn't say another word, and didn't cast another glance in her direction as he retreated toward the bedroom.

"I'll find out one way or another," she said, when he was out of earshot and as she entered the kitchen.

Lorraine Krag could not resist having another last word.

Chapter 63

 of Monday, October 2, April Fielding dropped a crate of plants to one side of a metal table in the stockroom of Pike Nurseries. Her head swayed while she mouthed the words to the song "Stressed Out" by Twenty One Pilots playing on an iPod Touch on a docking station on a metal shelf in a corner of the room. The duties were not that difficult, and one of the perks that came with the job was the manager gave her permission to play her tunes at a low level when there were no customers in the store.

She lifted a potted plant from the wooden crate, removed it from its tissue-paper wrapping and placed it on a shelf. Then she grabbed another plant, repeating the process. It was something she enjoyed doing and this was a happy change from making deliveries with the company truck. She felt at ease handling plants and considered a career in the horticulture industry after university — if she goes to university. Now at the beginning of her upper sixth form level of education, she hadn't made any definite plans to attend university.

If people wanted to say she was a little odd, that was fine with April. She lived in her own world. Always did. With her tattoo of a vampire on her arm that she loved, and her bleached blonde hair, which she dyed on purpose, she wore mostly black outfits. Today she had on black jeggings and a satin black buttoned-down, long-sleeved blouse opened to her chest, conspicuously revealing a sterling silver chain with a dagger pendant. It was her style, and suited her interests.

Removing the last potted plant from the crate, she hurriedly tore off the wrapping and placed it on the shelf with the others. She put the empty crate on the floor by the waste basket and carried another wooden crate full of potted plants to the table. All the while she'd been thinking that she wasn't afraid to wear her weirdness on her sleeve. She was comfortable with herself and comfortable displaying it for the world to see. After all, she was young, and could get away with it.

From an early age she liked reading scary stories, enjoying the whole creepy aspect and suspense. As she got older, she developed a taste for the supernatural and eventually settled on the subject of the vampire. She couldn't get enough of it. At times she even wondered if it was possible for the supernatural existence of a vampire.

She hoped so. It was too early to say that she was going through a phase — so, at least, she believed.

The song "Suedehead" by Morrissey playing on the iPod Touch reminded her of her last date. Sadly, it wasn't what she'd thought.

April had met Tommy Taylor some months after her sixteenth birthday. He had transferred to her school at the beginning of the semester, and he caught her eye. Tommy was particularly sensitive and wore punk-style clothes. That was what attracted her to him. When he invited her to a Morrissey concert at Metro Radio Arena, she had to say yes. She felt this kind of music, classic as it might be called, captured her moods.

The arena bounded to the south by the River Tyne and situated on the south-western edge of Newcastle upon Tyne was a perfect place for live music. At the time she had thought the Saturday night concert would give her an opportunity to get to know him better and possibly lead to something more. Little did she know that to make a girl he liked jealous, he'd asked her out with him just like that!

That Monday in school she knew something was up when she tried to start up a conversation with him and he brushed her off. Eventually she heard through a friend of a friend that he threw her over for a blonde chick, probably the one he liked, but she didn't know, for sure. She didn't bother trying to find out.

He didn't try anything on her. *Better yet*, she thought, she didn't do anything with him.

"C'est la vie," April mumbled, ending her mental meandering.

She'd gotten tired of listening to the same songs from her playlist. Before removing the last potted plant in the crate, she turned off the iPod Touch and returned to her duties.

The sound of the telephone ringing interrupted her thoughts. With no one else around, it was up to her to answer it, another one of her duties.

"I've got it," she called out to no one in particular, jubilant, as she left the stockroom.

She picked up the phone by the counter and asked, "Hello, Pike Nurseries. How can I be of assistance?"

"May I speak with April Fielding?" a woman's voice asked.

"This is April," she answered, not recognizing the voice.

"Good afternoon, this is Ileana Vladislava. I'm calling to invite you to visit my greenhouse here at the castle."

"Sure, I would love to come over."

"There is more to tell you."

Ileana went on to tell her that she was leaving the entire contents of her greenhouse to her. Wightwick Hall had been put up for sale. She was moving from the area. April found a piece of scrap paper on the counter and copied down a phone number Ileana dictated to her.

"I'm sorry I didn't get to spend more time with you."

"A key to the castle for you is with the estate agent. Call the number I gave you and arrange to get it."

"Well, I need to go but I will get it after school tomorrow. And thanks again," she said, bewildered by it all.

April hung up the telephone and leaned back against the wall. She was going to see the greenhouse in Wightwick Hall, like she had wanted to for so long. Yet, a sense of loss welled inside her. In some strange sort of way, part of her suddenly felt like she was going to miss Ileana Vladislava. The eccentric lady had captured her interest. Another thought or two, and the young girl found herself shrugging her shoulders.

"C'est la vie, once again," she said aloud as she opened the door leading into the stockroom.

Chapter 64

A LITTLE MORE THAN A WEEK after the shooting incident of the werewolf, I found Ileana in her study. White sheets were draped over the furniture. She had just finished a call, picked up the telephone again and made another call. I stayed by the door waiting, not meaning to eavesdrop, but it sounded like she was talking to her estate agent.

With all the recent drama, it was reason enough for us to leave Newcastle upon Tyne. It was reasonable for Ileana to assume that werewolves would come seeking vengeance. Though there was no proof that there were any more werewolves. Still, we couldn't take the risk.

Ileana hung up with a satisfied expression on her face. As I came into the room, she told me the good news that she would make a pretty penny on the sale of Wightwick Hall. A potential buyer wanted to convert it to a hotel, which meant a couple of million pounds minimum. That was how she had earned her wealth: buy, renovate, sell, and repeat. Over a period of so many years, she had managed to accumulate over three million pounds in her savings account at Barclays, which included the earned interest on the deposits. The estate agent would handle all the details of the sale and direct deposit the money into her bank account.

The long flowing sleeves of her maroon knee-length dress made of gossamer fabric, swayed as she walked to the window and pulled aside the burgundy curtain to peek outside. Something caught her eye.

I couldn't help but ask, "See something else you want to take with you besides me?"

On my way toward her, I caught a glimpse of myself in the window. Actually, the only thing I saw was the long-sleeved, emerald-green velvet knee-length dress with sheer sleeves that I was wearing. My body cast no reflection. There was only a faint silhouette of my body, standing before me like an apparition.

"No, I suppose not, Myrna. It's just Lorraine Krag. She is working in her garden. She's on her knees and clawing at the soil with a hand hoe."

"Strange of her to do that at almost five o'clock on a Monday afternoon. That old busybody's spying on you never ceases. In some crazy way, she just can't get enough of you," I said approaching her and stopping to brush her hair with my hand.

"When I see her, it makes me cringe to core of my supernatural being."

"Is everything you need in that suitcase?" I asked and walked over to check it out.

"All that I require."

"It's rather light," I said as I lifted the dark gray suitcase and put it back down.

Turning away from the window, she asked, "You ready to head out?"

I came around to her side. "Yeah, let's get out of here."

"I'll bring the car around to the front door," she said with satisfaction.

"While you do that, I'll make a quick call to my aunt," I said, grabbing my smartphone out of my brown canvas backpack.

The call had lasted only three minutes. As I walked down the spiral staircase, I was feeling guilty about what I'd told Aunt Eowyn. Basically, I told her I accepted a job with Nursing Beyond Borders in a clinic in Bangalore, India. That I'd be gone for a couple of years and return home to England. The next thing I heard was the sound of her crying softly. I asked her to call Siobhan Mulcahy and tell her this. The last thing I told her was that I loved her. I had to tell her something so she wouldn't worry. Even if it was a fabrication.

The front door was open. So, I just stepped outside, closed it behind me, and stood there, and waited. I heard the trunk of Ileana's Bentley Continental GT slam shut. That was when Lorraine Krag turned her head to the direction of the noise. She stood up and dusted the soil off her tan pants. When she saw the FOR-SALE sign in front of the castle, she dropped the hand hoe on the ground and put her hands on her hips.

"Well, isn't that something," Lorraine said out loud, looking right at me.

Ileana drove the Bentley out of the garage and into the driveway. Before entering the passenger's side, I shot Mrs. Krag a chilly glance. She glared back with a look of outrage.

Before I sat down, I tossed my backpack into the backseat. After closing the door, Ileana noticed the smirk on my face.

"What now?" she asked me.

Then I raised my right hand and made a claw with it and growled then gestured with my head toward Lorraine Krag. She laughed. Then I laughed.

"You didn't tell me where we are going," I said rather curiously.

We exchanged a look and without a word I knew. I would like to think we came to a silent agreement, the way vampires could read each other's minds.

"You know the Black Forest in Baden-Wurttemberg, Germany is a place with hordes of deer. Ruins of medieval castles stud the banks of the Rhine," I said, matter-of-fact.

"Some parts of the autobahns in Germany have no speed limit," Ileana said with a quiver of excitement in her voice.

She picked up my glance and returned it and we smiled at one another.

"Wherever we end up is fine with me. I have the utmost faith in you," I said as the car started to move.

Giving Lorraine Krag a sinister look, I formed my hand into a claw and pointed it in her direction.

"Well, of all the nerve!" Lorraine said in her most indignant tone, rolled her eyes and then bellowed at the top of her lungs, "Arthur honey, you are not going to believe this."

After pulling out of the driveway, Ileana headed northwest on Jesmond Dene Road. Now we were on our way to the Newcastle International Airport. The rays of the sun fell on me. I relaxed into the seat and flipped the sun visor down. Without explaining, I grabbed two pairs of sunglasses from the glove compartment and passed her one.

"Put these on," I said, suddenly feeling the need to say something.

I started thinking it was possible that we were the only vampires in the world. That was a lonely feeling. If not, was there a chance we would run into other vampires in our travels? What were the odds of that happening? Still, I didn't want to get my hopes up. There was the possibility, and that was if Ileana and I worked together, and if the opportunity presented itself, we could create more vampires, easily. It was something to discuss later.

Everything was perfect. For better or worse, the two of us made a good team. What we shared as vampires was stronger than anything I had ever felt before.

By some strange chain of events, all the planets and stars had lined up perfectly, that day I first saw Ileana Vladislava at the Newcastle City Library. When I look back on my life, what I remember the most was how I became a vampire.

Epilogue

2019. Norwich, England

"YOU DIDN'T TELL ME YOUR NAME," the salesgirl said sweetly.

"No, I didn't," I said quietly.

I was looking out the front window while she talked. Whatever I'd come for, it wasn't here. My mind was consumed with the sky being overcast. The grayness of the late afternoon made the Jarrolds home furnishings store look rather dismal. It was a good thing I wore my H&M blue hooded rain jacket over my light brown camisole and matching jeggings. Best to get a move on and get going; the rain might come at any moment now.

"I told you mine."

"Rachelle Spratlin, right?" I asked whimsically, turning to her cordially.

"That's right," she said, staring at me with anticipation.

"Myrna Ivester. I am delighted to make your acquaintance," I finally told her.

Rachelle stepped out from behind the wooden counter and we laughed at the awkwardness. I kept my blushing eyes to the floor. Being very drawn to her, I could feel the blood running through her veins.

Last week I had come into the store for home decorating ideas. That was when I met Rachelle. With raven-hair, she had a somber beauty and the same pale skin tone as Ileana. I sensed a darkness in her. On that day, she had on a sleeveless blouse with a floral pattern and a black pleated skirt. The colorful vampire tattoo on her shoulder had caught my attention. I asked her about it, and she told me about her lifelong fascination with vampires, even though she considers it to be fantasy.

After talking with her further, I realized she wasn't cut out for the life of a vampire. She came from a stable and loving home and was attending the University of East Anglia studying international relations and politics. How odd, I thought. A loner who longed for a different way of life was the type of person who would want to live as a vampire. If anyone would know, it would be me.

"I have enjoyed our talk, but I must go."

"There are no other customers around, and the building is eerily quiet," she said, then asked in an enticing tone, "Must you leave now?"

"Yes, I must."

"Please, come back anytime."

It was the proper thing to say, but I think she truly meant it.

"I may," I said as I walked toward the door to leave.

At that moment, a familiar voice came from outside the door. Through the glass door, I saw the back of the head of a woman wearing a plain outfit consisting of a dark brown skirt and matching blouse under a tan cardigan.

"I just have to go inside. I haven't been there in ages," said the woman's voice.

"I'm going to go get the newspaper from the store down the street. I'll meet you there in five minutes," came a man's voice.

The woman's voice came stronger. "Surely, dear."

The door swung open — and there stood Lorraine Krag. What was she doing in Norwich? Despite the lighter color of my hair and my very pale skin, she recognized me immediately. There was no doubting the look on her face. It was a shock to both of us.

"Myrna Ivester? Is that you?" she asked, as if she really wasn't sure.

"Excuse me, madam," I said, and walked out the door, right past her.

"Arthur! Come here quick. You're not going to believe who I just saw," she shouted to him down the street.

That was the last thing I heard her say as I walked off, hurrying down the sidewalk in the opposite direction. Wanting to get away from her fast, there was no looking back. In my memory, Lorraine Krag was a very meddling woman. I certainly had no intention of talking to her.

After securing my helmet, I climbed on my black Suzuki Burgman 400 scooter parked at the corner of Bedford Street and Swan Lane. Two weeks ago, Ileana surprised me on my birthday with this latest model released in early 2019. I started it up and headed toward Thorpe Road.

For the past four months Ileana and I had been living in Norwich in the English county of Norfolk. I loved the United Kingdom, not just the memories, but the good of things that could still happen here.

Ileana purchased a mansion on Holmwood Rise near Woodrow Pilling Park. The woods surrounding the park was filled with wild animals including deer. It was suitable to our needs. There was nothing more enchanting than the French floor-to-ceiling windows, and stone terrace with a walled garden. The cellar was pretty big and was a very important part in Ileana's decision to buy the place. I loved it on sight.

Vampires, living side by side with humans, who would have imagined it?

Our time in Germany had been brief. For almost two-years we lived in a two-bedroom guest house in the middle of the southern part of the Black Forest near St. Margen. What Ileana liked best about Germany was driving on the autobahns. It was such a thrill for her. Anyway, we had trouble with the German language. Though, I surmised the area was too secluded.

I drove the scooter onto Harvey Lane making my way toward Holmwood Rise. Still, I felt Ileana and I were the only vampires on earth. Yet I didn't feel lonely. Someday I would like to bring others into our fold. I was often on the lookout for the right candidate, and Ileana was aware of it. She instinctively knew that I wouldn't do anything without her consent. My respect for her was profound. The bottom truth was that she was the head of this family.

Sometimes I could barely remember who I used to be. Yet, somewhere inside I missed my old home in Newcastle upon Tyne. Missed my Aunt Eowyn. And occasionally I missed my old friend Siobhan Mulcahy, who saw the world in such a black-and-white way. But now I was really missing Ileana.

After parking the scooter in the garage, I went inside the house. I had barely closed the door when the rain came down in roaring sheets.

"Ileana! I'm home!" I called out, anxious to tell her about my day.

ABOUT THE AUTHOR

ANN GREYSON is the author of the 2019 novel *Never-DEAD*. Other writing credits include book reviews for *Goodreads* website, poetry for *The Muse* literary & arts magazine, and theatre reviews for *Talent Magazine*. She has a passion for creating fictional characters for television, acting in the programs: *i Citizen*, *SpaceWoman Light-years Apart*, *Birdwatcher*, *PuRR*, *The Out World,* and *Never-DEAD*. Ann portrays Ileana Vladislava in *The Lonely Vampire* short television program broadcast on Manhattan Neighborhood Network's Lifestyle Channel 2 in 2017. She is the producer of *Pompilia* broadcast on Anne Arundel Community Television, and *The Watchers*, a nominee for a VOLLIE Award for Best Local Documentary from Community Media Center TV of Westminster in 2014.

With many dancing credits on stage, she also sings and acts in the music videos: *Shine, O Christmas Tree, House of the Rising Sun, Motherless Child,* and *Buffalo Gals.*

Ann Greyson has an Associate of Arts degree in English from Howard Community College. She is a member of Actors' Equity Association, SAG-AFTRA and the Alpha Alpha Sigma chapter of Phi Theta Kappa. She has the honor of receiving the Albert Nelson Marquis Lifetime Achievement Award from Marquis Who's Who in 2017.